# BULLET POINT

ALSO BY
# PETER ABRAHAMS

Reality Check

PETER ABRAHAMS

BULLET
POINT

HARPER TEEN
*An Imprint of HarperCollinsPublishers*

Many thanks to my editor, Kristin Daly

HarperTeen is an imprint of HarperCollins Publishers.

Bullet Point
Copyright © 2010 by Pas de Deux

Library of Congress Cataloging-in-Publication Data
Abrahams, Peter, date
    Bullet point / Peter Abrahams. — 1st ed.
        p.    cm.
    Summary: The only thing seventeen-year-old Wyatt knew about his
biological father was that he was serving a life sentence, but circumstances and
a new girlfriend bring them together, and soon Wyatt is working to prove his
father's innocence.
    ISBN 978-0-06-122769-1 (trade bdg.)
    [1. Fathers and sons—Fiction.   2. Prisoners—Fiction.   3. Criminal
investigation—Fiction.]   I. Title.
PZ7.A1675Bul 2010                                                         2009025440
[Fic]—dc22                                                                      CIP
                                                                                 AC

Typography by Sarah Hoy
10 11 12 13 14  LP/RRDB  10 9 8 7 6 5 4 3 2 1
❖
First Edition

*For Anthony: none better*

# 1

TIMES WERE BAD. Baker Brothers Iron and Metal Foundry went bankrupt. They fired everybody, including Rusty Halenka, who'd worked the seven-to-five on the main furnace for fourteen years. That meant he was around the house a lot. Rusty was Wyatt Lathem's stepdad. They hadn't gotten along when times were good.

The family—Rusty, Wyatt, Linda (Wyatt's mom), and Cameron, Wyatt's little half sister—lived in Lowertown. Lowertown was actually on a hill, the highest part of East Canton, getting the name from the fact that it lay farther down the river from the rest of the town. That was an interesting fact all the local kids learned in school. Another interesting fact was that there was no West, North, South, or just plain Canton, and no one knew why. The settlement dated back to Indian times, but no one famous had ever visited except for Mark Twain, who'd boarded the wrong train on a speaking tour. No one famous had ever come out of the town, either, with the possible exception of Wyatt's real dad, *famous* maybe not being the right word.

"Off to work," Linda said from outside Wyatt's door. "Take Cammy to the bus stop. Wyatt? You hear me?"

"Yeah."

"Then say something."

Wyatt, lying in his nice warm bed—his mom left for work at six, the sky still dark in winter—raised his voice and said, "Yeah."

From the other side of the wall came Rusty's voice. "Fuck sake, keep it down."

The house went silent. Wyatt heard a car engine turning over but failing to start, not far away. Then the door opened and Linda stuck her head in, backlit from the hall light. She looked strange, even a bit scary. It took Wyatt a second or two to figure out why: she was in the middle of her eye makeup, had done one eye but not the other; he saw the tiny brush in her hand. In a low voice she said, "And stay with her till she gets on the bus."

"Yeah."

She glanced around. "Your room's a pigsty."

"Oink."

She smiled; a little smile, gone in a flash. She wasn't smiling much these days. That quick smile made her look younger for a moment, thinner, happier, almost like a different person. She closed the door. Wyatt rolled over, tried to get back to sleep—he didn't need to get up till six-thirty—but couldn't. He heard Linda in the kitchen, opening a cupboard, pouring coffee, jingling keys. It was the kind of house where you could hear just about everything.

The front door opened and closed, closed with a little

thh-chunk; something was wrong with the latch and you had to give it a good strong pull. Now that Rusty was out of work he had time to make repairs like that, and Linda had handed him a list a few days before, a list he'd crumpled up and tossed back, not quite at her. Rusty was a big red-haired guy—some of that red hair turning gray—with freckles on his forehead. He had freckles on his big meaty hands, too. Wyatt didn't want to lie there thinking about those freckles and that crumpled-up list zipping past his mother's face. He got out of bed, walked down the hall—cold, because the hall radiator had stopped working—and into the bathroom, spending a minute or so. A second door off the bathroom opened into Cammy's room. He knocked.

"Time to get up."

"One more page."

Wyatt entered her room. Cammy lay on her side in bed, reading by the bedside light, her fine blond hair fanned out on the pillow. No freckles on Cammy—she had Linda's coloring. Wyatt was darker. Cammy didn't even glance at him, her eyes never leaving the book—a big thick book, no illustrations. Cammy was only in second grade. Had he even been able to read in second grade? She turned the page, an automatic kind of movement with her hand, like she was a reading machine.

"You said one more."

"Two. I meant two." Her eyes sped up, back and forth, back and forth.

"Come on."

"I don't want to go to school."

"Tell me about it."

Now she took her eyes off the page, looked at him. "Okay," she said. Cammy threw back the covers. She was wearing flannel pajamas with a bear pattern—friendly-looking bears, tumbling around—the sleeves frayed and a couple of buttons missing.

Wyatt returned to his room, did fifty push-ups and fifty crunches, like every morning, then showered, dressed, and went into the kitchen. Cammy was at the table, eating some kind of chocolatey-looking cereal and reading her book. He made toast, opened the peanut butter jar and a jar of raspberry jam. Someone had used the same knife in both, mixing peanut butter in with the jam and jam in with the peanut butter. It all got mixed together anyway once you started eating, so what was so annoying? Maybe just because of who the someone was. Wyatt ate his toast with butter and nothing else.

Not long after, Wyatt walked Cammy to the bus. It was light now, but no sun, just a low, unbroken ceiling of cloud. A cold wind blew from the west, buffeting the bare branches of the trees, of which there weren't many in Lowertown, and scouring away what was left of the last snowfall, leaving frozen brown earth and some icy patches. The school bus stop was halfway down the next block, and some kids were already waiting, most of them bigger than Cammy and all wearing gloves or mittens.

"Where are your mittens?"

"Forgot."

"Put your hands in your pockets."

Cammy put her hands in her pockets. Wyatt's hands were bare, too, but not from forgetting: Once the boys of

Lowertown reached middle-school age, they stopped wearing gloves, also wore their jackets unzipped even in the coldest weather, or abandoned jackets altogether for hooded sweat-shirts, which was what Wyatt was wearing now.

They stood at the bus stop. A FOR SALE sign swung back and forth in the wind. One kid's nose was running. No one said anything. The bus came and the kids got on, Cammy last. The driver was an old guy named Mr. Wagstaff; his nose was running, too. He looked at Wyatt over Cammy's head and said, "Hey, Wyatt, stayin' in shape?"

"Pretty much."

"Keepin' those grades up?"

"Yeah." Which was stretching the truth a little.

"Gotta stay eligible," Mr. Wagstaff said. "Need that bat in the lineup." East Canton High had a strong baseball tradition, and a lot of geezers like Mr. Wagstaff came to every game. Wyatt, now a sophomore, had made the varsity as a freshman, had ended up starting in center field and leading off. He loved baseball, had always loved it and been pretty good, but mak-ing the varsity and then doing so well—he'd hit .310, stolen twelve bases without being caught once, and gone errorless in the field—Wyatt still had trouble believing it; the best thing that had happened in his life, by far.

"I'll be eligible," he said.

"Atta boy," said Mr. Wagstaff. The door closed with a hiss and the bus drove off. A little kid in the back made a face at Wyatt out the window.

Wyatt walked back to the house, turned the knob on the side door that led into the kitchen, found he'd forgotten to leave it unlocked. He went around to the front door; also locked. He felt in his pockets. No keys, meaning he was locked out of his car as well.

"Christ." A breath cloud rose from his mouth, got torn apart by the wind. He walked around to the bathroom window—sometimes left open a crack, even in winter—but it was closed. He tried it: closed and locked, as he knew all the other windows would be, too. This wasn't the kind of street, or neighborhood, or town where people left their houses unlocked. Wyatt returned to the side door and did the very last thing he wanted to do, which was knock. Rat-a-tat.

He listened. The house was silent. Wyatt tried again, harder this time, and listened again. Still nothing. "God damn it," he yelled, and pounded on the door. It swung open, just like that, and there was Rusty.

Rusty wore a ratty old robe, held together over his beer gut with one of those meaty, freckled hands. His hair stuck up from his head in clumps, and one of his eyes was partly crusted over. He gazed down at Wyatt, but not as far down as in years past, with how Wyatt was growing; gazed down without saying anything, also without moving aside, blocking the entrance with his big, barrel-shaped body. Wyatt knew him, knew he was waiting for "Sorry," or "Excuse me," or at the least Wyatt looking down, unable to meet his gaze. Wyatt didn't look down. No telling how long this could have lasted, but after only a few seconds Wyatt caught a break, the wind rising suddenly, driving a cold blast through the doorway, making Rusty flinch. He shook his head like it wasn't even worth it to waste a word on Wyatt, and backed away.

Wyatt went inside, found his keys, looked around for his backpack with no success, finally realizing he'd left it in his locker at school. Had there been any homework assignments? For sure in geometry, his favorite subject—he was carrying a B in it so far, had even gotten an A in math once or twice— it was the only subject he liked at all, but he always tackled geometry homework in some other class, English, history, environmental studies, health, none of which interested him. As for those others: he had to do enough to stay eligible. First practice was only a month away. As he went out, he heard Rusty pissing in the bathroom.

Wyatt's car sat in the driveway: Mustang, twenty-two years old, bought for $450 from Mannion's Salvage, fixed up by Wyatt and Dub Mannion, varsity catcher and Wyatt's oldest friend, even though Dub was one year ahead in school. Maroon, with tinted windows and brand-new alloy rims: a thing of beauty. Wyatt scraped ice off the windshield with the tips of his fingernails, got in, turned the key. Rumble rumble, va-voom. He loved the sound of that engine, 225-horse V-8. Wyatt backed out of the driveway, looking both ways, felt the iciness of the street under the tires. He had a feel for this car, for driving in general—even the driver's ed teacher had said so. Wyatt sped up, still going backward, turning the wheel just so. He whirled through two perfect backward dough- nuts, never touching the brake, then eased out of the spin and drove the two miles to East Canton High, staying under the speed limit the whole way and coming to a full stop at all the stop signs.

Dub was already in the student parking lot, standing

beside his ride, an F-150 with MANNION'S SALVAGE on the side in gold letters. Dub had a big round face that almost always looked happy, but not now.

"Heard the news?" he said as Wyatt got out of the Mustang and locked it.

"Guess not."

"No baseball."

"What are you talking about?"

"School committee met last night. They cut it out of the budget."

"They cut baseball?"

"Cut everything—baseball, football, basketball, even marching band."

"Why? What's going on?"

"Town's out of money."

"How can the whole town be out of money?"

Dub shrugged his big shoulders. The school bell rang.

COACH BOUCHARD MET all the baseball players after school that day in the gym. The coach was a little white-haired guy with big hands and cold blue eyes that never seemed to blink. He'd coached baseball at East Canton High for forty years, won many district championships and six state championships. But before that he'd had a long career in the minor leagues, finally making it to the majors for the last week of his last season, and going one for seven at the plate, that one being a triple, as Wyatt and the whole team knew from looking him up online.

The players sat in the stands, Coach Bouchard on his feet before them. "Any of you guys not heard the news by now?" he said. No one spoke. "Pretty straightforward—we got the ax. Not just us, all sports, all what they call extracurriculars." The coach had a way of dragging out certain big words, like *extracurriculars*, resulting in a tone Wyatt thought was sarcastic. "Excepting for the marching band—that got saved at the last minute. What're they gonna march for, that's my goddamn question." Coach Bouchard glared at the team, like they'd done something wrong. "How about you guys? Any questions of your own?"

The boys were silent.

"This ever happen to you before?" the coach asked. "Don't think so. Then there gotta be some questions."

A kid said, "Why? Why is this happening?"

"Town's broke," said the coach.

"How can the whole town be broke?" said another.

"State's broke, too," the coach said. "School budget comes part from the state, part from property tax here in East Canton. But when folks is in foreclosure—you all know what that means? Foreclosure?" Nods here and there. "When the bank's taking your house away—that's foreclosure." Wyatt knew already: he'd seen it happening on his own street. "And when folks are in foreclosure, do they keep on paying their property tax?"

"Why should we?"

Wyatt glanced back up in the stands, saw that question had come from Willie Garcia, a senior, the backup middle infielder. He didn't remember ever hearing Willie speak before, never seen much expression on his face, either. Plenty of expression now: he looked angry.

"I hear you," said Coach Bouchard. "And it's not just folks' houses. When a business goes under, say a business like Baker Brothers, then they stop paying taxes, too. Not many businesses that size in East Canton. Town can go broke in a hurry." He gazed at the boys. "Any other questions? If there ain't, those of you what got equipment belonging to the team, go on and keep it, far as I'm concerned. Other'n that—"

"I've got a question," Wyatt said.

"Shoot," said the coach.

"Where are we going to play baseball?"

Coach Bouchard closed his eyes and shook his head slowly from side to side.

The coach left the gym, walked down the hall to his office, and went in, leaving the door open. The boys hung around for a few minutes, saying how fucked-up this all was, and how much the school sucked and the town sucked, "and the whole stupid planet," Willie said. And because that was funny, or maybe because Willie was suddenly talking, everyone started laughing, and they left the gym, pushing and shoving a bit, but in a better mood. As they went down the hall, Wyatt, toward the back of the crowd, glanced in and saw that Coach Bouchard was packing stuff in boxes. He looked up at Wyatt.

"See you for a sec?"

Wyatt nodded, entered the coach's office.

"Close the door."

He closed the door.

"I'd say take a seat," the coach said, "but Herman already took the chairs." Herman was one of the janitors.

"Where are you going?" Wyatt said.

"Home."

"I mean how come you're packing up?" No more baseball, but coach doubled as a health teacher.

"Handed in my resignation, effective"—he checked his watch—"eleven minutes ago."

Wyatt gazed at him, didn't know what to say.

"Thinkin' I'm a rat?" the coach asked. "Deserting a sinkin' ship?"

A rat? Wyatt could never think of Coach Bouchard that way. The coach wasn't exactly what you'd call a warm person, but he was straight up, gave each kid a fair shot—no one ever complained about favoritism—and besides, he'd taught Wyatt so much: how to be patient at the plate, wait for his pitch, even set the pitcher up a bit, plus all the intangibles like being relaxed and alert at the same time, and putting the team first, and playing hard until the last out. "Oh, no, Coach, I wasn't thinking that. I was thinking, you know, what about health class?"

The coach paused, his hand on a trophy he was taking from a desk drawer. "Not gonna help them sugarcoat this," he said.

Wyatt didn't understand. Who was "them," for starters? He remembered something from history class, how even the Great Depression had finally come to an end. "The economy's going to get better, right, Coach? What if it gets better soon, like by the summer? Then we could have a team again next year."

The coach gazed at him. Those cold blue eyes didn't look quite so cold. "Yeah, sure, anything's possible. And I'm the last one to run my mouth on any of this. But we got complicated problems, maybe more complicated than people can handle."

"But people made the problems in the first place, didn't they, Coach?"

The coach smiled. His teeth were yellowish plus a couple

were missing, but there was something nice about his smile. "Got a head on your shoulders," he said.

Wyatt didn't get that at all. Except for math—and not that he was great at math, B's, yes, but he wasn't in the top stream—he was an average student, maybe below.

"You're a smart kid, is what I'm saying," the coach explained, perhaps because Wyatt was standing there with his mouth open. Wyatt came pretty close to arguing the point. "Want some advice? About playing ball, I mean. An old dumbass like me ain't qualified to opinionate about nothin' else."

What was going on? Wyatt had never heard the coach talking like this; he was always confident, teaching the team, Wyatt figured, how to be confident by example. "Yeah," he said, "sure."

"Reason I'm tellin' you this," Coach Bouchard said, "is you've got some talent for the game, maybe the kind, if it keeps developin' and you grow some more, that'll take you to a college. Not sayin' D-One, you understand, no promises on that score, and notice I'm not breathin' a word about pro ball, but—somewheres. Meaning scholarship money, son, and the chance to get a real education. You follow?"

Wyatt nodded. College: that would be something. How much more did he have to grow? Wyatt was a hair over five ten and built solid, weighing one seventy-five.

"My advice," said the coach, "is for you to get out of here fast."

"Get out of where, Coach?"

"This school, this town. Got to establish residence in some

other town, a town that's got a high school with a good baseball program."

Establish residence? What did that mean? He named the only team from their district that had given them trouble last season. "Like Millerville High?"

The coach snorted. "Think Millerville's in any better shape than us? Same thing could happen there, if not this month then next, or next year. No, where you gotta go is someplace more prosperous, the kind of town that'll have baseball no matter what, even in a crappy economy."

Wyatt tried to think of towns like that. He hadn't traveled much, had been out of state only once, last year when the four of them—he, Cammy, Linda, Rusty—had taken a trip to Disneyland. He'd seen prosperity on that trip—they'd spent an hour or so driving around Beverly Hills—but the coach couldn't be meaning somewhere like that. Was there even a high school in Beverly Hills? That would be like transferring to the moon.

"I'm thinkin' Silver City," the coach said.

"Silver City?" It was at the other end of the state, four hundred miles away.

"Know any folks down that way?"

"No."

"Not an issue—I got some contacts at Bridger High. I'll make some calls—just say the word."

"So, I'd be, like, living in Silver City?"

"Exactly. Living there. Residing. Can't just parachute in and suit up. That's only in The Show." Coach Bouchard laughed.

Wyatt didn't get the joke. "But, uh, Coach, living with who?"

"Some family that likes baseball. Boosters, kind of thing. Coach down there's Bobby Avril—should be able to set you up, no problem. Bobby sent a kid to Tulane last year, full ride, and another one to Arizona State."

*Full ride:* sounded like words to make a magic spell. This was all so much. Wyatt tried to line it up in his mind the way the English teacher did on the blackboard, using—what were those marks called? Bullet points? Yeah, that was it. Wyatt lined up the most obvious bullet points, like living in a new place, a booster family, Bobby Avril, and leaving home.

"Well?" said the coach.

Wyatt took a deep breath. "Yeah," he said. "I'll do it."

"Smart man," said the coach. "All you got to do is keep doin' what you're doin'. Play hard, stay relaxed."

Wyatt nodded. Yes, he could do that. He was going to miss things, his mom, of course, and Dub and the team, and other kids at East Canton High, but: yeah. And Cammy. He was going to miss her, too. Wyatt held out his hand. "Thanks, Coach, thanks a lot."

"Don't thank me," the coach said. They shook hands. The coach's hand was hard and rough, the big fingers twisted. Wyatt turned to go. He was almost at the door when the coach called him back. "One more thing," he said. Wyatt walked back into the room. The coach opened a filing cabinet under the window, searched through the bottom drawer. "Here you go," he said. "Might as well have this. Everything's just gonna end up in boxes in my garage, moldering away."

He gave Wyatt a photograph, six by nine or so.

"What's this?" Wyatt said. A black-and-white photo and obviously kind of old, the edges yellowish and turning up, it showed two guys in baseball uniforms with East Canton on the chests, although the lettering was different from the lettering on the uniforms now. One of the guys, the unsmiling, older one, had a salt-and-pepper mustache. The other was a kid, maybe about Wyatt's age, a good-looking kid with a big white smile on his face. Wyatt didn't recognize either of them. "Who are these guys?"

Coach Bouchard jabbed his finger at the older one. "That's me, for Christ's sake."

"Oh," said Wyatt. "Sorry." The mustache had fooled him, plus how young the coach looked; his face—now deeply grooved—had hardly any lines at all. But those cold eyes were the same; he should have seen that. "Who's the other one?"

"Take a guess."

Wyatt had no idea. "The team captain, maybe?"

"Woulda been, if he'd stuck around for another season."

"Uh-huh," Wyatt said. Why did the coach want him to have this picture?

"No idea who that is?" Coach Bouchard asked.

"Nope."

"Look closely."

Wyatt looked closely, shook his head.

The coach gave him a long stare. "Maybe this ain't such a good idea," he said. He reached for the photo, got a corner of it between his fingertips, but Wyatt didn't let go.

"Why not?" he said. "Who is this guy?"

Coach Bouchard sighed. "Ah, Christ," he said. "It's a slick-fielding shortstop I had way back when. Name of Sonny Racine."

The photo trembled slightly in Wyatt's hand. "My father?" he said. "My real father?"

The coach sighed again. "Biological, I guess they say these days, 'stead of real."

# 3

WYATT HELD THE PHOTO in both hands, kept it steady. He'd never seen a picture of his father before; they'd been separated, if that was the way to put it, prior to Wyatt's birth. First had come six or seven years of ignorance, then his mom—it was just the two of them then, pre-Rusty—had sat him down and told him the story. After that came a year or two of intermittent questions, and since then he'd pretty much stopped having any thoughts at all about his—how had Coach Bouchard put it?—his biological father. Had he ever asked to see a picture? Maybe, long ago, because he had a faint memory of his mom telling him there were no pictures. Now, with this photo in his hands, one thing was clear: the son looked a lot like the father, at least the father as a young man.

Wyatt glanced up. The coach was watching him, eyes narrowed. "How come you never told me about this?" Wyatt said. "I never even knew he . . . he played ball."

"You never asked," the coach said. "And it was all a long time ago. Maybe a mistake, like I said. Give it back. I'll put the damn thing in a box. End of story." He reached out.

Wyatt drew the photo away. "I want to keep it."

The coach raised his hands, palms up. "Okay. It's all yours. And as far as I'm concerned, might as well tell you I had no problem with him. Never in trouble that I knew of, fine fielder, fast, like you, but nowhere near the hitter. Didn't have your pop. Don't know whether that's information you want or not."

"I—I don't have much information at all," Wyatt said. "About him."

The coach nodded. "Prob'ly best. But I figured at least you knew he went here, East Canton High."

"I guess I should have realized," Wyatt said. "But I never really thought about it."

"That's prob'ly best, too."

Wyatt took another look at the picture. That flashing white smile: this kid—wearing number eleven, Wyatt noticed, his own number, an observation that gave him a sudden strange feeling in his gut—seemed pretty happy. "How come he stopped playing?"

Coach Bouchard shrugged. "Stopped lovin' the game, maybe? Lots do, no idea why. Don't recall the details in this case, not like he was the star of the squad or nothin'. Mighta dropped out of school. Lots more did that back then. Now, drop outta high school and you haven't got a chance."

"How come?"

"How come? Lookit the world out there."

Wyatt swung by Dub's place on the way home. The Mannions lived in a big farmhouse just outside of town;

they had chickens, a couple of horses, and a mule they'd named Wyatt. As Wyatt drove past the corral, Wyatt the mule curled back his lips, showing huge yellow teeth; he was a mean bastard. That was the joke: the Mannions were fond of Wyatt—Wyatt the kid—and almost treated him as one of their own.

Wyatt parked beside Mr. Mannion's car—a shiny black Caddy, three or four years old. Mr. Mannion could probably afford a new one every year, but the Mannions weren't like that. Wyatt knocked on the front door.

"It's open," Mrs. Mannion called from inside.

Wyatt went in, saw her in the kitchen, slicing a big red tomato. "Hi, Mrs. Mannion."

"Hi, sweetie. I think he's downstairs."

Wyatt found Dub and Mr. Mannion in the TV room. The Mannions called it the TV room but really it was a cool home theater, with a huge flat-screen TV, surround sound, soft leather couches, and an old-fashioned popcorn machine. But the TV wasn't on, and Dub and his father were talking, Dub on a stool, his father behind the bar. They stopped as Wyatt came in.

"Hey."

"Hi, Mr. Mannion."

"Lousy goddamn news," Mr. Mannion said. He was a big bald guy, once a Big Ten linebacker, now twenty or thirty pounds overweight.

"Yeah, I know," Wyatt said.

Dub glanced at his father. "Can I tell him?"

"Don't see why not," said Mr. Mannion.

"Tell me what?" said Wyatt.

"The thing is," Dub said, "my dad's kind of, you know, like, arranged, uh—"

Mr. Mannion interrupted. "Listen to him, Wyatt. Seventeen years old and he can't string two words together. What he's trying to say is that starting next week he's going to be living with his aunt in Silver City."

"Silver City?" Wyatt said.

"I'm transferring to a school down there," said Dub.

"Bridger High?"

"How'd you know?"

Wyatt laughed. "I'm doing the same thing."

Mr. Mannion gave him a quick, sharp glance.

"You are?" said Dub.

"Yeah," Wyatt said. "When did the coach talk to you?"

"He, uh, didn't," Dub said.

"Coach didn't talk to you? I don't get it."

"My dad—"

"The Bridger AD and I went to college together," Mr. Mannion said.

Mr. Mannion was a smart businessman, as everyone said, knew how to get things done. "Cool," Wyatt said. "We'll be there together." He laughed. "Maybe the whole team'll move down."

Dub laughed, too. Then he said, "Hey, Dad—any chance Wyatt can live with Aunt Hildy, too?"

"One thing at a time," Mr. Mannion said. He checked his watch, then went upstairs.

*  *  *

Wyatt and Dub made popcorn, cracked open some sodas, watched *SportsCenter.* "Ever been to Silver City?" Dub said.

"No."

"Pretty nice town," Dub said. "Practically in the mountains. They got elk there."

That sounded good.

"We could take up bow hunting," Dub said,

"Nah," Wyatt said.

"Ice climbing?"

"Yeah," Wyatt said. "We'll need crampons."

"What's that?"

"Kind of spikes for your boots."

"How do you know that?"

Wyatt shrugged. They were showing highlights on TV. A skinny guy with full-sleeve tattoos on both arms drained a long three-pointer. "The coach gave me something."

"What?"

Wyatt had the photo in the big inside pocket of his jacket. He handed it to Dub.

"Is that the coach?" Dub said. Dub was pretty smart, although hardly anyone seemed to know; he was an even worse student than Wyatt.

"Yeah," Wyatt said.

"Looked just as mean back then," Dub said. "Who's the kid?"

Wyatt gazed at that big smile for a moment; a confident smile, even cocky. "My father," he said.

Dub's eyebrows—bushy and expressive—went up. "Whoa," he said.

"Yeah, I know."

"He played ball for Coach Bouchard?"

"News to me, too."

"He looks kind of . . . you know, normal," Dub said. "Where is he?"

"I don't know."

"I meant like which prison."

"Got that," Wyatt said. "And the answer's still I don't know."

Dub took another look at the picture. "What position did he play?"

"Short."

"'Cause he's wearing the same number as you—would have been amazing if he was a center fielder, too."

"I guess."

They sat on the couch, feet stretched out on footrests, ate popcorn, drank soda, watched more highlights.

"Can you believe that pass?" Wyatt said. "Sick."

"You never, uh, talk about him, huh?" said Dub.

"Who?"

"Your father."

"Gone before I was born—you know that."

"Yeah."

"So there's nothing to talk about."

They lapsed into silence, not an uncomfortable one. Wyatt and Dub had spent lots of time together, just like this.

"Play some Madden?" Dub said after a while.

"Sure."

"Gonna beat your ass," Dub said. They played Madden.

Wyatt was up by two touchdowns—Dub never won—when Mrs. Mannion called down, "Wyatt? Staying for dinner?"

"Thanks, I better get going," Wyatt said.

He drove home, stopping for gas when he noticed the needle quivering down near empty. He put in three dollars' worth, all he had on him. Standing at the pumps, cold wind whipping through under the overhang, sky dark, he tried to find the right words for telling his mother about Bridger High. Nothing came to mind. He decided to just wing it. Why not? She was his mom.

She was in the kitchen, still in her office clothes except for slippers, thawing a frozen red block of spaghetti sauce on the stove.

"Hey, Mom."

"Hi, honey. Dinner'll be ready in fifteen minutes."

"I—"

"And Coach Bouchard called."

"Yeah?"

Wyatt went into his bedroom, closed the door, called the coach on his cell phone.

"Hi, Coach. Wyatt."

Silence on the other end. Then came what might have been ice cubes clinking in a glass.

"Coach? You called me?"

The coach cleared his throat. "Yeah, hi. I did." The coach sounded a little strange—like he'd been drinking. Wyatt rejected that idea immediately.

"What's up?"

"Kind of a—what would you call it?—bump in the road. That's it—bump in the road. We've hit a little bump in the road."

"Who?" said Wyatt. "What bump?"

"About Bobby Avril. Seems like the school committee— talkin' about Silver City, not East Canton—has these rules I didn't know about, rules—what's the word?—governing, rules governing transfers. Transfers and sports, is what I'm referrin' to. Anybody else can transfer, of course. But for playin' sports, don't matter varsity or JV, there's only one transfer who can play on a team each year, meanin' the year of transferrin'. After that, why, you'd be resident, so no problem for the next year. Get what I'm sayin'?"

Coach Bouchard was taking fast, and again Wyatt got the feeling he'd been drinking, but he thought he grasped the general idea, and it led to a bad thought: Dub wasn't going to be able to play for Bridger.

"So, um," Wyatt said.

"Bottom line—you can transfer to Bridger, no problem, but you can't play ball for Bobby Avril, not this season."

Wyatt's heart began to beat way too fast. "Coach? I don't think I heard you right."

Coach Bouchard's voice sharpened a bit. "There's nothin' I can do. Rules is rules."

"But I don't understand."

"Don' understand? Chrissakes, by the time I called Bobby Avril, first thing I got in the door, that one transfer space was already taken."

"Someone else transferred first?"

"Exackly. Turns out his dad goes back a ways with the AD, just like I go back with Bobby. Only thing is he beat me to the post."

The post? What post? Wyatt didn't get that, maybe didn't get any of it. "Whose dad?" he said.

"Dub Mannion's," said the coach.

"Dub got the position?" Wyatt thought back to that sharp glance Mr. Mannion had shot him down in the home theater. What had Wyatt said just before that? *I'm doing the same thing.*

"What I'm tellin' you," Coach Bouchard said. "First come, first served basis."

Silence. And then the ice cubes again.

"Coach? Can I stop by your office tomorrow? Talk about this?"

"Tomorrow? Not gonna be there tomorrow or any other goddamn tomorrows. I resigned. Done, all through. Weren't you listenin' today?"

**"SUPPER'S ON,"** his mom called from the kitchen.

Wyatt heard her but stayed where he was, standing in his room. He'd laid the photo on his desk and was now examining it under the light of the lamp. He noticed little things he'd missed before, like how big his father's hands were—bigger than Wyatt's, just about the same size as the coach's—and a light-colored metal chain, maybe gold, that his father wore around his neck. He bent closer, gazing into the photo image of his father's eyes. They began to look not like eyes at all, but simply ovals of light and shade, mostly shade.

"Wyatt? I've been calling and calling."

He turned. His mom was in the room, a red-tipped wooden spoon in her hand; he hadn't heard her enter.

"Sorry, I—"

Her glance went right to the photo. "What are you looking at?"

"Nothing, Mom."

"I hope it's not something you shouldn't be—" By now she'd moved in closer; his mom was kind of unstoppable when she got curious about something. "Who are— Oh, my God." She grabbed the photo, stared at it, then whipped around toward Wyatt. "Where did you get this?"

"I, uh, the coach gave it to me."

"The coach? Why would he do a thing like that?"

"On account of the economy, Mom. He was packing up. All the extracurriculars are gone."

His mother's eyes opened wide, and her face seemed to soften. "Baseball, too?"

"Yeah."

"Oh, dear."

"Yeah." Was there any point in going into the whole Bridger idea? None that Wyatt could see: The Bridger idea was gone, too. "So the coach had this and he gave it to me." He pointed to the photo, still in her hand. They were standing close together now, their eyes on the photo. "Did you know him back then, Mom, in high school?"

"Hey," Rusty called from the kitchen, "what's the holdup with dinner?"

Wyatt's mom didn't seem to hear. "Not really," she said, her face still soft, and now her voice as well. "He was two years ahead of me. I knew who he was, of course. All the girls—" She stopped herself.

"All the girls what?" said Wyatt.

Cammy came in. "Dad says what's the holdup with dinner."

"Can't he serve himself?" Wyatt said.

"Wyatt, hush," said his mom. "Tell him we'll be right there."

"Roger," said Cammy, and left the room.

"All the girls what?" Wyatt repeated.

Linda's lips turned up the slightest bit, as though she were about to smile, but she did not. "He was popular with the girls, let's put it like that."

"So when did you get married?" Wyatt said. "After you graduated from high school?"

His mom turned to him. "We actually never did get married," she said. "We were going to, what with you coming along, but then—"

"You never got married? I'm finding this out now?"

"There wasn't time—he did that terrible thing and got arrested and then—"

"Hey!" Rusty was in the room. "What's going on?" His face had pink patches here and there, a sign that he'd had a few drinks.

"Sorry," Linda said. "We're coming."

"What's so interesting?" Rusty pointed with his chin at the photo.

Linda lowered the photo to her side, the back of it facing out.

"Let me see," Rusty said.

"It's nothing, not important."

"I like not-important things," Rusty said, and then he moved with surprising quickness—Rusty was one of those people capable of surprising you from time to time, never in a good way—striding across the room and snatching the photo out of Linda's hand.

"Don't," Linda said.

Rusty turned his back on Wyatt and Linda, hunching over the photo. A moment or two passed and then his back stiffened. "What the fuck?" He whirled around, said to Linda, "Where have you been hiding this?"

"I haven't—" Linda began.

"It's mine," Wyatt said.

"Yours? Where'd you get it?"

"Coach Bouchard. It's mine." Wyatt reached out. "Give."

Rusty held the photo out of Wyatt's reach. "Have to think about that," he said. "Might not be good parenting, letting it into your possession."

"Huh?" Wyatt said.

"Not exactly what you'd call a role model, this pretty boy," said Rusty, tapping the photo. "Gotta look out for your moral development."

"What the hell are you talking about?" Wyatt said.

"Rusty, please," Linda said.

"'Rusty, please'?" said Rusty. "Now you're gonna defend him? Defend the convicted murderer?"

"Of course not," said Wyatt's mom. "There's no need for any of this. Let's all calm down."

"That picture's mine," Wyatt said. "The coach gave it to me."

"'That pikchew's mine,'" Rusty mimicked. "Listen to him—Cammy's more mature, for fuck sake."

Wyatt lunged forward, tried to grab the photo. Rusty whipped it out of reach.

"Please," said Wyatt's mom. "Let's all—"

"Calm down?" Rusty said. He smiled, the kind of smile

where the eyes don't join in. "Okay," he said, "since he wants it so bad, he can have it." Rusty tore the photo to shreds, real quick, zip zip zip, and flung them at Wyatt.

Wyatt and Rusty had had some nasty arguments, but things had never gotten physical, at least on Wyatt's part: Rusty had whacked him upside the head the odd time back when Wyatt was younger. Wyatt didn't think about any of that, didn't think about how Rusty was still a lot bigger than him, didn't think at all. He just charged at his stepfather, knocking him into the wall. A cheap wall—the whole house was cheap—and Rusty made a big hole, breaking through the drywall and splintering one or two of the slats underneath.

"Fucking son of a bitch," Rusty said, looking astonished, dust raining down on his wiry red hair.

"Oh, God, stop, stop," said Linda, coming up behind Wyatt and gripping his upper arms. At that moment, when Wyatt couldn't quite defend himself properly—not his mom's intention at all, he was aware of that in real time—Rusty wound up and threw a roundhouse punch, his meaty, freckled fist landing square on Wyatt's nose. Then came a cracking sound, like a wishbone on Thanksgiving, followed by pouring blood and a sharp pain radiating from Wyatt's nose across both sides of his face; sound coming first, pain last.

Wyatt sagged backward, knocking his mom, not a big woman, to the floor, although he didn't fall himself. He glanced around to see if she was all right, and Rusty got him again, this time on the jaw, but not dead on. Not dead on, but Wyatt went down anyway, hot and raging inside, and the next thing he knew his vision had a reddish tinge and he welcomed it, might even have growled like an animal. He rolled over and dove at Rusty's legs.

Rusty toppled backward, cracked his head against the edge of the doorframe, and spun into Cammy, who'd suddenly reappeared in the doorway, holding the handle of the pot of spaghetti sauce in both hands. Cammy flew across the hall. Rusty fell and lay still, spaghetti sauce splattering everything: walls, floor, each member of the family. Then Cammy and Wyatt's mom were both in tears, wailing, really, and Rusty was rising to his knees. "Gonna fuckin' kill him," he said. Wyatt thought of the small automatic Rusty kept under the bed in the master bedroom and took off. In seconds he was outside and in the Mustang, peeling away from home, rubber shrieking in the night.

Wyatt drove, fast at first, and with no plan, no idea where he was going, and then slower, out of town and down a narrow lane to a beach by the riverside, where kids went swimming in summer. No swimming tonight: in his headlights he saw that the river was frozen over, except for a narrow black channel in the center. For a moment, a pathetic moment—as he realized while it was happening but let happen anyway—he wondered how it would be to slip down into that icy dark water. Wyatt shook his head, clearing it of shit like that, at the same time setting off a sharp pain in the middle of his face.

He switched on the interior light, checked his face in the rearview mirror. Two or three smears of blood on his cheeks, but his nose had stopped bleeding. The problem with his nose was its new shape and location. Wyatt's nose, to which he'd never paid much attention, had always been straight, not too big, not too small. Now it was big and swollen, and worse, crooked, bent one way in the middle, then angling off in the other direction at the tip.

Wyatt leaned forward so he could see better. There were tears in his eyes. That made him angry at himself. *Suck it up*, as Coach Bouchard always said. Wyatt spoke the words aloud: "Suck it up." Then he got a good grip on his nose, thumb on one side, fingers on the other, took a deep breath, and yanked it back into place. Another cracking sound, more blood, more pain, and he might have let out some cry—but when he checked the mirror, his nose was straight again. The thought hit him that maybe Coach Bouchard wasn't really an authority on the subject of sucking it up.

Wyatt sat in his car, parked in this place—familiar, except he'd never been here in winter; kind of like a stranger in his own hometown. At first he ran the engine to stay warm, but the needle was dipping down toward empty—a great car and he loved it, but not good on gas—and he switched it off. Then it was quiet, the sky full of stars, the only movement that black rippling out in the middle of the river. It got colder and colder in the car. Wyatt was wearing only jeans, sneakers, a short-sleeved T-shirt. He could see his breath. It fogged the windshield. He didn't like that, wanted to see out, so he kept a little porthole-sized circle of glass clear. After a while he started shivering and couldn't stop. He felt alone. That was new.

"What's the goddamn point?" he said.

Wyatt started the car, backed away from the river, U-turned, and headed into town. By the time he got to his house, he was nice and warm again. A light shone in the kitchen, and in Linda and Rusty's bedroom, but otherwise the house was dark. Wyatt slowed down, almost turned into the driveway, but instead kept going, not from fear of Rusty's little automatic, or fear of anything, really: he just didn't want to go there. He drove down Main Street, all closed up for the night, gradually began to feel more like himself. His cell phone rang. He saw his mom's number on the screen and didn't answer.

Wyatt ended up parked outside the Mannions' farmhouse. An upstairs window opened and Mrs. Mannion looked out. A minute or so later, Dub came outside, wearing a ski jacket and pajama bottoms. He opened the passenger-side door and slid in.

"Hey," he said.

"Hey."

"I'm real sorry about that Bridger thing. I didn't have a clue about them only having one spot."

"Didn't think you did."

"My old man's so fucking organized."

"That's good."

"I don't even want to go anymore."

"That just proves you're dumb."

"You go. You take the position. You're better anyway. I can't hit the curveball for shit, and that means I'll wash out sooner than later."

"Shut up."

Dub glanced over. "Hey," he said. "What's with your face?"

"Nothing."

"Don't look like nothing."

Wyatt took a deep breath and shivered all of a sudden, even though he was no longer cold.

"C'mon inside," Dub said. "It's cold."

"Nah."

"I'm freezing my ass off."

"Then go."

"Nope," said Dub, sitting back, like he was actually getting comfortable.

Dub was very stubborn, always had been. They ended up going into the Mannions' house together.

# 5

MRS. MANNION, wearing a quilted pink robe, her round face glistening with some sort of clear cream, made hot chocolate. They sat around the Mannions' kitchen table—Wyatt, Dub, Mrs. Mannion. It was warm in the Mannions' house, much warmer than home, and Wyatt felt no drafts; his place was full of drafts.

"Hot chocolate okay?" said Mrs. Mannion.

Dub grunted.

Wyatt said, "Yeah, thanks."

"Not too hot?"

"No," Wyatt said. "Just right."

"So," said Mrs. Mannion, "first thing would be a call to your mom, right?"

Wyatt shook his head.

"She'll be worried," said Mrs. Mannion. "You know that."

Wyatt knew, but he didn't admit it out loud.

"Can't he stay here for the night?" Dub said.

"Of course. Longer if he wants. But he still needs to call his mom."

"She'll be asleep," Wyatt said.

"No she won't," said Mrs. Mannion. "Proves you've got a lot to learn about mothers." Wyatt gazed into his hot chocolate, thinking: *Rusty will answer for sure.* "Tell you what," Mrs. Mannion said. "I'll call."

"Aw, Mom," said Dub.

"Don't 'Aw, Mom' me." Mrs. Mannion reached for the phone and dialed. Rusty had the kind of voice that carried through the phone speaker, and Wyatt clearly heard: "Yeah?" Mrs. Mannion stuck her jaw out a little. "Linda, please. It's Judy Mannion." A second or two went by and then Mrs. Mannion said, "Linda? Wyatt's over here. He's fine." She listened for a few moments and said, "Good idea." Then she hung up and turned to Wyatt. "Your mom's coming over."

"Why?"

"Why? What kind of a question is that?"

"I'm going to bed," Dub said.

Mrs. Mannion washed the mugs and stood them upside down in the drying rack. "I'll be pushing off, too," she said. "Invite your mom inside when she gets here."

But when Wyatt saw the headlights coming, he went out to the driveway to meet her. His mom drove an old Cherokee— old and wrecked, rusted out and burning oil, but not yet quite paid off. Wyatt got in the passenger side and sat down. Linda's face was puffy from crying, and she was no crier.

"I'm staying at Dub's," Wyatt said.

His mom nodded. "Okay, I understand. I just wanted to

make sure you were all right."

"Yeah, I'm all right."

"No, you're not," said his mom. "Look at me."

He looked at her. He was all cleaned up now, blood washed off, hair combed, nose a bit swollen but straight.

"I'm so sorry," she said. A tear formed in one eye, rolled down her cheek.

"You didn't do anything."

"Oh, I did."

"What, Mom? I don't get it."

"I only wanted—" Her face started to crumple up. She got control of herself and continued. "I hate what just happened. It made me sick. And there's no excuse, none at all. But for someone like Rusty—his whole life has been about hard work, and now getting canned like he did, sitting around all day, useless, stewing in his . . ." Linda went silent for a few moments. "He's his worst self right now."

*This is how he always is.* That was Wyatt's response, but he held back, caring too much about his mother to say it.

Linda gazed at the Mannions' house. Dub's big flat screen glowed in his second-floor window. "I wanted this—want this to work so bad."

"Wanted what to work?"

"A family. This family."

Wyatt shook his head.

"Nobody's perfect, Wyatt."

"And a bird in the hand is worth two in the bush." A nasty thing to say, and he regretted it at once.

Too late, of course. His mom actually winced, as though

he'd thrown a punch. "This jealousy of his—it's just so stupid," she said.

"He's jealous of me?"

Wyatt's mom gave him a long look that made him even more uncomfortable than he already was but that he couldn't interpret. "That's not what I meant," she said. "I meant—" She paused, as though making some effort, then licked her lips. "I meant Sonny. Rusty's always been a bit jealous of him."

"He knew him?"

"Not really. Rusty was a bit older, went into the service as soon as he could, got posted out to the Coast. He was jealous sort of after the fact, jealous that Sonny and I were—had once been . . . an item."

"An item?"

"A couple. We . . . we were so young."

Wyatt didn't want to hear about that. Wasn't he the young one right now? Her job was to be the older one. "Where is he?"

"At home, asleep. I don't think he even—"

"Not Rusty. I'm talking about my real father."

"He's in prison. A life sentence, you know that." The TV light went off in Dub's bedroom.

"Everyone keeps saying I know things," Wyatt said, "but I don't. What prison?"

"I'm honestly not sure. They sent him to Sweetwater originally, but he might have gotten transferred since then."

"Sweetwater? That's the name of a prison?"

"Sweetwater State Penitentiary. From the Sweetwater River, downstate."

"Did you ever visit?"

His mom nodded. "Once, a few weeks before you were born."

"Only once?"

"It . . . it was horrible. And he didn't want me to come back."

"Why not?"

His mom shrugged. "Life sentence. It was pointless." She sighed. "Plus, what he did—I could never think of him the same way again. That made it almost easy, letting go. Maybe a harsh thing to say, but true."

"What was the crime?"

"You know all—" She stopped herself. "It was a robbery gone bad. Sonny swore he didn't fire the shots, but even if that was true, it's the same as if he did, under the law."

"Who fired the shots?"

"They ended up pinning it on Sonny, all on the testimony of some lowlife."

"What was his name?"

"I don't remember," his mom said. "So long ago, and besides, none of this—"

"Come on, Mom." Wyatt raised his voice. He was tired of this fogginess, a fogginess he hadn't even realized was there till this last few minutes, but now he wanted clarity, a simple understandable story from A to Z, all the blanks filled in.

"What do you mean, 'Come on'?" his mom said.

"I want the story."

"But—"

"Just give it to me in bullet points."

"Bullet points?"

"The important parts."

His mom nodded. "The most important part was how stupid it all was. Sonny had a good job, working construction for this company in Millerville, but he got involved with the wrong people and—"

"What wrong people?"

"Art Pingree was one of them—the nephew of Sonny's boss."

"Was he the lowlife?"

She shook her head. "The real bad one was a friend of Art's they called Doc. It was all his idea—I'm certain of that. Sonny never said a word to me about any of it. The whole thing hit me like a bomb. For ages I kept thinking there was a mistake, like Sonny had a twin he didn't know about, and they'd gotten the wrong guy."

"What was the idea?" Wyatt said. "What happened?"

"The idea—if you can call it that—was to rob these drug dealers in Millerville."

"Drug dealers? I thought it was a bank."

"Sorry. I may have said that way back when. In order to . . . make it better, somehow."

"That makes it better?"

Wyatt's mom didn't answer, just stared straight ahead. Chimes hanging by the Mannions' garage door gleamed in the night.

"They were planning to steal the drugs?" Wyatt said.

"The money," his mom replied. "They thought drug dealers would have lots of money and would never go to the police—a kind of perfect crime. But it all went bad."

"How?"

"They went breaking into a house on Cain Street in Miller-ville, the very worst part. Shots got fired. A . . . woman died."

"A woman?"

"The girlfriend of one of the drug dealers. And her baby got shot in the eye. She was in a coma for a long time, but I think she lived."

"God almighty."

"What nobody knew was that the state police were on to the drug dealers and patrolled the street every night. They burst in and arrested everyone. I never saw Sonny again, not as a free man."

"What if he didn't fire the shots?"

"Same as if he had."

"But it's not."

"In the eyes of the law."

"But in real life."

"Real life?"

"Yeah—it's not really the same. You know, like morally."

"I'm not so sure of that," his mom said.

She had the engine running in the old Cherokee and the heat blowing full blast; still, Wyatt felt cold.

"Does he ever write or anything?"

"No. Life goes on, Wyatt. We—" She cut herself off, resumed more softly. "We've got our own problems." They sat in silence for a while. Then she turned and touched his shoulder. "We can make this work. We've got to." Her gaze moved to his nose, and she quickly looked away.

"I'm staying with Dub."

"For tonight, fine. But I know Rusty will feel bad about this in the morning. He'll want to square things up."

"You're dreaming."

"Don't say things like that."

"I'll say what I want. He's a pig and now he's living off you."

"That's what's killing him—don't you understand? And he's not a pig—he's basically a good person."

"Bullshit."

"You can't talk to me like that."

Wyatt opened the door, got out.

"Wait," said his mom, fumbling with her purse. "I've brought you some money."

He slammed the door, went back into Dub's house. The basically good person, even better than that, was his mom, of course, and he wished he hadn't slammed the door. As he entered the Mannions' house and felt the warmth inside, he realized she had had no real expectation that he'd be coming home anytime soon, maybe didn't even want it, possibly fearing what might happen. Why else would she have brought him money?

Wyatt climbed the stairs and entered Dub's room, a pigsty like his, except much bigger, fancier, airier, with a spare bed for overnight guests. No lights were on but Dub was awake.

"Hey."

"Hey."

"My mom called her sister, Aunt Hildy. You know, down

in Silver City. And she's cool with you living there, at her place."

"Huh?" Wyatt said.

"No baseball, I know, but there's no baseball here, either. And you could kind of get away, if you want. From Rusty, I'm talking about. Plus next year you'll be a normal resident, so you can play. You'll only be a junior."

Wyatt lay down, closed his eyes. They wouldn't stay closed.

"How much does she want?"

"How much does who want?"

"How much rent. Your aunt."

"Rent? Zip, for Christ's sake."

"I'll think about it," Wyatt said. His eyes closed. His nose hurt for a while and then he was asleep.

DUB'S AUNT HILDY had two kids, both grown and living on their own. Aunt Hildy, who worked as a paralegal at Weiner and Moor, the biggest law firm in Silver City, looked a lot like her sister, Mrs. Mannion, except older, thinner, and not as happy. She'd been married and divorced a couple times, now lived by herself in a white clapboard two-story, three-bedroom house just outside of town, up on a hill with a view of the Sweetwater River and mountains in the distance. Wyatt and Dub slept in the rooms vacated by Dub's cousins, Dub in the big one over the garage, Wyatt in the small one on the ground floor.

Aunt Hildy—that was what she told Wyatt to call her—gave him his own key. It was a much nicer house than home, but Wyatt didn't care too much about that. What he really liked was a kind of absence, namely the absence of tension, when he unlocked the door. Was Rusty inside? What kind of mood was he in? How was he treating his mom? None of that mattered anymore. Except the treating mom part: that was still on Wyatt's mind, but he told himself that his departure must have raised Rusty's baseline mood.

The departure: Wyatt, his mom, and Cammy, all standing around the Mustang in the driveway. Rusty stayed inside; Dub was in his truck on the street, engine running, the plan being to ride down in tandem. A cold wind blew. His mom's face was very pale, Cammy's, too. Cammy had a sleep seed at the corner of one eye. Wyatt fought off an urge to wipe it away.

"Take this," his mom said, holding out an envelope.

"What is it?"

"Just a little money."

"I'm set for money." Wyatt had cleaned out his bank account, had $356 in his pocket.

"I want you to have it."

*Send it when Rusty gets a goddamn job.* That was Wyatt's thought; he kept it to himself, instead just saying, "Don't need it, Mom."

The envelope remained in the space between them, wavering in her hand, and then she slowly withdrew it into the folds of her coat. His mom stood there, the wind ruffling her hair, revealing more gray than he'd ever noticed, plus it seemed thinner, too. She looked a bit confused.

Wyatt stepped forward and hugged her. "Bye, Mom."

She squeezed him close, then took his face in her hands—hurting his nose by mistake, a pain he ignored—and kissed him three times, almost angrily, if that made sense.

"Bye, Mom," he said again, letting go of her and backing away; her arms were reluctant to disengage, almost clinging to him. And down below, Cammy *was* clinging, clutching his legs with her little hands.

"Don't go," she said.

He patted her head. "See you soon."

"When?"

"I don't know. Soon."

She didn't let go. Linda pried her away. Cammy was crying when Wyatt drove off, behind Dub in the truck. Wyatt checked in the rearview mirror and saw his mom was waving, her other arm around Cammy.

It took about twenty minutes to get to Bridger High from Aunt Hildy's. Wyatt and Dub took turns driving, a pretty drive that paralleled the river for a while and then cut through downtown Silver City—a much nicer downtown than East Canton's, with some restaurants, a coffee shop, and a few stores with gold-lettered signs—and up a hill to the school, bigger and newer than East Canton High and surrounded by well-groomed playing fields that went on and on. The very first day, Wyatt noticed something at the bend in the road, just before it left the river: a sprawling, earth-colored complex on the other side.

"What's that?"

"The pen."

"Pen?"

"State pen. The prison."

"Sweetwater State Penitentiary?"

"Think that's the name."

Wyatt would see Sweetwater State Penitentiary twice every school day. Had Sonny Racine been transferred somewhere else? Wyatt preferred to think so.

As for Bridger High, Wyatt soon realized it was better than East Canton High, meaning the classes were harder.

"You believe all this homework?" Dub said one evening, about three weeks after their move, the two of them at opposite sides of the kitchen table. "What's *obsequious* mean?"

"Like a sequoia tree, maybe?" said Wyatt.

"Big, you mean?"

"Gigantic."

Dub stuck the end of his pen in his mouth, gazed at the page. "Yeah, that fits." They worked in silence for a while and then Dub said, "First practice is tomorrow."

"I know," Wyatt said.

The next day, first baseball practice, Wyatt and Dub drove to school in their separate rides, since Dub would be staying late. But Wyatt didn't go right home. He came close, walking out to the upper parking lot, reserved for students, with his books under his arm. But as he neared the Mustang, his footsteps slowed, as though some magnetic effect was holding him back, and after a moment or two he came to a stop and just stood there. The upper parking lot was at the highest point of the campus, looking down over most of Silver City, the river, and in the distance, Sweetwater State Penitentiary. Wyatt gazed at nothing for a minute or so, then turned, walked around the school, and headed for the baseball diamond.

A beautiful diamond: the base paths reddish just like in the big-time, and perfectly groomed; the outfield grass amazingly green for the time of year, the fence a smooth blue curve about six feet high, topped by a bright yellow stripe. Two coaches, one old, one young, stood at home plate, watching the players jog around the field. They all wore gray baseball pants, blue stirrups, blue warm-up jerseys, and white caps with a blue B. The caps, especially, were very cool, and Wyatt couldn't help wanting one.

A few parents sat down low in the stands, huddled together against the wind. Wyatt climbed to the top row and moved toward the very end, past third base, as far from the action as possible. He spotted Dub, dead last in the line of joggers—somehow he'd been getting slower every year—wearing number 19. At East Canton, he'd always worn 9. That meant someone else had 9. Wyatt ran his gaze over the players, found 9 in the middle of the pack—a short, blocky kid with thick legs, a catcher for sure. Last year's starter? Or last year's backup to a senior, expecting to be the starter this season?

The team took infield, the older coach standing at the plate and hitting grounders, the players fielding them—or not—and firing to first, the first baseman then throwing home, where Dub and number 9 took turns catching the ball and handing it to the coach. Once in a while the coach laid down a bunt, and whichever catcher was up had to scramble out, scoop up the ball, and snap it to first. This was maybe the moment when everyone began to see what Dub could do, because despite how slowly he ran, he was much quicker than number 9 at the scrambling part; and as for their arms, no comparison—Dub had a cannon.

The coach began hitting line drives and fly balls to the

outfield. Three kids were playing center, Wyatt's position; it was easy to pick out the starter, a tall kid, number 1, maybe taller than Wyatt and leaner, whose long legs didn't seem to be moving fast but who easily got to every ball and hit the cutoff man every time with throws just as good as Wyatt's, if not better.

The sun, still looking pale and wintry, sank behind a cloud, and the wind rose a little more. Wyatt slipped his arms out of the sleeves of his sweatshirt, tucked them against his chest for warmth. The younger coach rolled a screen out to the mound, started throwing batting practice, each batter getting six pitches. Dub hit the first one he saw over the fence in center, then crushed a few more. Number 9 couldn't get the ball out of the infield. Number 1 batted last. Wyatt was shivering by that time, but he had to see what this kid could do. Swing and a miss; chopper to third; one-hopper to short; blooper to right; foul down the right-field line; swing and a miss. Wyatt rose, clambered out of the stands, headed for the parking lot. Anyone could have a bad day, but Wyatt knew he could start for this team, could have started on opening day, next week. He missed baseball so bad.

Wyatt didn't watch any more practices. The next day he found a batting cage beside a bowling alley in a run-down part of town. No one was around. He went into the bowling alley: about a dozen lanes, snack bar, popcorn machine with popcorn popping, and only one person in view, a girl his own age or a bit older, stacking bowling shoes on shelves behind the counter.

She turned, came closer. Yes, a bit older. She was good-looking, with long shiny black hair and a silver eyebrow ring. "Hey," she said, "looking to bowl?"

"How much for the batting cage?" Wyatt said.

She raised an eyebrow, not the one with the ring. She had shiny dark eyes, almost as dark as her hair. "You want to buy it?"

"No, uh, just use it," Wyatt said. "For hitting."

"Sorry," she said, "just pulling your leg." She had a throaty kind of voice, like someone who'd smoked for years, but Wyatt didn't smell any smoke on her. "It's five bucks per half hour," she said, "but tell you what—since you're the first customer of the year, you can hit for free if you help me set up."

"Hey, thanks."

She put on a short leather jacket with thick silver zippers and led Wyatt outside. The wind was blowing again.

"It's not a little cold for baseball?"

"No." Wyatt opened the trunk of the Mustang, took out his bat, a thirty-four-inch, twenty-nine-ounce thin-handled Easton Reflex he'd bought last summer from a graduating East Canton senior for forty dollars.

"Your car?" said the girl.

"Yeah."

"Nice."

"Thanks."

They walked over to the cage and the girl unlocked it. The pitching machine had an arm-style delivery and a hopper with twenty or thirty balls on the side. Wyatt plugged it in, and it started humming right away.

"Liftoff," said the girl. Her hand moved to the dial. "Slow, medium, or fast?"

"Fast," Wyatt said.

She turned the dial, went out the door, and closed it.

Wyatt took his stance at the plate. Hands up, weight back, balanced, still, eyes on that steel arm. It swung back, took a ball that rolled in from the hopper, and came whipping forward. Wyatt saw the ball clearly—those spinning red laces clearer than anything he'd seen for days, weeks, months—and swung. He hit the ball on the screws, rocketing it to the far end with a force that shook the whole cage. And the next one just the same. And the next and the next and the next, smashing every ball in that goddamn hopper. He realized he was stronger than last year, maybe a lot stronger.

"Hey," said the girl, watching from the safety of the other side of the chain link.

# 7

WHEN WYATT WENT BACK after school the next day, the bowling alley was closed even though the hours-of-operation sticker on the door read 11 A.M. TO MIDNIGHT. But the day after that it was open. Wyatt entered, bat in hand. The girl was alone again, behind the desk. She watched him approach.

"More BP?" she said.

"Yeah."

"Have to charge you this time."

Wyatt laid a five-dollar bill on the counter. She was wearing a black bowling shirt with GREER stitched in white over one breast.

"Can you see that all right?" she said. "Greer—with two *E*s?"

He quickly raised his gaze up to her face, nodded a little too vigorously.

"The problem is everybody always spells it *I-E*," Greer said. "I've had to correct them maybe a million times."

"You know a lot of people," Wyatt said, a not completely unfunny remark that maybe surprised both of them.

Greer laughed. "What's *your* name?"

"Wyatt."

"Wyatt. Never met a Wyatt. Sounds like a gunslinger riding in from the old West."

This might have been a place for another not completely unfunny remark, but none came to mind. Wyatt's mouth seemed to open on its own, and out popped something really stupid. "How old are you?"

Greer raised the non-ring eyebrow. "How old am I?"

"None of my business," Wyatt said, backtracking as fast as he could.

"It's not a state secret," Greer said. "Nineteen. And you?"

"Me?"

"Yeah, you. Now that we're minding each other's business."

"Seventeen," Wyatt said. "Just about."

"When's your birthday?"

"August."

"So what you mean by 'just about' is that you'll be seventeen in, like, four or five months." Greer's eyes, so dark and shiny, seemed to get even brighter, like she was about to laugh, but she didn't.

"Yeah."

"What date?"

"The second."

"Me, too."

"August second?"

"November," Greer said. "You believe in astrology?"

Wyatt had never really thought about that; did now, real fast. "No," he said.

"Me neither," said Greer. "It's complete bullshit. For example, suppose we were living on another planet."

"Then, um, uh . . ."

"The angles would be different, of course," Greer said.

"And?"

"So the stars wouldn't line up the same way. The constellations would be gone. No Gemini, no Aquarius, no Taurus the bull. No constellations, no astrology."

A silence fell in the bowling alley. "Are you in college?" Wyatt said.

"Nope," said Greer. "I'm in the bowling alley business."

"How's that working out?"

What was this? A second not completely unfunny remark? Yes, because Greer laughed again. Wyatt had gone out for a month or two with a girl in the freshman class last year, and been to a few drunken parties in houses when the parents were gone, parties where there'd been some pairing off to various bedrooms, but other than that he had little experience with girls, so . . . so actually this was going pretty well.

Greer stopped laughing, very sudden. "It's working out like shit," she said.

"Oh, um."

Greer's eyes narrowed and she looked like she was about to, say something negative, but then the phone rang. She picked it up. "Torrance Bowl," she said. Wyatt heard a man on the other end. He sounded irritated. The brightness went out of Greer's eyes. She took a key off the wall and handed it to Wyatt, not really looking at him. He went outside, let himself into the cage, turned the dial up to fast, and crushed baseballs for half an hour.

Back inside, Greer was still behind the counter, punching numbers on a calculator. "Time's up already?" she said, not taking her eyes off the little screen. "You can hit some more if you like. How much does the electricity cost? A few cents?"

"There's wear and tear on the machine," Wyatt said, a concept that came directly from one of Rusty's diatribes. For the first time, it occurred to Wyatt that maybe Rusty had had a role in shaping him; a very unpleasant thought.

Greer's fingers went still; she looked up. "Yeah," she said. "You an accountant in training?"

"No." But—supposing he didn't make it to the big leagues, an idea he knew to be a fantasy yet still hadn't abandoned completely—he'd need a job someday and he wasn't bad with numbers.

"What are you?"

"What am I?"

"Like, in school, or what?"

"Yeah, in school."

"Where?"

"Here."

"Bridger?"

"Yeah."

"Go, Bears. Rah rah."

"You went there?"

"My whole life."

"Huh?"

"Just feels that way," Greer said. She gave him a long look. "Or are you the kind who fits in?" Wyatt didn't answer; but yes, he was. Wasn't he? "Yeah," she said. "I believe you are. When's the first practice?"

Wyatt took a deep breath.

"For baseball, I mean. You're on the team, right? Got to be—I saw you hit. Hardest thing in sports, according to Ted Williams—hitting a baseball."

"How'd you know that?"

"Know what?"

"Ted Williams, all of it."

"My dad was a huge fan. He could spout off stats ad nauseam."

"Sorry," said Wyatt.

"For what? He's not dead, if that's what you're thinking."

"Oh, good."

"Yeah, great."

"So he just stopped being a fan?"

"Got involved in other things," Greer said. "Other games, let's say."

"Football?"

She gave him another look. "Know what I like about you?" she said. "Besides your batting stroke?"

Wyatt felt himself reddening, hoped it didn't show; in fact, she'd somehow sent a charge through his whole body.

"Your sense of humor," Greer said. "That's what I like— no one's got a sense of humor in this town."

"I'm actually not on the team," Wyatt said.

"That one I don't get."

"It's not a joke."

Greer put a finger to her chin: a nice-looking chin with a tiny cleft. "Not on the team but you can hit, so let me guess. I got it—booted off for getting caught with a six-pack."

"No."

"A crack pipe."

"C'mon."

"You're right. No doper, obviously. You don't have that look in your eye."

"What look?"

"Absent," Greer said. "So that brings us down to something weird, like you were caught with the coach's wife."

"It's nothing like that," Wyatt said. "I just moved here and they've got rules about transfer students."

"Of course they do. They've got rules for everything, rules that only they can break."

Wyatt shrugged.

"Must be frustrating," Greer said.

"It's all right."

"Where were you living before?"

"East Canton."

"A dump worse than this one."

"It's not so bad."

"Your dad got transferred or something?"

"Huh?"

"Or your mom? To a new job—your reason for moving in the middle of the year."

"No," Wyatt said. "I came myself."

"On the lam?"

"You got it."

Greer laughed. "Your way of saying no more questions, I bet." She glanced at the clock. "How about a cup of coffee, a Coke, something?"

"Um, okay."

There were Cokes in the drink machine behind her, but Greer didn't open it. Instead she grabbed her leather jacket from under the counter and said, "Let's go in your car."

"Yeah?" He glanced around, saw no one else to take care of the bowling alley. By that time, Greer was practically at the door. He followed her. She held the door for him, then locked it. "It's okay to close early?"

"Why not?" said Greer.

"What if someone wants to bowl?"

"They can scratch that itch elsewhere."

Wyatt and Greer walked to the Mustang. A gust of wind rose and blew her against him.

"Sorry," he said.

"For what?"

They got in, Wyatt hurriedly gathering books and papers off her seat and tossing them in back.

"First time in a Mustang, believe it or not," Greer said.

Wyatt turned the key. "This one's real old," he said. He started backing out of the space, glanced at her. "Seat belt."

Greer grinned. "That's what my grandmother always says."

"She's right," Wyatt said, at the very moment they came to a big icy patch in the middle of the empty lot. Without thinking—but even with thought he might have done it anyway—Wyatt spun the wheel hard and goosed the pedal. The Mustang spun around once in a tight doughnut, Greer suddenly screaming and gripping his right forearm so hard it hurt, at the same time making it not so easy to bring the car out of the spin. But he did, straightening perfectly and driving out of the lot at five miles per hour, using the turn signal and looking both ways. Greer's grip loosened on his arm, but she didn't let go completely, not for ten or fifteen seconds, although it felt much longer than that.

High Sierra Coffee was a shadowy little coffee shop off the main drag in Silver City with worn wood floors, shelves full of books, a few people hunched over laptops. Wyatt and Greer sat at a small round table in the back corner, Coke for him, espresso for her. He'd never actually seen an espresso before, must have been staring at it a bit too long, because she said, "Want a taste?"

"One taste and it'd be gone."

Greer smiled, sat back in her chair; teeth very white, skin very smooth, eye makeup a little smeared. "I'd like to own a place like this someday."

"Yeah?"

"That's my dream, anyway. One of my dreams."

"How much would it cost?" Wyatt said. "The rent, equipment, all that?"

"Who knows?" Greer said. "Too much."

"There'd probably be insurance, too."

Her face darkened. "I've had enough of goddamn insurance."

"What do you mean?"

Greer was silent for a few moments. Clouds must have shifted, because a sudden golden shaft shone through a skylight, illuminating their table and everything on it—Coke slowly fizzing, steam rising from the little espresso cup, Greer's right hand, a strong, finely shaped hand, the nails all chewed down to the quick. "It's a long story," she said.

"There's time," said Wyatt. "Unless you have to get back to work."

She took a sip of espresso. Her lips weren't very full but were, like her hands, finely shaped. "That's the point," she said. "I don't. We're in receivership, so who gives a shit?"

*Receivership:* a word Wyatt was all too familiar with, from the unfolding of the Baker Brothers bankruptcy.

"You own the bowling alley?" he said.

"The bank owns it now," Greer said. "Some bank in San Francisco. But before that my father owned it. Plus a whole big amusement center across town."

"That's in receivership, too?"

Greer shook her head. "Turned to ashes instead."

"I don't understand."

She finished what was left of the espresso, put the cup down, rattling the saucer. "Last year, when things started to go bad—the economy, all that—the amusement center burned to the ground. My dad was found guilty of arson in a court of law—so it must be true, right?" Her eyes welled up, very briefly, but she didn't cry. "My father, who built the amusement center from scratch, I'm talking about he even did the framing, the Sheetrock, the painting—guilty of burning it all down for the insurance money." Her voice had risen; one or two people glanced over.

Wyatt, his voice very low, said, "You don't think he did it?"

"Who cares what I think? The fact is he's stuck in Sweetwater for five years, minimum."

"Sweetwater?"

"The prison across the river," Greer said. "Number one employer in the county. Haven't you seen it?"

WYATT WASN'T PREPARED for things happening fast, but somehow when Saturday rolled around he had a date with Greer. The plan was to pick her up at her place, go to lunch, and then drive around while she showed him the sights of Silver City. Aunt Hildy always did her shopping on Saturday morning, and Dub had practice. Wyatt slept in, woke to a quiet house. He found himself looking forward to the day ahead for the first time in a long time; and he wasn't thinking about baseball at all.

Greer lived in an old apartment building a few blocks north of the main street, meaning away from the river. He sat in the car, waiting outside. It was a four-story building, kind of grimy outside but with fancy little details under the grime, like two Greek temple–type columns framing the front door, and the stone head of some aggressive-looking creature sticking out of the wall above it, fangs bared.

The door opened and Greer came out. She wore the short leather jacket and jeans, wasn't carrying a purse, not even a little one. In his experience, girls always carried a purse when they went out. But no time to think about that. She opened the passenger door and slid inside.

"Hey, cowboy," she said.

"Hi," said Wyatt. Her smell reached him, a really nice smell, flowers and something else. He glanced over, caught the gleam of her eyebrow ring and a quick smile.

"Cut yourself shaving?" she said, touching the tip of her chin.

Wyatt touched his chin, checked his fingertip. Yes, a little red smear; he wiped it off on his jeans.

"If I was a vampire you'd be in trouble," Greer said.

"I'm not worried," Wyatt said. "I had garlic for breakfast."

Greer laughed. "Vroom vroom," she said. "Let's see what this baby can do."

For some reason, Wyatt had a mature thought at that moment: *She's already seen what this baby can do, on that icy patch in the Torrance Bowl parking lot.* He stepped lightly on the gas and drove sedately down the street. Greer's eyes were on him: he could feel them.

"Is that your own place?" Wyatt said, nodding back toward the apartment building.

"Yeah. I've got a one-bedroom."

"Cool," Wyatt said. Having your own place: what would that be like? "So you don't, uh, live with your mother, or anything?"

"Correctamundo," Greer said. "Hang a right at the top of the hill."

Wyatt hung a right, followed a tree-lined street overlooking the river. The houses, big, old, nice-looking, but a little run-down, were spaced far apart.

"Pretty much the oldest surviving part of town," Greer said. "Dates from back when there was still silver in the mine. The mining directors lived here, plus doctors, lawyers, that kind of thing." She pointed. "My mother grew up in that one."

Wyatt pulled over. The house was tall, with balconies, a screened-in porch, and a conical tower at one end.

"I think it was white back then," Greer said.

Now it was yellow with brown trim, the paint peeling here and there; and a blue tarp covered one section of the roof. "Who lives in it now?" Wyatt said.

"No idea."

Curtains parted on an upper floor and someone looked out. Wyatt eased off the brake, let the car roll forward. "So, uh, where's your mom living now?"

"An even sweller place," Greer said. "Sweller than this was in its heyday."

"Yeah? Are we going to see it?"

"Depends on whether you're planning a trip to Seattle."

"Your mom lives in Seattle?"

"Check."

"Your parents are divorced?"

"You do a dynamite Q and A, you know that?"

"Sorry."

"Nothing to be sorry for." She patted his knee, sending a small electric charge up his leg. "What would happen to human conversation if we didn't have Q and A? Long silences, baby, end of story."

Way over his head. Wyatt realized that he was out of his league. Greer was smarter and older, and had more of something else he couldn't even label. But the next moment, right after all that was hitting home, some part of him, possibly the competitive part, rose up, refusing to simply fold. Driving down this fading street where local silver barons had once lived, he forced his mind to wrestle with what Greer had just said, to really understand.

"I don't know," he said.

"You don't know what?" said Greer. "Hang another right."

"Well," said Wyatt, turning onto a long street that slanted down, away from the river, "there's communication in silences, too."

"Hey," she said. And then more quietly. "Point taken."

And not just good communication, either. Entering his silent home—home back up in East Canton—and sensing Rusty's mood: that was communication, too. "Good and bad," he said.

"Communication?"

"Yeah."

"You're so right," Greer said. "Take my stepfather."

"So your parents *are* divorced." For some reason, he wanted to nail that down.

"Hard to come by a stepfather otherwise, unless you know something I don't."

That stung a bit. Greer's words often seemed to do that, Wyatt thought, but he didn't mind. In fact, he found himself laughing.

"Gonna let me in on the joke?" she said.

"No joke."

"Then what's funny?"

He glanced at her. She was gazing at him; no eye makeup today—she looked younger, closer to his own age. *You* was the answer, *you're funny, and lots more than that,* but he kept the answer inside, instead saying, "What about your stepfather?"

"He's the biggest asshole in the world," Greer said, "but the worst—"

A gray squirrel darted into the road, just a few yards in front of them, moving right to left. Wyatt swerved to the right, away from oncoming traffic, if there'd been any, and hit the brakes, steering behind the squirrel. But at the last instant, the squirrel paused and then did the dumbest thing possible, darting back the way it had come. Next came a feeling like passing over the tiniest speed bump, a soft one.

"Christ," Wyatt said, looking back in the rearview mirror. The squirrel—what was left of it—wasn't quite lying still. He stopped the car and got out. "Christ." The squirrel's head was motionless and so was its body and three legs. But the fourth leg was twitching—more than that, really, the tiny paw making little scrabbling movements on the pavement, as though trying to get the rest of the animal up and on its way. Wyatt walked over, looked down. The squirrel's eyes were open, at least the one facing up, but was the squirrel seeing him, taking him in? Wyatt couldn't tell. All he could tell for sure was that the squirrel's guts were all over the place and that one leg—rear, left side—was trying to get the animal up and on its way.

Which wasn't going to happen. The squirrel was beyond hope, finished, the only question being when. *Misery:* the word for describing the squirrel's condition at that moment, and what did you do for creatures in misery? You put them out of it. Wyatt's first thought was to get back in the car, turn around, run over the squirrel again. But he couldn't do that: overkill, right? He now completely understood the meaning of that word; and not just overkill, but detached and cold-blooded—their meanings were clear, too. That left what? Stomping on the squirrel? To stomp on a living thing, and not in anger: he couldn't do that, either.

Wyatt went back to the car, hearing the scritch-scratch of that one paw on the pavement the whole way. Greer sat in the passenger seat, her head turning to follow his movements. Wyatt opened the trunk, found an old, soiled towel used for wiping off his bat during drizzly games, and also took out the bat itself.

He returned to the squirrel, lying in a small but growing red pool. That one paw was still trying to do things, more feebly now. And that soft brown eye: on him for sure. Wyatt bent down, laid the towel over the body, at the same time hearing the car door open. He rose, took a deep breath, raised his bat, and brought it down on the lump under the towel, just as hard as he thought necessary, and no harder.

He felt Greer beside him. She gripped his upper arm, squeezed so hard it hurt, even made him gasp out loud. Nothing moved under the towel. Greer let go, squatted down, carefully rolled up the towel so no part of the body showed, and took it to the ditch that ran beside the road. Greer placed the bundle in the ditch.

She turned and approached Wyatt. He realized she wasn't as tall as he'd thought, a good half foot shorter than him. Without a word or any preliminaries, she took his head in her hands, pulled it down to hers, and kissed him on the mouth, hard at first and then softer. Not the first girl he'd kissed, but this was on another level, so much more knowledgeable. Wyatt felt the power of the person behind the kiss.

He heard a car coming and backed away. The car—a black-and-white cop car—pulled out of a side street and drove up the hill, slowing down and then stopping beside Wyatt and Greer. The window slid down and a cop peered out, a gray-haired cop with baggy eyes and a fleshy pink face.

"Some problem?" he said.

"Uh," said Wyatt.

"Ran over a squirrel," Greer said. The cop's gaze went to her. "Put it in the ditch."

The cop nodded. A moment or two of silence went by. "You Bert Torrance's daughter?"

"Yeah," Greer said, more grunt than verbal reply.

"Recognize you from the lanes." Greer looked him in the eye, said nothing. The cop looked right back. "Drive safe," he said. The window slid back up and he drove off.

Wyatt and Greer stood together by the roadside. "Isn't small-town living grand?" Greer said. "That's enough adventure for one day."

"What do you mean?"

"Take me home."

He looked at her. Her face was flushed, her eyes a little blurry. "You're mad about the squirrel?"

"What would I be mad about? It was an accident."

"But, you know, what I did after."

"What you did after?" Greer said. "That couldn't have been better, you blockhead." She laughed. "So damn good it got me hot."

Wyatt's mouth went dry; his knees got weak. He found those weren't mere figures of speech.

Greer's one-bedroom apartment was on the top floor of the building with the strange stone head over the door. Wyatt didn't get to see much of the living room—just barely taking in some musical instruments—electric guitar, acoustic guitar, mandolin—before Greer took him by the belt buckle and drew him into the bedroom.

"First time?" she said, now on the bed.

"Well, I wouldn't exactly say—"

"No problem," Greer said, working on that buckle. "Just relax."

"Don't think I can."

She laughed.

Some time later, Wyatt felt more relaxed than he ever had in his life, and not just relaxed but something far greater than that, like the world was all right after all, and so was his place in it.

"So," Greer said. They lay side by side, her head on his shoulder, in a slightly awkward position, in fact, even hurting

a bit, but Wyatt felt no hurry to make any changes whatsoever. "Where were we when we were interrupted?"

"Your stepfather," Wyatt said.

"Right," said Greer. "The biggest asshole in the world."

"Not so sure about that."

"There's competition?"

"Yeah." And Wyatt told her about Rusty, and a story or
two about his home life back in East Canton, and how he'd
come to Silver City.

"Wow," Greer said. "We got parallels here, sports fans.
Where's your real father?"

"That's the most amazing part," Wyatt said.

# 9

THE NEXT DAY, Sunday, rain slanting by in sheets outside the window, Wyatt back at Greer's, the two of them in her bed.

"Normally I hate the rain," Greer said. "But today I can't think straight."

"How come?"

"How come? If you don't know, who does?"

"What do you mean?"

"I mean it's your fault, you blockhead. You're making me spacey."

Then came a period of relative quiet, interrupted by the ring of Wyatt's cell phone. He reached down to the floor, groped the phone out of the pocket of his jeans, checked the number on the screen: his mom. "Have to take this," he said.

"Why?" said Greer.

He held his finger over his lips, pressed the answer button. "Hi, Mom."

"Hi, Wyatt. How are you doing?"

"Great. Uh, fine. I'm all right."

"Well, good. You sound happy."

"Yeah, you know."

Greer got a mischievous look on her face and reached for him under the covers. Wyatt left the bed, stood by the window.

"Where are you?" his mom said.

"In Silver City, Mom—you know that."

"I meant now—are you at ho—at Dub's aunt's?"

"On my way."

"In the car?"

"No." Wyatt didn't like lying to his mom, or to anyone, really. "At a friend's."

"So you're making friends?"

"Uh-huh." Wyatt felt Greer's eyes on his back. He turned. She was sitting up in bed, making no attempt to hold up the sheets. Her finger made a quick pattern in the air: QA? He almost laughed.

"That's great, Wyatt. And school?"

"Fine, Mom, everything's fine. How's Cammy?"

"She misses you."

"I miss her, too." Greer's face changed; he saw a new expression on it, new to him, at least—eyes narrowed, two vertical grooves on her forehead, just above the nose. She came close to looking ugly, surely impossible for such a beautiful girl. Had he mentioned Cammy to her? No. Wyatt held his hand down, palm to the floor, at about Cammy's height level. Greer's face returned to normal. "And how are you doing, Mom?"

"No complaints, except for . . ." She went silent for a moment or two, maybe choked up. Then she cleared her throat and went on. "Except for you being away, and all. How are you doing for money, by the way?"

"Fine."

"You sure? I could send you a money order."

"Don't need it, Mom. I can always get a job."

"Schoolwork comes first."

"I know."

"But, uh, speaking of jobs—there may be some news about that."

"Oh yeah?"

"Too early to say, so maybe I shouldn't have brought it up at all."

"Come on, Mom."

His mother took a deep breath; such a close-up sound—she might have been right there in the room. Wyatt moved nearer to the window. Outside, it was raining even harder, water spewing out of the drainpipes on the houses across the street. "Promise to keep it under your hat," his mom said, "but Rusty may have a job lined up."

"Yeah?" That had to be good. "What kind of job?"

"A good-paying job. Not like at the foundry, and no benefits, but good-paying for times likes these. Rusty'll be—if he gets it—driving a truck for Secondary Metals Services."

"What's that?"

"They're out of Fort Collins, but the route's all over the place."

Wyatt didn't get it. Fort Collins was three or four

hundred miles from East Canton. "You're—we're moving to Colorado?"

"Oh, no, certainly not now. I'd have a hard time getting a better job than what I've got now, and this is the worst possible time to sell the house. For now—this is if it all comes through—Rusty will be back home every second weekend, maybe a bit more often after they see him settling in. So, uh . . ."

Silence. The implication was pretty obvious: if Rusty got the job, he'd be pretty much moving out for the next while, meaning there'd be no reason for Wyatt not to move right back in. "Sounds good, Mom. When will you know?"

"Any day. I'll call soon as I know."

Another silence.

"I'll let you go."

"Okay, Mom. Bye."

"Love you."

"Love you, too. Say hi to Cammy."

"You can say hi yourself. She's right here."

There was a little rustling sound, followed by Cammy. "Hi," she said.

"Hi."

"Wyatt?"

"Yeah?"

"Is that you?"

"Of course it's me. Who does it sound like?"

"It's raining."

"Here, too."

"When are you coming home?"

"Not sure. I—"

His mom came on. "Okay, Wyatt, take care."

"Bye."

Wyatt clicked off, turned to Greer, still sitting up. She didn't have a single tattoo on her body. That surprised him, surprised him in a good way, although he couldn't have explained why. There was just the eyebrow ring; maybe the absence of tattoos made the eyebrow ring's statement more special, or powerful, or something: he couldn't take it any further, and as for what the statement was, he didn't know that, either.

"When will your mom know what?" Greer said. "If you don't mind me being nosy."

"Rusty's trying to line up a job."

She thought about that, nodded. "Have you got any pictures of Cammy or your mom?"

He sat beside her on the bed, ran through some pictures on the phone.

"Who's that?"

"Dub."

"And that?"

"Just this girl I used to know."

"She's pretty. What's her name?"

"Didn't really know her that well. She was in my English class."

"You like the apple-cheeked blond type? That's not me."

"I like your type. Here's Cammy."

"She's adorable."

"And here's my mom."

Wyatt's mom hated having her picture taken. This one showed her all dressed for work, makeup on, having a last sip of coffee by the stove and trying to wave Wyatt off at the same time. Greer gave the photo a careful look. "She has beautiful eyes. They're just like yours."

"Yeah?"

"But the rest of your face comes from somewhere else." Wyatt remembered Coach Bouchard's old photo: there was no doubt about that. Greer handed back the phone. "Enough chitchat—come here."

Dub and Aunt Hildy were in the middle of dinner when Wyatt got back. Spaghetti with meatballs and garlic bread, probably Wyatt's favorite meal, and a place was set for him. They looked up. Something was wrong: Wyatt knew Dub very well, had been reading that face practically all his life.

"Hi, sorry I'm late."

"No problem," Aunt Hildy said. "Just a call would be nice."

"Sorry."

"I can heat this up if you want."

"It's fine like this." And it was. Wyatt was starving. He realized he hadn't eaten a thing all day, maybe a first. "How was practice?" he said, putting down his fork at last just out of decency.

"Not bad," Dub said. "It's such a piss-off."

"Dub," said Aunt Hildy.

"But it is, Aunt Hildy. They—we've got nobody close to

Wyatt in the outfield. He'd be starting in center and leading off, maybe even batting third."

"I didn't mean that," Aunt Hildy said. "I meant your language."

"Language?"

"Piss-off," said Aunt Hildy. "We're at supper."

"Oh."

All of a sudden, Wyatt started laughing, couldn't stop. He covered his face with his napkin.

"What so funny?" Dub said.

"Drink some water," said Aunt Hildy.

Wyatt drank some water, pulled himself together. "Thanks for dinner, Aunt Hildy. It was great."

"You're more than welcome. Seconds?"

"Yeah. Please."

"You boys have homework tonight?"

"Not much."

"Hardly any."

"Meaning plenty," said Aunt Hildy. "One of you go up and get started, the other helps me wash up first."

Wyatt and Dub flipped a coin. Dub won and went upstairs. Wyatt got a dish towel and stood by the sink. Aunt Hildy believed the dishwasher used too much water, tried not to use it. She had a two-part sink, filled one half with warm, sudsy water, the other with plain, washed and rinsed the dishes, then handed them to Wyatt, in charge of drying and stacking in the cupboard. Aunt Hildy's hands were small, square, efficient; Wyatt spotted a few faint liver spots on them.

"How's everything going?" Aunt Hildy said, eyes on her work.

"Good."

"School all right?"

"Yeah."

"Holding up without baseball?"

"Yeah."

"Dub told the coach all about you."

"I know."

"Next spring'll be around before you know it."

For a moment, opening the silverware drawer—Aunt Hildy's knives and forks so much heavier than those at home—Wyatt felt a sharp sudden pang, like a real pain in his chest, from missing baseball. Then his mind moved on to Greer, and the pain was gone.

"Meeting new people?" Aunt Hildy said.

"Yeah."

"I wanted to talk to you about that." She turned to Wyatt, handed him the last dish. "Not my business, goes without saying, but you're new in town, couldn't possibly have learned the lay of the—how things are yet. Know what I'm talking about?"

"Not really." Aunt Hildy hadn't let go of the dish, meaning they each had a hand on it.

"I understand you're seeing Greer Torrance."

Wyatt felt himself turning red. He hadn't told Dub, hadn't told anyone. It was all so new. "How do you know that?"

"I just do." Aunt Hildy let go of the plate. Wyatt lost his grip on it, snatched it out of the air with his other hand just before it would have hit the floor. He turned, put the dish in the cupboard.

"Do you know her?" he said, his back to Aunt Hildy.

"Not face-to-face," she said. "This is a small town, Wyatt—maybe not as small as East Canton, but small enough so nothing stays secret for long. I just feel your mom wouldn't be too comfortable with you and someone like Greer Torrance."

Wyatt turned. Sometimes he got stubborn, and when he did his chin tilted up, pretty much on its own. It was doing it now. "I don't see anything wrong with her."

"No, of course not. She's very attractive—maybe a bit too old for you, what with girls being more mature to begin with, no offense—but there's no way you'd be aware of her reputation."

Wyatt's chin tilted up a bit more. "Which is?"

"For one thing, I'm sure you don't know that her father's an arsonist. A firefighter of my acquaintance got burned that night."

"Greer told me."

"Told you about the firefighter?"

"Not that part, but about her father, yes."

"And what about her role in it?"

Wyatt felt himself turning redder. "What role?"

"It was pretty clear that she was involved, too—they couldn't prove it, is all."

Wyatt didn't believe that. He just stood there, shaking his head, not trusting himself to stay calm if he replied. He was starting not to like Aunt Hildy.

"And before that, she was into drugs—very lucky she

didn't get thrown in jail herself."

Into drugs—that could mean a lot of things. What did it mean to someone like Aunt Hildy, a middle-aged, small-town woman?

"I'm talking about serious drugs, like heroin," Aunt Hildy said. "The police knew."

Serious drugs? He'd seen no sign of that—her apartment was tidy, her skin unmarred, no mention of drugs, not even once, in any context. A thought came to him. "Do you have friends in the police?"

Aunt Hildy nodded. "A coworker is married to one of the sergeants."

"This sergeant," Wyatt said, "a beefy guy with a pink kind of face?"

She nodded again.

"He ran my plate?"

"It's a small town, Wyatt, but with rough edges. I wouldn't want anything to happen to you."

He gave her a long look, not friendly. She blinked a couple of times. "I'm going for a walk," Wyatt said.

The rain had stopped but the wind still blew, very cold. Scraps of cloud raced fast across the moon. Wyatt found shelter behind a tree, called Greer, got put straight into voice mail. He wondered about driving over to her place. Not cool. But he still hadn't rejected the idea when his phone rang.

"Hello?" he said.

Not Greer, but a man. "Hi, there," said the man. "This Wyatt?"

"Yeah—who's this?"

"Sonny."

"Sonny?"

"Sonny Racine," the man said. "Your father, to one way of thinking."

# 10

WYATT HAD NO IDEA what to say. He stood in the shelter of the tree, halfway down the block from Aunt Hildy's house, the cell phone pressed to his ear.

"But that's not my way of thinking," came the voice from the other end, a fairly deep, pleasant-sounding voice. "Father's got to mean a lot more than getting a girl pregnant." Silence. "Agree or disagree?"

Wyatt stood there, phone pressed to his ear. The wind curled around the tree, rippled the hems of his pants.

"Hear me all right?"

"Yeah."

"Don't mean to ask questions I've got no right to. Got no rights at all, where you're concerned. No illusions on that score." A long pause. "The right to ask questions is all yours."

Wyatt didn't speak.

"Or not, up to you. I can just hang up, that's your preference."

Wyatt cleared his throat, suddenly thick feeling. "Where are you?"

"Right now? The pay phone in B pod, why?"

"In prison?"

"That's right. Sweetwater—thought you knew."

"I wasn't sure. How—" Wyatt stopped himself. How had his fa—this man, better stick to that—how had this man found him, gotten his number? Not hard to connect the dots. Dot one, Greer. Dot two, Bert Torrance, doing five years for arson behind the same walls. So obvious, and so infuriating, like he was being manipulated.

"You were about to say something?"

"No," Wyatt said.

"It, uh, it's good to hear your voice."

Wyatt remained silent.

"And it's, uh, good to know you're in the neighborhood. No mystery there—Bert Torrance is what you might call a casual acquaintance of mine in here, as you probably figured out already, sounding like a smart young man the way you do."

"Yeah," Wyatt said. Did that give the idea he considered himself smart? "About the Bert Torrance part," he added.

His—the man laughed. He had a soft little laugh that sounded like it came more from the front of his mouth than from the throat, chest, or belly. "Smarter than the old man, that's for sure."

Wyatt didn't like that, not at all. "You're not my old man," he said.

"Sorry I—"

"And all that about getting a girl pregnant—were you talking about my mother?"

"My apologies. So sorry. So sorry twice. Meant the smart thing as a compliment, nothing more. I see my mistake now. As for your mother, long time out of touch with her, but I had the greatest respect, way back when. And thanks for standing up for her. Lesson learned. I can tell she raised a fine young man, not easy for a single mom. Or even if she's not single— been no communication since . . . since the events."

Wyatt was silent, sharing no details of his mom's life. Then it hit him that this man might already know—he'd told Greer about Rusty, Cammy, lots of other details. Had Greer passed on all that, too, to her father? Prisons had high walls to keep bad people separate from good, but now Wyatt realized voices went back and forth, no problem, as though the walls were sieves.

"But you don't have to accept apologies in this life. May even be the wrong thing to do sometimes."

"Like when?" Wyatt said.

Then came that soft little laugh again. "I—" The man stopped himself. Wyatt heard voices in the background, maybe speaking Spanish. "Good question. I'll have to get back to you on that. Unless you don't want me to call, of course. Up to you."

Wyatt said nothing.

"Got to go. Nice talking to you."

More Spanish, louder now.

Click.

Wyatt stood behind the tree, wind blowing, the moon now hidden. He was wearing jeans, sweatshirt, sneakers, should have felt cold but was sweating instead. He tried to sort things out, tried to think, didn't really know where to start. What he really wanted to do was call his mom, tell her what had happened. He overcame that impulse, a weak, unmanly one, kind of pitiful. His mom had her own problems. He tried Greer's number again, again got put straight into voice mail. This time he left a message.

"Give me a call. No matter what time it is." He thought about the impact that might have and toned it down some. "No emergency or anything. Just call."

But she didn't, not that night. Wyatt tossed and turned for hours, finally fell into a sleep full of unpleasant dreams, all forgotten in the morning.

Greer called at lunch period the next day. Wyatt and Dub had different lunch periods. Wyatt was sitting in the cafeteria with some kids from his last class, English, who were talking about *Hamlet*, which they'd just started and which he didn't understand at all.

"Hamlet's a wimp," one kid said. "No guts."

"What?" said another. "Just because some ghost appears and says this and that, he's supposed to start killing people?"

"You're missing the point," said a girl named Anna who sat next to him in class, a blond, apple-cheeked girl whom up to very recently he would have considered beautiful. "It's not even a real ghost."

"Huh?" said the first kid.

"The ghost just represents thoughts in Hamlet's head," Anna said. "He's actually very brave, because he's the only one in the whole play who's concerned with acting morally."

"You're not making sense," said the second kid, and he tossed a Frito in the air and caught it in his mouth.

Anna shook her head. "It's hopeless." She turned to Wyatt. "What do you think?"

That was when his phone rang. He checked the number, excused himself, moved toward the window, clicked on.

"Yeah."

"You're pissed," Greer said.

"Huh?"

"Pissed off at me, annoyed, angry, furious, fit to be tied. I could hear it in the message. Can hear it right now."

"Why would I be pissed off?" He glanced around, saw Anna unwrapping a stick of gum, watching him at the same time. He moved farther away.

"We're going to play that game?" Greer said. "All right—you're pissed off, annoyed, angry, furious, fit to be tied, because on my weekly visit to the old man I mentioned you."

"You did a little more than that."

A long pause. Behind him, Wyatt heard Anna say something about ghosts and Hamlet's father. Then Greer spoke. "Guilty," she said. "Guilty as charged. But my father knows me—he could tell I was excited about something from the look on my face."

"Excited about what?"

"You, you block—you. The rest just came out, an amazing coincidence, no? I couldn't help myself. My mistake, I see that now—those goddamn inmates gossip all the time, worse than a sewing circle." Another pause. "You're so mad."

He didn't answer.

"This is over?" she said. "Over before it's even started?"

*Yeah, I guess it is.* Wyatt came very close to saying that. But he didn't. Why not? Was he too nice a guy? Or—thinking about her bedroom and more of that—not nice enough? He didn't say it was over; also didn't say it wasn't.

"How bad was the talk?" Greer said. "With your—I don't even know what to call him? DNA supplier? I'm sorry if it was real bad."

"I don't want to talk about it."

"Fine," she said. "Let's not talk. Why don't you come over—I'm off till two."

The bell rang. "I've got math," Wyatt said. "Right now."

"It's your best subject. One little cut won't hurt."

"Yeah," Wyatt said. "It would."

"Okay," she said. "No problem."

"Bye."

Wyatt went to math class. The teacher—a real old guy with little scabs on his bald head—surprised them with a pop quiz, first of the term, just one single question. Two trains left two different stations at two different times, traveling at two different rates. Mark the point where they meet.

"Crash, you mean?" said a kid at the back.

Not that hard a problem: Wyatt had solved many similar ones, usually didn't mind the work too much, sometimes came close to enjoyment. But this time his brain refused to grapple with it.

"Pens and pencils down," said the teacher.

Wyatt handed in a blank sheet.

● ● ●

After school, Wyatt walked to the student parking lot with a few other kids, one of whom happened to be Anna from English class.

"Hey, Wyatt," she said, dropping back beside him.

"Hey."

"You're new in town, right?"

"Yeah."

"How do you like it so far?"

He caught Anna's scent on the breeze, fresh and a bit like apples. "Well," he said, turning to look at her, and as he turned he saw Greer across the lot, leaning against the Mustang. "It's, uh . . ." Anna followed his gaze, took in the sight of Greer in that short leather jacket, tight jeans—a smooth crescent of her bare belly showing—and also wearing big sunglasses. Anna's eyes opened a little wider. "Good, um," Wyatt continued. "Good so far."

"Uh-huh," said Anna, taking one more look at Greer and drifting off.

Wyatt approached the car. Greer stuck her sunglasses up on her head. Her eyes were puffy, as though she'd been crying.

"How was math?" she said.

"Could have been better," Wyatt said. "What are you doing here?"

"Thought maybe we could go for a ride," Greer said. "Unless you've got other plans."

"Don't you have work at two?" The dismissal bell at Bridger High rang at 2:27.

"I switched shifts."

"At the bowling alley?"

Greer shook her head. "My other job."

"I didn't know you had another job." He opened the door, started to get in.

"I'm not coming?" Greer said.

He glanced around. "How did you get here?"

"I got a ride."

They gazed at each other over the top of the car. The wind blew a wisp of her hair, curled it around her ear. "Okay," Wyatt said. "Come on."

Greer climbed into the car. Wyatt backed out of his space, turned, drove out of the lot.

"Anyplace special?" he said.

"Up to you."

Wyatt drove aimlessly, ended up on a road by the river, with abandoned warehouses on one side and rusty train tracks on the other.

"You're angry," Greer said. "I can feel it, like it's coming right off your skin."

"What right have I got to be angry? I don't even know you."

"What did you say?"

"You heard me," Wyatt said.

"You don't even know me? After the weekend?"

"That's not what I mean."

"What do you mean? What other kind of knowing is there?"

Wyatt pulled over, parked in a weedy patch by the train tracks. Broken glass lay all over the place. He turned to her.

She was watching carefully, her eyes, eyes that he'd looked into so deeply yesterday, now almost unfamiliar. "There's more to knowing someone than—" Wyatt stopped himself, started over. "I didn't know you had another job, for example."

"And that's important?"

Wyatt shrugged.

"My other job is reading to blind people in this old folks' home for three hours, twice a week. It pays fifteen dollars an hour on account of some long-ago grant. There. Enough information?"

Now she was angry, too, and yes, he could feel it coming off her skin. That put Wyatt off balance, and he blurted the next thing that came to mind. "What about the heroin?"

Her head snapped back as though he'd hit her. "Fuck you," she said. "You know that? Fuck you. What are you, some kind of police informer?"

"Of course not, I—"

"That's a complete bullshit lie." Her voice rose fast, practically a shriek by the time she got to *lie*. She pounded her fists in her lap.

"All right, all right, take it easy. I wasn't accusing you of anything, just asking the—"

"Who have you been talking to?"

"No one, really—"

"Kids at school? That blond bitch in the parking lot?"

"I hardly know her, and—"

"Just like you hardly know me, so you must be fucking her, too."

"For God's sake, you're talking crazy. Calm down." He reached toward her, meaning to touch her arm.

"Don't touch me." Greer turned, very quick, ripped open the door, and started running away, up a strip of cracked pavement that led to the warehouses.

"Christ," Wyatt said. He watched her run. She was fast. In a few moments she'd disappeared beyond the warehouses. Wyatt could see a street on the other side, light traffic going by. He drove around the block, went slowly down that street. No sign of Greer. On the next block, a bus was just pulling away from a stop. He followed it for a while. Greer didn't get off. Back in town, the bus ran a light that was just turning red, and Wyatt, seeing a cop on the corner, stopped and waited. By the time the light changed, he'd lost sight of the bus. He called Greer's cell, got put straight to voice mail. Then he went home—that is, to Aunt Hildy's—and dug out his homework. He finished all his assignments, checked his work twice, making sure there wasn't a single mistake.

# 11

WYATT HAD JUST READ Act One of *Hamlet* for the third time—a real ghost? or a voice in Hamlet's head, as Anna was saying?—when his mom called.

"Wyatt? How are you doing?"

"Fine."

"Yeah? You're sure?"

"I'm sure."

"Uh, good. That's nice. I'm calling with some news—Rusty got that job. Remember I was telling you? Driving a truck for—"

"I remember."

"Not the greatest job, but in this economy it's nothing to shake a stick at. Means he'll be away a lot—did I mention that? Only every second weekend here at home, at least to start. Company puts him up in motels on the on-weekends, and he'll be sleeping in the cab most other times, till we get some savings going again. Next Monday's his first day, meaning he'll be gone for two weeks after that." She paused, maybe waiting for him to say something.

"Sounds good," Wyatt said, the only comment that came to mind.

"Yeah, well, it'll be tough on him, of course, and on . . . but I was thinking this might be a good time for you to, uh, come on home."

That made sense. Wyatt knew it right away.

"Up to you, Wyatt. But since there's no baseball in either place, why not?"

"Yeah, Mom, I think you're right."

"Oh, wonderful. I was really hoping you'd say that. And Cammy will be so happy—she misses you something terrible."

"Don't tell her right away."

"Oh? Why not?"

"Just want to think about it for a day or so. I wouldn't be coming back till Monday anyway." Eliminating the slightest chance of seeing Rusty, even just coming and going at the front door.

"All right," his mom said. "Think it over, for sure. But doesn't it make sense?"

"Yes."

"Great. Be seeing you, then. Drive safe."

Aunt Hildy got delayed at work. Dub came home with pizza. Wyatt was at the kitchen table, *Hamlet* open in front of him. If the ghost was just in Hamlet's mind, how come these other guys, like Horatio and Marcellus, saw it? On the other hand, the ghost didn't talk to them, talked only to Hamlet, so maybe Anna was right. The ghost went on and on, kind of understandable phrase by phrase—except for impossible words here and there, some sort of explained in the margins—but not at all understandable in its entirety. Whatever was on the ghost's mind got Hamlet upset, although for some reason he didn't tell Horatio and Marcellus anything about it. Weren't they Hamlet's friends, Horatio especially? There was no Shakespeare in sophomore English at East Canton High—a good reason to go back, right there. That was kind of a joke: he wanted to tell it to Greer.

Dub slid the pizza box across the table. "How was practice?" Wyatt said.

"We suck."

"Can't be that bad."

"We scrimmaged Southern High—sixteen–zip before they stopped it. Can't hit, can't pitch, can't field, can't do shit. Nobody's heard of the cutoff man."

"Bad days happen."

"Bad as this? Guess who had to pitch the ninth."

"You?"

Dub nodded.

"That's bad. Did you get anybody out?"

"Hell no." Dub tore a slice of pizza from the box, downed it in two bites, a string of melted cheese hanging off his chin. "This all sucks."

"What does?"

"Everything—coming here, you not playing, Coach Bouchard getting shafted."

Wyatt shrugged.

"Come on—you don't miss baseball?" Dub said.

"Yeah, I miss it."

They ate more pizza, got down to the last slice, flipped a coin for it.

"Tails," Wyatt said.

Heads. Dub finished the pizza. He was still chewing when he suddenly looked up at Wyatt and said, "So tell me about this babe."

"Babe?"

"That's what everyone says."

"Who's everyone?"

"People," Dub said. "Is it supposed to be a secret or something? How come you didn't tell me?"

"It just happened. And what was I supposed to say?"

"What were you supposed to say?" Dub said. "Whether you were getting any, of course. What else?"

A good reason for secrecy, right there. Dub was his best friend, didn't mean any harm, but Wyatt got angry anyway, so angry he was a bit taken aback himself. He pushed away from the table, knocking the pizza box to the floor. "It's nobody's goddamn business."

"Hey. Calm down."

"Don't tell me to calm down. I am calmed down."

Dub laughed.

"I'm not joking," Wyatt said.

Dub held up his big hand—his left, catching, hand, two fingers taped. "Ease off, Wyatt. Just trying to look out for you, is all."

"I don't need looking out for. And wipe your goddamn chin."

"Huh?" Dub wiped his chin, glanced at the cheese on the back of his hand, smeared it on his pants, then glared at Wyatt. Now he was angry, too. Was the cheese responsible in some way? "Not so sure about that," Dub said, "the not-needing-looking-after part."

"Oh? How come?" Wyatt's chin was up. He felt the kind of thing that was coming, even if he couldn't have said exactly what.

"'Cause maybe you've gotten in over your head. This girl has a reputation, according to Aunt Hildy. No way you could have known, so new here."

"What reputation?"

"Don't make me spell it out."

"Spell it out."

Wyatt's chin came up a little more. Dub was red in the face. They'd somehow closed in on each other, even though the table was still between them. Getting into a fistfight with Dub? Something that had never happened, had never come close to happening, in all the years they'd been friends. Was it about to happen now? Dub would kick the shit out of him, no doubt about that. Wyatt got ready.

Dub took a deep breath, backed away. "Naw," he said. "Gossip sucks. You do what you gotta do." He turned, picked up his books, went upstairs.

Wyatt put the pizza box in the trash, sponged off the table, and then went down the first-floor hall to his bedroom at the end. His cell phone rang. He checked the number: Greer. Wyatt didn't answer. He was going home.

A few hours later, as he was falling asleep, he had a crazy

thought: What would have happened if, after the talk with his father's ghost, Hamlet had just said fuck it and left town, starting life somewhere else and ending the play in the middle of Act One. He wondered what Anna would think of an idea like that.

Wyatt was fast asleep when a distant tap-tap reached down into his consciousness. Tap. Tap. He rolled over, opened his eyes. Tap. Tap. The sound was coming from his window, a sound a lot like the tapping of a sharp fingernail. He got up, went to the window, drew the curtains apart a few inches.

Wyatt saw a face outside the window—a pale oval that seemed to hover in the night, unconnected to a body. The sight scared him for a moment; then his eyes adjusted and features took shape on the oval face—Greer's features. She wore dark clothes, merging with the night. He opened the window. They spoke in quick, urgent whispers.

"What are you doing here?"

"Seeing you."

"Why now? What's wrong with you?"

"You're not taking my calls. That's what's wrong with me."

"I'll call you tomorrow."

"Don't be silly—I'm coming in."

"That's not a good—"

But Greer already had a leg through the opening, and a second or two later she was in the room. It was a night like the last, clouds racing across the moon, allowing just enough flickering light in the room to pick out the bright things: the eyebrow ring, Greer's teeth, her eyes.

"What the hell's going on?" Wyatt said, still whispering.

She looked him up and down. "Always sleep in your boxers?"

"Shh."

She lowered her voice, although not much. "You must be freezing your ass off. I am." She turned and closed the window very quietly.

"You can't stay here."

She faced him. "That's the last thing I need, present company excluded. A few hours will be fine."

"I don't want you here."

"No?" she said. She put her arm around his neck, pulled him close, kissed his mouth. Her free hand slid down the front of his shorts. "You're a liar," she said, her lips now right at his ear.

Wyatt awoke with Greer in his arms. The wind had died down, and steady moonlight came through the gap in the curtains, illuminating her sleeping face. She looked younger asleep, peaceful and beautiful. He was all mixed up inside. His mind kept doing a lot of on-one-hand, on-the-other-hand stuff. A toilet flushed upstairs and then footsteps moved on the floor of the hall above, light footsteps, Aunt Hildy's. A bedspring creaked. Silence. Wyatt pulled Greer a little closer.

She mumbled something that sounded like "Five more minutes."

"You're awake?"

"No."

They were so close they hardly had to make any sound at all to communicate, almost like telepathy.

"Then how come you're talking?" he said.

"Because I love you." Her eyes fluttered open. "Oops. Way too soon for that kind of revelation." She met his gaze. "Promise you didn't hear."

"I heard."

"And?"

And what? Was he supposed to say he loved her, too? How did you know if you did? Who did he love? His mom, and Cammy, too, but that was different. This, whatever was going on with Greer, provoked strong physical feelings, not just the obvious kinds, but others in his head and in his gut, like he was in a constant state of excitement, could live on nothing but water and air. Was that a type of love? He had no idea.

"And?"

"And it's fine," he said.

"Fine?"

"You know, like okay."

"Okay?"

"Not a deal breaker."

Greer laughed, a little too loud. He put his finger over her lips. She bit him, not hard but not softly, either. Things started heating up. Wyatt almost missed the sound of footsteps in the hall, not the upstairs hall but the hall outside his door. He squeezed Greer's arm, trying to get her to be still. She went still, a lucky break: he wasn't sure how she'd react to anything.

Knock-knock at the door. Greer slipped under the covers. This was almost like a comedy he'd seen at the East Canton fourplex, like lots of comedies he'd seen there, except it wasn't funny.

"Wyatt?" Aunt Hildy called through the door. "Are you all right?"

"Yeah, fine."

"Were you on your phone just now?"

"No."

"I thought I heard you talking."

"No. Maybe, uh, maybe I made some sound in my sleep. Sorry if I woke you."

"You didn't. Can't sleep myself tonight for some reason." Then came silence, but she didn't go away.

"Try not thinking about anything," Wyatt said.

Aunt Hildy laughed, actually more of a snort. "If only," she said, and padded away.

Greer came up from under the covers and lay quiet, head on Wyatt's chest. "Everything you do, everything y—"

"Shh."

She started again, very soft. "Everything you do, everything you say . . . I like."

"Shh."

Time passed. Was it starting to get light outside? Wyatt wasn't sure. "Greer?" he said. She was asleep. He slipped out from under her, went to the window. Still fully night. He took his cell phone off the desk, checked the time: four forty. How to handle this? She could stay till everyone left and then—

Greer sat up. "I better get going," she whispered.

He sat beside her. "How did you get here?"

"Drove."

"You have a car?"

"My dad's. It's not insured and the plates are gone, so I don't like to drive it much, you know?"

Nothing funny about that, but Wyatt had a hard time not laughing.

She got out of bed, pulled on her clothes. Wyatt stood naked beside her. When she was all dressed, she put her arms around him. "I'd like a picture of us, just like this," she said.

"Not a good idea," Wyatt said. "Doesn't everyone know that by now?"

"You're no fun." She kissed him, opened the window, stuck one foot out. "I meant to tell you something," she said, "but it's so hard with all this whispering."

"What?" he said.

"I met him," she said. "He's really nice."

"Who?"

"Your—Sonny, Sonny Racine. I went to see my dad today—yesterday—and he was there, in the visiting room. He gets a lot of respect."

"What the hell?" Wyatt raised his hands, the kind of gesture that goes along with not knowing where to begin. Greer climbed out the window and disappeared in the darkness.

# 12

"HEY. WAKE UP, FOR CHRIST'S SAKE."

Wyatt opened his eyes. Dub was in the room. He grabbed a pillow and tossed it at Wyatt's head. Greer's smell was on it; and everything, the whole night, came back to him. Dream-like, but not a dream. Wyatt tossed the pillow aside. Dub gazed down at him.

"You look like shit."

Wyatt rubbed crust from the corners of his eyes, saw no sign of last night's unpleasant conversation on Dub's face. "Not as bad as you," he said.

"Ooo, that hurts, pretty boy," Dub said. A big grin spread across his face, always a sign of some fun idea taking hold. Dub lifted the far side of the mattress off the springs and upended it like it was nothing, dumping Wyatt, bedding, mattress on the cold floor.

"What the hell?"

"Wakie-wakie."

Dub left the room. Wyatt would have gotten the shit kicked out of him, no doubt about that at all.

Wyatt should have felt sleepy at school but did not, in fact found himself tremendously alive and engaged. In English class, he suddenly had his hand up in the air, very unusual for him to be volunteering a question, probably a first. The teacher, Ms. Grenville, wearing a brightly colored neckerchief—she had lots of them—glanced down at her seating chart and said, "Wyatt?"

"I, uh—" Too late, lowering his hand, this whole idea maybe not such a good one.

Ms. Grenville gave him an encouraging smile. "Go on."

"What if he, um, Hamlet, would have just said forget it?"

Some guy at the back of the room guffawed, but Ms. Grenville leaned forward at her desk, looked interested. "Forget it in what way?" she said.

"Like figured it was all too complicated and left town."

"And gone where?"

"I don't know."

"Remind us, someone, where the story takes place."

"In a fort," someone said.

"In Elsinore Castle in Denmark," said Anna.

Ms. Grenville nodded. "Denmark," she said. She turned to Wyatt, raising her eyebrows.

"I guess he'd have to leave Denmark," he said.

"Because?"

"It probably wouldn't be safe to just leave the castle, go to some other town in the same country. What with, um, Claudius being the new king, and all."

"Very interesting," Ms. Grenville said. "Your whole idea.

Has anyone read ahead yet?"

Anna raised her hand.

"And does Hamlet ever consider Wyatt's idea?"

"Not directly," Anna said. "But he thinks about suicide—isn't that what the whole to-be-or-not-to-be thing is all about?"

"Yes," said Ms. Grenville. "And Hamlet rejects suicide. In the end, he figures out a very clever way to get at what Wyatt calls the complications—in other words, to find out if the ghost has told the truth—and then he faces up to what he has to do."

"But what about when Claudius tries to send Hamlet to England?" Anna said. "He kind of does leave the country after all."

Ms. Grenville gave Anna a frown. Anna was the smartest kid in the class by far, and Wyatt had always assumed teachers loved having kids like that around; now for the first time, he wondered. "That's a secondary complication," Ms. Grenville said, "that we'll get to in due course."

After school, Wyatt drove to the bowling alley: closed. He called Greer, got sent straight to voice mail. He drove down the main street, keeping an eye out for a car with no plates. He stopped at High Sierra Coffee, looked in, saw Anna there with a few kids from school. She saw him and waved. He backed out of the coffee shop and drove to Greer's apartment building. Cars were parked on both sides of the street, all with plates.

Wyatt went to the front door, standing under that strange

stone animal head, and checked the buzzer panel. All but one single buzzer had a plastic typestrip with a name beside it, none of the names being Torrance, G. Torrance, Greer Torrance, or even simply Greer. He was gazing at that unlabeled buzzer when his phone rang. The screen read UNKNOWN CALLER.

"Hello?"

"Hi, Wyatt. It's, uh, Sonny. Sonny Racine."

Wyatt had already recognized the voice, regretted answering. "Yeah," he said. "Hi."

"Hope I'm not bothering you. Got a chance to make a quick call, thought I'd take advantage of it."

"Uh-huh."

"Wanted to see how you were making out—in a new town, and all."

"Fine."

"Good to hear." A long pause. "School okay?"

"Yeah."

Another pause, this one maybe longer. "Got a favorite subject?"

"Not really," Wyatt said.

"I used to like math the best."

Wyatt said nothing.

From the other end came the sound of throat-clearing. And then: "Funny thing, I happened to meet your girlfriend."

*Girlfriend?* The word—maybe because he wasn't thinking of Greer like that yet, maybe because of who was uttering it, or uttering it first—disturbed Wyatt.

"Talking about Bert Torrance's daughter. Poor old Bert,

but that's another story. As for Greer, she's a charming young lady. And she seems crazy about you."

This was disturbing, too; why, he couldn't say. He remained silent.

"But maybe not my place to be making all these personal comments. Just a nice happenstance, that's all, meeting her. I'll let you go."

"Okay."

"If there's anything you need, being close by now, and all, don't hesitate."

"Uh, sure. Bye."

"Take care."

Wyatt clicked off. If there was anything he needed? What was that about? How could Sonny Racine help even if Wyatt did need something? He was behind bars.

Wyatt glanced up and down the street. It was cold out, not a cloud in the sky, a sky bright enough to make his eyes water. He could see the tops of two smokestacks in the distance, but nothing was coming out of them. Things were different by day. That expression—as different as day from night—hit home. It wasn't simply a matter of astronomy, the Earth spinning on its axis, but an internal difference, the way you thought and felt. The same person could arrive at different answers, depending on where he stood in relation to the shadow line moving across the face of the Earth. What if all the important things happened at night? Maybe they did.

Wyatt's gaze went to the buzzer, the one with no label. He was a free agent. Nothing was stopping him from jumping in his car and driving up to East Canton. If he got started right away and the weather held, could he make it by Cammy's bedtime? Wyatt pressed the buzzer.

No answer. He didn't press it again. He took one look—perhaps one last look—at the snarling stone creature over the door, and turned to go. Then a voice—Greer's voice—came from the speaker by the buzzer panel.

"Who's there?"

"Me."

"That's funny—I was just dreaming of you."

Bzzz.

Wyatt went inside and up the stairs to the top floor. Greer was waiting with the door open. She wore a white terrycloth robe with RITZ-CARLTON SHANGHAI stitched on the front in blue.

"Just got up?" she said.

"No." He closed the door behind him. "I went to school."

"You did? But you look great, like you had a full night's sleep. And I've been sleeping all day and I look like shit—what's up with that?"

"You look fine," he said. But in fact she didn't—there were dark circles under her eyes, her skin looked ashy, and a tiny scab had formed under her eyebrow ring.

"You're a liar," Greer said, "but we already established that." She took his hand; hers felt hot. "The funny thing is I may look like shit but I feel absolutely fantastic. And hungry. I'm ravenous. How about something to eat?"

"Sure. Okay. You want to go to the coffee shop, or—"

"Nah. I'll fix something right here."

"You can cook?"

"How do you like your eggs?"

"Well, um."

"Scrambled, poached, soft-boiled, hard-boiled, over easy?"

"Scrambled, I guess. About last night, I—"

"Coming right up. Wait in the living room—I don't like being watched."

"No?"

"Not when I'm cooking."

Wyatt sat in the living room, separated from the kitchen by a wide arch; Greer moved back and forth across the opening, different things in hand—eggs, spatula, pan, salt and pepper, an onion. He turned to the musical instruments—electric guitar, acoustic guitar, mandolin—but didn't pick any of them up. Wyatt had no musical ability whatsoever. "Can you play these?"

"Some," Greer called from the kitchen. "What do you like—besides rap, I mean."

Besides rap? Wyatt didn't know much about any other kinds of music. "My mom likes Bruce Springsteen."

"Cool." Greer came into the living room. She fumbled behind one of the cushions on the couch, found a metal tube—a slide?—that she slipped on the third finger of her left hand, and then picked up the guitar. "How about this kind of music?" she said, sitting beside him and starting to play. Hey! She was good. The guitar made sounds a lot like moaning and crying. Then she sang: *When things go wrong, so wrong with you, It hurts me too.* Her voice was hard but somehow beautiful at the same time. She broke off in the middle. "Bacon's gonna burn," she said, and hurried into the kitchen.

Wyatt followed. "Hey. You're so good."

"I'm a saint," she said, flipping bacon in the pan. It smelled great.

"I meant your song."

"It's not my song," Greer said. "Copied it note for note from Elmore James."

"Who's he?"

"Was," said Greer, putting eggs and bacon on two plates and bringing them to the table. "Siddown. Eat."

They sat at the table, a tiny rickety table, so small their feet had no choice but to touch under it. Wonderful smells rose in the air. "This is great," Wyatt said. "And you can really play."

"I fake it, that's all."

Wyatt shook his head. "And sing, too."

"Shows you've got a tin ear," Greer said. "I'm flat pretty much the whole time. My dad can sing, hits every note dead center. And he's the one who can really play. He had a band, way back when. They came pretty close to getting a record contract."

"He taught you to play?"

"Bingo." Greer slid her bare foot up under his pant leg. "The bacon's too crisp."

"No. It's perfect." And the scrambled eggs: so light and tasty, with onion and pepper flavors, and something else he couldn't name. "So, uh, how did your dad get from the band to, um—"

"Prison?"

"I wasn't going to say that, but yeah." He laid down his knife and fork. "I want to talk about the prison." He could hear the tone of his own voice changing, growing harder. "What's going on?"

"Meaning?" Greer said, cutting a bacon strip, not looking up. "How my father got there? Did he really do the arson?"

"That, too," Wyatt said. Greer withdrew her foot. "But first, what's the story with you and—" Kind of weird to be calling him by his full name, but no alternative was acceptable. "—and Sonny Racine?"

Greer raised her head. Yes, she looked terrible; beautiful, but terrible for her. "He was in the visitors' room. My dad waved him over. End of story."

"They're free to move around like that?"

"Depends on what pod they're in. The visiting area for the real bad-guy pod is one of those talking-on-a-phone-through-a-glass-wall deals. But they're not bad guys, our dads."

"He's not my dad," Wyatt said; his voice rose. "You know I don't think of him that way, so why are you saying it?"

"Sorry," Greer said. She cut her bacon into little pieces but didn't eat any. Wyatt picked up his knife and fork. "He's very popular," she said.

"Who."

"Mr. Sonny Racine. Everyone likes him."

Wyatt put the knife and fork back down. "You're talking about the other criminals?"

"They're human beings, too," Greer said. "You're not giving him a chance."

"A chance to do what?"

"To get to know you a bit."

"Why would he want to do that?"

"I just know he does, that's all. He said he'd like to meet you."

"Like I'd visit the jail?"

"Yeah."

"Forget it. I told you what happened. He committed a horrible crime."

Greer stuck her fork into a bacon piece, popped it into her mouth, started chewing. "The thing is, my dad thinks he's innocent. It's the consensus in there, in fact."

"I don't understand what you're saying."

"Sonny Racine may be serving a life sentence for something he didn't do. I can't put it any simpler than that. I've actually started doing some research, if you'd like to take a look."

GREER WENT INTO THE BEDROOM, came back with a sheet of paper. "I got this at the library." She laid it on the table: a copy of a seventeen-year-old newspaper clipping from the *Millerville Beacon*. In the top right-hand corner was a picture of the sun with heat lines radiating off it, and the words SUNNY AND MILD. Below that was a headline: THREE GUILTY IN NORTH SIDE BREAK-IN.

> *A Superior Court jury rendered a guilty verdict yesterday in the trial of three men for January's North Side home invasion that resulted in the death of a woman and the wounding of an infant.*
>
> *Found guilty on charges of murder, assault with a deadly weapon, and other lesser offenses were Arthur Pingree of Millerville, Sonny Racine of East Canton, and Norbert "Doc" Vitti, also of Millerville. Pingree and Racine were given life sentences without parole. Vitti, who testified for the prosecution, received a 15- to 25-year sentence, with the possibility of parole.*

The jury deliberated for just under three hours, delivering the verdict shortly before lunchtime.

The charges stemmed from a home invasion at 32 Cain Street on January 17. The house was occupied at the time by Luis Dominguez and his brother, Esteban, both of whom had long criminal records for various drug offenses.

The plot, as outlined in the prosecution's case and seemingly corroborated by the testimony of Vitti, involved stealing the large amounts of cash that the three men believed were kept in the house. On the stand, Vitti said, "Guys like that, heroin dealers and such, they're not the type to go crying to the cops."

What actually occurred after Pingree, Racine, and Vitti broke into the house became the subject of conflicting testimony during the trial, which lasted three days.

Millerville police captain William Mack testified the department had been aware for months of the activities of the Dominguez brothers and patrolled Cain Street on a regular basis, including on the night of the break-in.

Police entered the house just at the finish of a wild gun battle, finding the Dominguez brothers both wounded, eight-month-old Antonia Morales, daughter of Esteban Dominguez and his girlfriend, Maria Morales, shot in the head, and Maria Morales, the mother, dead.

Pingree and Vitti were arrested on the spot. Racine was found hiding in nearby woods shortly after. The murder weapon, a .22 handgun according to forensic evidence, was not found.

Vitti testified that Racine was the shooter, although all

*three of the convicted men are equally guilty under the law.*

*In a separate trial last month, the Dominguez brothers, both illegal aliens, were found guilty on drug charges and sentenced to federal prison in Colorado. On completion of their sentences they will be turned over to the INS for subsequent deportation to Mexico. The child, Antonia Morales, survived with the loss of an eye, and is now in foster care.*

Wyatt looked up from the page. He felt sick, that perfect home-cooked breakfast threatening to come back up. Greer stood behind him, reading over his shoulder. "That's some of the worst writing I've ever seen," she said. "The story barely makes sense."

"Horrible," Wyatt said. "The baby."

"Yeah," Greer said. "Take that away and it's almost funny."

"Funny?"

"In a dark kind of way. Like a Joe Pesci movie."

"I don't get the joke," Wyatt said. He ran his eye over the story again. "And there's nothing here about any possibility of Sonny Racine being innocent."

He turned to her. She still didn't look well, and maybe because of that—the chalkiness of her skin, the bruised smudges under her eyes—the beautiful underlying structure of her face was all the more apparent. "I didn't say he was," she said. "I'm just reporting the opinion from inside."

"From inside the prison, you mean?"

"Yeah."

"The opinion of criminals."

"I don't like that word. Not the way you say it."

"How do I say it?"

"So judgmentally."

"They've already been judged," Wyatt said, surprising himself with a not-too-stupid remark.

Greer laughed, a strange laugh, not amused. "I'm either going to end up loving you or hating you, no in-between."

"What are you talking about?"

"Nothing," she said. "It's just a feeling. But one thing I know is that one particular criminal, the criminal a.k.a. my father, doesn't claim to be innocent."

"So he did it? Burned down the amusement center?"

"Torrance Family Fun and Games—might as well get the name right." Greer went to the window, looked out. "He admits he did it," she said. "Whether he did or not . . ." She went silent.

Wyatt thought of what Aunt Hildy had said: *A firefighter of my acquaintance got burned that night.* And even more: *Pretty clear that she was involved, too—they couldn't prove it, is all.*

"The point is," Greer said, "they drove him mad, just out of his mind."

"Who did?"

"That bank in San Francisco. All he needed was more time, just to ride out this slump, but those bastards wouldn't do it." She turned, and now there was color in her face, coming back in patches. "They cut his balls off instead. And guess what I hear, irony of ironies—now the bank's in receivership, too."

"So maybe it was hopeless from the get-go," Wyatt said.

"What are you saying?" Greer's voice rose. "What the hell was the point of that?"

Wyatt wasn't really sure. Also, he didn't know why she was suddenly angry. Maybe because of all that uncertainty, he blurted out what was bothering him the most. "Did you help him?" he said.

"Whoa," Greer said, her voice much quieter. She backed up, bumped hard into the window. "Whoa. Who have you been talking to?"

"Nobody."

She came forward. "Liar."

Wyatt got up, faced her across the table.

"Let's get this straight," Greer said. "You're asking whether I helped my dad light that fire."

"You don't have to answer. But it's a logical question."

"Oh, really?" Greer said. "Here's one for you—friend or foe?"

"Me?"

"Yeah, you. One assumes friend after what we've been doing together, but a woman never fucking knows, does she?"

"Aw, come on," Wyatt said.

She mimicked him. "Aw, come on—Mister Almost Seventeen."

Wyatt felt himself reddening. "What's wrong with you? It's kind of . . ."

"Go on."

"Kind of understandable, if you did help him."

"Except what? Spill it. You're thinking something—it's all over your face."

"Except for the firefighter who got burned," Wyatt said.

Greer's cheeks flushed, one brighter than the other, as though she'd been slapped. "Who have you been talking to? And don't say nobody."

Wyatt said nothing.

"That aunt of yours?"

"She's not really my aunt."

"But it's her," Greer said. She smacked her fist into the palm of her other hand; a gesture Wyatt had seen lots of guys do, but never a girl. "Small towns suck so bad," she said. "She knows about you and me, right? This aunt-like figure, I'm talking about."

Wyatt nodded.

"And she doesn't approve."

"I don't care what she thinks."

"Has she introduced you to Freddie Helms yet?"

"Who's he?"

"The firefighter. Do you know how awful my dad feels about that?"

"No."

"It's why he pleaded guilty, didn't even put up a fight, even though the lawyer said he had a good case."

"Meaning he didn't actually do it after all?" Wyatt said.

"Christ," Greer said. "Meaning the case wasn't solid, was going to be hard to prove beyond a reasonable doubt. Don't you know how justice works?"

Wyatt was getting tired of her tone. "But it ended up working here," he said, "because your dad did it."

Greer tilted her head to one side, as if to see him from a new angle. "You don't care at all, do you? About me."

"That's a stupid thing to say."

"Maybe you should go."

Wyatt just stood there.

"Yes," she said. "No maybes. Go."

Wyatt nodded, his mind made up about lots of things. The most important: he was going home. He glanced down at the remains of his delicious breakfast, then headed for the door. All too much, nothing fitting together: Wyatt's mind was in a kind of silent uproar. He opened the door and looked back. Greer was standing by the table, arms folded across her chest.

"Did you help or not?" he said.

"Curiosity killed the cat."

"That's your answer?"

"Don't like it? How about this? I did the arson all by myself and my father took the fall for me. Like that better?"

"Is it true?"

"Sayonara," Greer said.

Wyatt walked out and closed the door. Halfway down the stairs, he heard a crash from above, the kind of crash a table getting overturned might make. He kept going.

Wyatt walked toward the Mustang, parked halfway down Greer's block. The wind blew between the buildings; from somewhere nearby came the sound of a baseball thumping into a glove. He glanced around, saw nobody. Not quite true: a man was sitting in a dented old car across the street. As Wyatt unlocked the Mustang, the man got out and approached.

"Hi, there," the man said.

"Hey," said Wyatt, pausing, one hand on the open door.

The man gave him a careful look. "Yeah," he said, "I can see it."

"See what?"

The man smiled; a normal-looking middle-aged guy, small and pudgy, with a double chin. "The resemblance," he said, "between you and Sonny."

Wyatt felt his heart rate speeding up.

"Name's Delino, by the way—Bob," the man said. "And you're Wyatt, no doubt about that. Sonny wants to know how things are going, settling in okay, that kind of thing."

"How do you know?" Wyatt said.

Bob Delino smiled again. "Got his smarts, clear to see." He reached into the pocket of his frayed denim jacket, took out a pack of cigarettes. "Smoke?"

Wyatt shook his head.

Bob Delino lit up, flicked the match into the gutter. "How I know," he said, pausing to inhale, "is that he asked me personally to check up." Smoke drifted out of Delino's nose and mouth. "He knew I was getting out, see? From Sweetwater. We were friends inside." He took another drag, squinted at Wyatt through the smoke. "I did sixteen months—all on account of a stupid misunderstanding about some copper pipe, but that's nothing you need to know. Important thing is the sixteen months was up yesterday, so here I am."

"Okay," Wyatt said.

"A free man," Delino said. "Feels not bad, the first few days. After that is when . . ." He tapped a cylinder of ash off the end of his cigarette, watched it disintegrate in the wind.

"Anyways, I'm heading back up to Minnesota, right after I get done seeing how you're making out."

"I'm fine," Wyatt said.

Delino stared at him. "How old are you?"

"Seventeen."

Delino shook his head. "Boy oh boy. Must be nice. School okay? Sports?"

"Yeah."

"This your ride?"

"Yeah."

"Sweet. Things are going good, obviously." He glanced at Greer's building, back to Wyatt. "That's it, then. Done my job." He reached into his pocket again, took out an envelope. "Sonny said to give you this. He's a good man, plus bein' a standup guy—don't see that combo every day."

Delino was holding out the envelope, but Wyatt made no move to take it.

"Not gonna bite you," Delino said.

"What's in it?"

"Money," Delino said. "Couple hundred bucks."

"No, thanks."

"C'mon, man." Delino shook the envelope.

"No."

"But I'm s'posed to give you this."

"I don't want it."

"Send it to the Salvation Army, then. Makes no difference to me, long as I do my job."

Wyatt shook his head. "You keep it."

Delino laughed, a harsh smoker's laugh. "That's a good

one," he said. Then, very quick, he leaned forward and spun the envelope like a Frisbee. It sailed by Wyatt and into the backseat of the Mustang.

"For Christ's sake," Wyatt said. He climbed into the car, couldn't find the envelope at first, finally spotted it under the front passenger seat. By the time he got back out, envelope in hand, Bob Delino was zooming past a stop sign two blocks away.

# 14

BACK IN HIS ROOM at Aunt Hildy's, Wyatt counted the money. Ten twenty-dollar bills = $200. They were all crisp, like they'd just come from a brand-new stack at a bank teller's window. He was holding one up to the light, seeing nothing obviously fake except Andrew Jackson's hair—could it possibly have looked like that in real life, so Hollywood?—when Aunt Hildy knocked on his door.

"How does Chinese food sound?"

"Great." Wyatt stuck the money under his pillow. Real money: kind of paranoid to think it might be fake. He didn't want this money, but no good plan for getting rid of it came to mind. He couldn't just throw money away, or burn it, or anything like that. Returning the $200 to where it came from seemed best. Could you mail money into the prison? Or—or maybe Greer could take it inside on one of her visits. But Greer was out of the picture. She'd said go, and he was going—back to East Canton and soon. Period, finito, end of story—except that at that moment nothing would have pleased him more than the sight of her walking through the door.

East Canton had no Chinese restaurants; Silver City had two. "This is my favorite," said Aunt Hildy as a waiter led her, Dub, and Wyatt to a corner table at the Red Pagoda, although they could have had just about any table, the place being pretty much empty. "I love the fish tank."

The fish tank stood nearby, a tall glass cube with coral fans and rocks at the bottom and three fish drifting through the water at different levels.

"Which one are you having?" Dub said.

"Very funny," said Aunt Hildy.

"Like in the Depression," Dub said. He had a reddish band across his forehead, pressed into the skin from wearing the catcher's mask. "Didn't people get so hungry they ate live goldfish?"

"You're thinking of the Roaring Twenties," Aunt Hildy said. "And those were prep school kids and Ivy Leaguers, not the poor." The waiter came. Aunt Hildy ordered a gin and tonic; the boys had soda. "My first husband," Aunt Hildy said, taking a sip, "was an Ivy Leaguer. Princeton, to be precise. He had a ratty old black-and-gold-striped robe. He was wearing it pretty much twenty-four/seven by the time I threw him out."

Wyatt and Dub looked at each other. Aunt Hildy took another sip, this one longer. "Go, Tigers," she said.

"How do you get into a place like that?" Wyatt said.

"Princeton?" said Aunt Hildy, making a dismissive wave. "It's overrated. They all are. He had beautiful manners, hubby numero uno, but no spine. Nothing beats spine, boys, and they don't teach that in college. How about we start with the Peking ribs?"

They had Peking ribs, moo shu pork, orange chicken, crispy duck, another round of Peking ribs, plus rice, egg rolls, fried wontons. Aunt Hildy ordered another gin and tonic. She described a trip to Cancún, where she'd met husband numero dos, who turned out to have had neither manners nor spine, though at first she'd been fooled on both counts. She also taught the boys how to use chopsticks, which Wyatt picked up right away and Dub had trouble with, actually splintering one by mistake. Wyatt was having a great time, just with all this great food, and being with Aunt Hildy, who turned out to be pretty funny, and totally forgetting his problems.

The check came. Wyatt dug out some money, his own, the $200 left under the pillow. "None of that, young man," said Aunt Hildy. "My treat, and besides, this is kind of a fare-well dinner, now that you're going home and all. I spoke to your mom today—she's so excited."

"So it's for sure?" said Dub.

Wyatt nodded. "Leaving tomorrow."

"But what about baseball?" Dub said. "Next year, I'm talking about."

"Maybe the economy'll pick up and we'll have it again in East Canton," Wyatt said.

"Think that's possible?" Dub said.

"Anything can happen," Aunt Hildy said. "And if not, Wyatt can always come back."

She paid the check. They rose and headed toward the door. Some men in navy-blue uniforms were on the way in. The two groups met by the fish tank. One of the men turned.

"Hey, Hildy," he said. "How's it going?"

"No complaints," said Aunt Hildy. "Yourself?"

"Not bad at all," said the man.

"I'd like you to meet my nephew, Dub," Aunt Hildy said. "And his friend Wyatt. Boys, say hi to Freddie Helms."

They shook hands with Freddie Helms. "Hey, guys," he said. "Did you check out those ribs?" Freddie Helms was a handsome guy with a strong grip; handsome except for one side of his face. It gleamed in the light of the fish tank like glass, a sheet of glass that had been broken and then melted roughly back together.

"Did they ever," said Aunt Hildy. "Take care."

"See you, Hildy. Nice meeting you, guys."

They went outside. Wyatt took a deep breath. All of a sudden he didn't feel so good, as though the meal wanted to come back up.

"What happened to him?" Dub said.

"Freddie?" said Aunt Hildy, answering Dub but looking at Wyatt. "He's the firefighter that got hurt when the amusement center burned down. Bert Torrance's place. Freddie thought he heard someone trapped inside and went in, but it turned out to be voices on one of the video games, something about a pulse through the wiring just before it melted."

"Is there anything they can do about it?" Dub said.

"Oh, Freddie's had a bunch of treatments," Aunt Hildy said, eyes still on Wyatt. "He looks much better now."

They got into Aunt Hildy's car, Wyatt in back.

"This was that arson thing?" Dub said.

"That's right," said Aunt Hildy, driving out of the parking lot.

"The father of, um . . . ?" Dub said.

Aunt Hildy nodded. They drove back to her place. Dub burped a few times but there was no more talk.

Not long after that, Wyatt was in his room, packing for the trip home, when his phone rang.

"Hello, Wyatt."

This time he recognized the voice right away. "Hi."

"Calling at a bad time?"

"No," Wyatt said, pausing over his open duffel bag, baseball glove in hand.

"Had supper yet?"

"Yeah."

"What was it, if you don't mind my asking?"

"Chinese."

"You went out?"

"Yeah."

"That's nice. Yangtze Palace or Red Pagoda?"

"Red Pagoda."

"I hear it's pretty good, the Peking ribs especially."

Hear from where? How? Wyatt didn't ask those questions, just said, "Yeah."

"Eat one for me next time."

"Eat one for you?"

"Or not. Just a suggestion. Kind of like having a thought for someone."

Wyatt didn't know what to say to that.

"Reason I'm calling—I wanted to make sure you got the package."

"Yeah, but—"

"And even though I'd trust old Bob with my life—well, wouldn't go that far—it's always prudent to verify, right? Can't imagine Bob would skim, but there's so much skimming in this society in one form or another—maybe how we got to where we are—that I'd just like to hear the figure from you."

"Two hundred, but—"

"Perfect."

"But I don't want it."

"Don't want money?"

"Not, um—you must need it yourself."

"I'm fine, and that's not your worry in any case. Why not call it an early Christmas present, or a late one? Word is you've got a fine set of wheels, and know how to handle them, too. Car like that sucks up money, in my experience."

"Word from Greer Torrance?"

"That's right."

"Does she know about this? The money?"

"No. But that's a funny question. Mind if I ask what's behind it?"

"Nothing."

There was a pause at the other end. Then: "She's an impressive young lady. Self-confident, if you know what I mean. A doer."

"A doer of what?" That popped out, irretrievably in the open before Wyatt could do anything about it.

Another pause. "Not sure I understand your question."

Wyatt plunged ahead. "The arson—was that her? Did

she have anything to do with it?"

"Don't know, but I can find out, if it's important."

Wyatt didn't say anything. This was going too far, too fast. What was the best way to—

"I get the feeling it is important. Call you back in half an hour."

"No, that's not—"

Click.

Wyatt dropped his glove into the duffel bag, picked up a T-shirt, couldn't decide whether it was clean or dirty, sniffed at it, still couldn't decide. The T-shirt slipped from his hands. He sat down at the computer, searched for the arson story. He got only one small hit, a few lines reporting Bert Torrance's conviction. But when he clicked on Images, he came upon a photo of Freddie Helms, a preburn photo. Freddie was wearing a firefighter's helmet, a coil of hose over his strong shoulder, a big smile on his undamaged face. Wyatt was still gazing at that picture when the phone rang.

"No involvement."

"Greer?"

"Exactly. She had nothing to do with it, had no foreknowledge, not even a hint. It was Bert by himself, start to finish. Sometimes a guy gets into a position, throws it all into the pot at once. Out of desperation, in Bert's case, and not too many men do their best thinking when they're desperate. Maybe not as true for women. But that's by the by. Also by the by, just a reminder that arson for the insurance score is not for amateurs—the prime suspect is usually pretty obvious."

"Why would I need a reminder on that?" Wyatt said.

Sonny laughed, a rich, joyful laugh, the kind that was sometimes contagious. "You're so right," Sonny said. "Whew. That's funny. The point is the girl had no involvement."

"You're sure?"

"Bert wouldn't lie to me, not to my face. I'm sure, one hundred percent. Don't worry about a thing."

"Okay," Wyatt said. And then: "Thanks."

"My pleasure."

Click.

Wyatt had a strange feeling, completely new to him, a kind of lessening of pressure inside, or the force of gravity seeming to weaken a little. Hard to describe: perhaps a feeling that came with receiving fatherly advice.

Wyatt finished packing and went to bed. He'd always been the type to fall asleep quickly, but not this night. A toilet flushed upstairs, water ran through the pipes—and was that a burp he heard?—and then the house was quiet. He rolled over, tried different positions, willed his mind to go blank. But his mind wouldn't go blank. Instead it occupied itself with thoughts of Greer. At the very least, didn't he owe her an apology? Wyatt went back and forth on that, finally felt for his cell phone on the bedside table and called her number.

She answered on the first ring. "Hey, there."

"Hi," Wyatt said. "Did I wake you?"

"Only if I'm sleepwalking."

"I don't get it."

"Meaning I'm walking across your yard as we speak,"

Greer said. Wyatt sat up fast. Then came a tap-tap-tap at his window.

Wyatt jumped out of bed, opened the window, smelled her. She smelled great. Greer climbed in. There was lots of moonlight, enough to see she still looked tired and drawn, and also wasn't wearing the eyebrow ring.

"What are you doing?" he said, his voice low.

"Had to say I'm sorry," she said. "The kind of thing you do in person."

Had she been crying? Wyatt thought he saw a tear track on her cheek. "I'm the one who's sorry," he said.

"You? What did you do?"

He'd doubted her, doubted his first intimate love; yes, these feelings he had for her had to be a form of love, might as well face that. "You had nothing to do with the fire," he said. "I should have known."

She gave him a long look. "You're the best," she said. Then she put her arms around him and kissed him on the mouth.

Soon they were in bed. She got on top of him, sat up, her head thrown back in the moonlight, maybe making a little too much noise, but Wyatt didn't care. The money got pushed out from under the pillow, scattering everywhere.

After, she slumped down on him, her damp hair against his chest; and was still in that position when the door burst open. The lights flashed on, and there was Aunt Hildy.

# 15

NO ONE, EXCEPT MAYBE DUB, was at their best in the next few minutes. Aunt Hildy used the word *whore* once or twice, Greer fired back a bad word of her own, Wyatt shouted at both of them to stop shouting, and finally Dub appeared in the doorway, his hair sticking up in strange clumps and rubbing his eyes. "Something wrong?" he said.

Wyatt and Greer left together, not through the window but out the front door, which slammed behind them. Wyatt, already packed, took his things.

Wyatt spent the rest of the night at Greer's. When he woke up, lying on his back, she was on her side, watching him. "You look so great when you're sleeping," she said. "I've never been this happy in my whole life."

"You look pretty good yourself," Wyatt said. And she did. The pallor, the circles under her eyes, the drawn expression: all gone. Her skin glowed, her eyes shone, the whites pure white, no hint of yellow, not a blood vessel showing. And again, no eyebrow ring, just the tiny hole, the surrounding skin healthy and unbruised. He considered asking why she wasn't wearing the eyebrow ring, couldn't come up with a cool approach. Did it even matter?

"No," she said. "My face is all wrong. But thanks anyway."

"Wrong? What's wrong with it?"

"Everything," she said. She pushed her face this way and that. "Here. Here. Here." Had he ever seen anything more beautiful? And right next to him, so close.

Some time later, while he was in a fuzzy state between sleeping and waking, Greer's lips brushed his ear, and she spoke. "Know what we should do today?"

Wyatt opened his eyes. She was smiling; and had been up to brush her teeth—he smelled mint. What they were going to have to do today was say good-bye. No going back to Aunt Hildy's, and besides, his mom expected him. "Well," he said, starting off in a way he knew was pretty lame, "the thing is I have nowhere to stay now, and—"

"Huh? You're staying here. I assumed that. You're a high school student, duly enrolled at Bridger High. Don't you want to make something of yourself? Am I missing something?"

Maybe he was the one doing the missing. Hadn't the situation changed? Yes, he'd decided to return to East Canton, but that was with Greer out of the picture. Now she was back.

"You're being a gentleman, right?" she said. "One of those guys with manners, too polite to ask? Don't have to be polite with me, pal. You can stay here, no thank-you notes necessary."

He laughed.

"That's settled," Greer said. "Now here's the plan. I think we should go see Morrie Wertz."

"Who's Morrie Wertz?"

"I looked him up. It's a matter of public record."

"What is?"

"Morrie Wertz was your—was Sonny Racine's lawyer. It turns out he's one of the oldsters. You know—at Hillside Breeze."

"I don't understand."

"Hillside Breeze—my other job, the old folks' home, where I read for fifteen bucks an hour. It turns out that Morrie Wertz has been in there the whole time, kind of like fate."

"Fate?"

"Waiting to happen. I haven't run across him yet—just about all the ones I read to are women. That's mostly what's in there. Men die younger. The crazy thing is a lot of these old biddies still want a guy, and any of the guys who's not drooling—and maybe even if he is—has his pick."

"But," said Wyatt, "how come you know all this?"

"I've got eyes."

"I meant about him being the lawyer, and in the old folks' home."

"Take a guess."

"Your dad told you."

"Bzzz," Greer said. "You win the prize. Claim it at any time. First, you've got to move your butt." She ripped off the covers.

"Hey!"

"Can't be late for school."

"School?"

"It's a school day. Accusations of screwing up your academic life—I'm taking them off the table."

Wyatt drove to school, calling his mom on the way. "Mom? The thing is the school here's a lot better, and all this changing back and—"

"Wyatt? Where are you?" In the background he heard Cammy asking for more sugar.

"In Silver City. I—"

"When are you leaving? The weather's supposed to turn nasty this afternoon."

"That's what I'm calling about, Mom. I've decided to stay a bit longer."

"But we've been through this. Rusty left last night. I called the office at the high school and told them you'd be back tomorrow."

"Sorry."

"Wyatt? What's going on?"

"I just think it's best for now."

"I don't understand. Are you in some kind of trouble?"

"I'll call later. Everything's all right. Bye, Mom."

Wyatt parked in the student lot at Bridger High, got one of the last spaces. He grabbed his books and hurried to the door, was almost there when his phone rang. He checked the number: home.

"Wyatt?" his mom said. "I just had a very disturbing conversation with Hildy."

"Look, Mom, I can't—"

"It's not clear to me that she'd even let you come back to stay there, if half of what she says is true. What were you thinking?"

Through the big glass door, a teacher was tapping his watch and motioning Wyatt to come inside. "C'mon, Mom. I've got, you know, a girlfriend. So what?"

"So what? You were a guest in Hildy's house. And from what I hear about this girlfriend—" His mom swallowed whatever was next. At the same time, the door opened and the teacher came out.

"Don't want to have to write you up," the teacher was saying, "but if you're not inside this building in—"

Wyatt missed the time element, because his mom was speaking again. "I want you home today," she said.

"No," Wyatt said.

"No?" said the teacher. "You're telling me no?"

"Mom? I'll call you later."

"But—"

Wyatt shut off his phone, went inside.


"Who," said Ms. Grenville, "do you think is the smartest person in the play?"

"Shakespeare," said the funny guy at the back.

"We can't really say Shakespeare is in the play, now can we?"

"He made up all the others, so he has to be the smartest. I read his IQ was 203."

"Where did you read that?"

"I didn't read it, exactly. Omar texted me."

"Who's Omar?"

"This kid in India. Don't know his last name."

Ms. Grenville sat down, a bit heavily, as though her legs had gotten weak. She adjusted her neckerchief. Anna raised her hand. Ms. Grenville looked relieved. "Yes?"

"Hamlet," Anna said. "He's the smartest. Isn't that the whole point? Sometimes he's so smart he overthinks."

"Can you give an example?"

Anna gave a bunch of examples.

"Anyone want to argue the case for another character being the smartest?" said Ms. Grenville.

No one did. For a moment, Wyatt thought of the grave-digger—he'd skimmed ahead, read that scene, not really understood it, maybe until now. And maybe not. He kept his mouth shut.

Anna's hand was up again. "But his smartness serves him well, too. He figures out a test to establish Claudius's guilt once and for all."

"The play within the play," said Ms. Grenville. "Act Three—that's our reading for tomorrow." The bell rang. "Please be prepared for a quiz on—" But the subject of the quiz was drowned out in the end-of-class din.

After school, Wyatt picked up Greer at the bowling alley. She was waiting outside, hands in the pockets of her short leather jacket. A sign on the front door read: CLOSED UNTIL FURTHER NOTICE. CONTACT PRESIDIO BANK AND TRUST, SAN FRANCISCO. "They changed the goddamn locks," Greer said, getting into the car. "No notice, no call, nothing."

"Is there anything inside you need?"

Greer turned to him, looked angry for a moment, then smiled. "Guess not. I was going to try to sell the popcorn machine."

"What's it worth?"

"I don't know." Greer sat back, reached for his hand without looking, held on.

Wyatt drove to Hillside Breeze, the old folks' home. It was an old brick building behind the hospital, also an old brick building but taller—in fact, the tallest building in Silver City—so Hillside Breeze stood in its shadow.

Inside, Hillside Breeze smelled like the bathroom at home after Wyatt's mom had cleaned it. The phone was ringing at the desk in the small, poorly lit lobby, but no one was there. Greer went behind the desk, studied a chart—looking at it upside down, Wyatt saw rows of numbered squares with names inside—and motioned toward the stairs.

They went up. The carpet was musty. The smells in general were now more like the bathroom at home just before the cleaning. At the top they turned right, passing some rooms and a lounge where old women were sitting in front of a television, a few with their eyes closed, to a door at the end. The name strip read WERTZ/COFFEE. Greer knocked. No answer. She opened the door.

There were two beds in the room. A bearded man slept on his back in the nearest one, toothless mouth open. The other bed was empty. A second man sat in a chair, back to the room, facing the window. An oxygen tank stood beside him.

"Mr. Wertz?" Greer said in a half whisper.

No answer.

She went closer and called the name again, louder this time.

"If you're selling, I'm not buying," the man said, not turning.

Wyatt and Greer approached him, stood on either side. He glanced at one, then the other, but with no interest. One of his eyes was droopy and teared at the corner. He had an oxygen tube under his nose, liver spots on his face, and breath Wyatt could smell from where he was standing.

"Mr. Wertz?" Greer said again.

"I told you—the money supply is cut off."

"We don't want money, Mr. Wertz," Greer said.

"No? What makes you so special?"

"It's not that," Greer said. "We just want to talk to you. If you are Mr. Wertz, that is."

Mr. Wertz turned to her again, this time looked longer. "Why would a pretty girl like you want to talk to me?"

"I'd like you to meet my friend, Wyatt."

Mr. Wertz turned to Wyatt. "What kind of friend?" he said.

"Boyfriend."

"Some people have all the luck," said Mr. Wertz. "Nothing beats luck and don't let anyone tell you different. If I'd had just the smallest bit of goddamn—" Then came a strange sound in his throat, like a gulp, and he just sat there. Wyatt could hear the hiss of the oxygen.

Greer squatted down beside Mr. Wertz, one hand on

the arm of his chair. "Wyatt here's father is Sonny Racine. Remember him?"

Oxygen hissed. Mr. Wertz closed his eyes for a long moment, then opened them and said, "I'm drowning."

"You're drowning?" Greer said.

"That's what it feels like. Didn't anybody ever put a pillow over your head, try to suffocate you?"

"No. Never." Greer shrank back a little.

"I defended guys who did that, got them off, more than one," Mr. Wertz said. "This was in my former life."

"You were a lawyer," Greer said.

"Top-notch," said Mr. Wertz. "Till the booze got me. Now I'm off it, can't stomach a drop, literal truth. Haven't got more than an inch or two of stomach left, if you're interested in stats." His eyes darted from Greer to Wyatt and back. The good one looked angry; with the other it was impossible to tell.

"Do you remember defending Sonny Racine?" Greer said.

"Who wants to know?"

"I do."

"What's your name?"

"Greer. And this is Wyatt, Sonny Racine's son."

"What the hell are you saying?"

"Just who we are," Greer said.

"There was no son. I don't remember a son."

"I—I wasn't born till later," Wyatt said.

Mr. Wertz grabbed Wyatt's wrist, his skin icy cold and papery. "Come here," he said, "here where I can see you."

Wyatt moved around the front of the chair, closer to Greer, wrenched his hand free. "Only one good eye," Mr. Wertz said. "Why no one around here can get that straight is beyond me." He gazed at Wyatt. "You're just a kid."

"I'm seventeen."

"Christ." Mr. Wertz went silent. The man in the other bed started snoring. "Knock it off, you son of a bitch," Mr. Wertz yelled, startling Wyatt. The man kept snoring. Mr. Wertz gestured out the window. "And where are all the birds?"

"They'll be back," Wyatt said.

Mr. Wertz grew calmer. "Sorry, kid," he said.

"Nothing to be sorry about," said Wyatt.

Mr. Wertz gazed out the window. "By then, the period in question, I was on the sauce pretty good," he said. "Somewhat reduced, if you know what I mean. Fired from North and Mulgrew, if you don't. Working as a PD."

"What's that?" Wyatt said.

"Public defender," said Mr. Wertz. He looked at Greer. "Doesn't he know the lingo?" Greer didn't answer. "I'll tell you both something, since you're two nice kids. Fresh faced. When they say the jails are full of innocent people, they're blowing smoke. Ninety-nine point nine nine nine percent of the guys inside deserve it, hell, deserve much worse. Then there's that teeny-weeny exception, irrelevant, if you're interested in stats. Sonny Racine was in that category."

# 16

"ARE YOU SAYING HE WAS INNOCENT?" Greer said.

"Wouldn't go that far." A tear rolled out of Morrie Wertz's droopy eye, but he didn't look sad, more annoyed, if anything. "No one's innocent—not even a newborn babe, don't fool yourselves. I'm talking about—" He made that gulping sound and went silent. His good eye got a faraway look; the bad one closed up even more. Oxygen hissed. Somewhere in Hillside Breeze a beep-beep-beep started up.

Wyatt and Greer crouched in front of Wertz's chair. "Maybe we should call somebody," Wyatt said.

Greer shook her head. "They're like this," she said.

Wertz gulped again. His bad eye quivered open a bit. "Reasonable doubt—that's all I'm talking about. Understand the concept of reasonable doubt?" He looked at Greer. "You do, but what about Mister Handsome over here?" He turned his head, glared at Wyatt. "How come my goddamn legs hurt so much if I can't even use them?"

"I don't know," Wyatt said.

"You should be a doctor," said Wertz. He nodded to

himself. "Booze destroys brain cells, but are they still in there, dead and black, or do they get flushed out? Am I pissing brain cells? I ask myself these questions."

Greer rose, leaned against the wall. "What about reasonable doubt?"

"That's an easy one," Wertz said. "Reasonable doubt means inventing some crackpot story and making sure there's at least one crackpot citizen on the jury to swallow it."

"So what are you saying?" Greer said. "He wasn't innocent, but you couldn't come up with the crackpot story or a crackpot citizen?"

"Finding crackpot citizens is a snap," Wertz said. His good eye blinked a few times. "Who are we talking about?"

"Christ," said Greer, her voice sharpening; Wertz flinched. "Sonny Racine."

"You blame me for losing that one?" Wertz said.

"Is that what happened?" Greer said.

Wertz shook his head. "Sonny Racine lost it himself."

Wyatt didn't understand any of this. "So he was guilty?" he said.

"I thought so when I first looked at the file," Wertz said. "But then he insisted on taking the stand, testifying. Which was how he lost the case—a crazy thing to do, against counsel's strong advice, although counsel wasn't at his strongest at the time. The DA was practically salivating, tore him apart on cross. Sonny Racine gave himself a life sentence. See what I'm saying?"

"No," Wyatt said.

"Nurse! Nurse!" The man in the other bed suddenly cried

out. Wyatt jumped up, his heart pounding. The man was still on his back, eyes still closed, looked as though he hadn't moved.

"Lid on it, you sack of shit," said Wertz, not turning to look. The man began to snore again.

"I jumped a mile," said Greer.

"That's Mr. Coffee," said Wertz. "Just ignore him."

"What did that mean," Wyatt said, crouching down again, "Sonny Racine gave himself a life sentence?"

The good eye was back on him. "You're not completely stupid, are you?" Wertz said. "Course the girlfriend here's smart as a whip, nothing could be more obvious. Two of you making big plans?"

They didn't answer.

"And if you were, why tell me, right?" He made a gravelly sound in his throat that might have been laughter. "Okay, it's simple. You tell a guilty guy, stay off the goddamn stand or you're done, and he stays off. You tell an innocent guy the same thing, and he has a tough time buying it. He thinks, hey, I'm innocent, I'll tell my story and this will all go away. Usually a ticket straight to the pen, but . . . oh well."

"Oh well?" Greer said.

Wertz shrugged. "Sometimes there's nothing you can do."

"But you've admitted you didn't handle it well," Greer said.

"I'm starting not to like you," said Wertz, "despite how easy you are on the eyes. I never admitted any such thing. And you know what? I've had enough. So here's your takeaway, children—Sonny Racine was covering up for someone."

"Who?" Wyatt said.

"Don't know," said Wertz, his gaze fastening on Greer. "But if I had to guess, I'd say a girlfriend."

Girlfriend? Wyatt didn't understand. There was no girlfriend, just his mom. And then he remembered that his mom had never married Sonny; a wedding was in their plans but the crime had come first. Things shifted in his mind, and suddenly came a scary question: his mom was the girlfriend?

"What girlfriend?" Wyatt said.

"Show's over," Wertz said. He turned to the window. A dark bird swooped by.

"What does that mean?" Greer said as they drove away from Hillside Breeze. "Your mom was involved?"

"No way," Wyatt said. The idea was out of the question, impossible, unthinkable.

"Then what's he saying?"

"I don't know. Probably nothing. He's kind of out of it, right?"

Greer nodded. She took his hand. Hers was trembling a bit. "If I ever get like that, shoot me," she said.

"You? Get like that?" He glanced at her, couldn't imagine her any different from the way she was right there in the passenger seat, her hand on his.

Greer was quiet for the rest of the ride back to her place. As Wyatt pulled up in front, she said, "Doesn't it make sense to pay him a visit? I'm talking about Sonny Racine."

No explanation necessary: Wyatt had been thinking the same thing. "Don't want to," he said.

"Why not?"

"I just don't."

"But then we'll never know what really happened. Don't you want to find out? I do."

"Why?"

"For your sake," Greer said. "I care about you, in case you've missed that somehow."

Wyatt parked the car, shut it off, and turned to her. Her lips were slightly parted. "What's it got to do with me?" he said.

"It's part of your past."

"I wasn't even born."

"Yeah," said Greer. "But."

The next day, when Wyatt got to school, Dub was waiting for him in the parking lot. He had a red welt on the side of his powerful neck. Catcher was a tough position: Wyatt could even see the imprint of stitches left by the ball.

"That hurt," Wyatt said.

"Huh? What are you talking about?"

Wyatt pointed to the welt.

"It's nothin'," Dub said. "What's going on with you?"

"Headed for class," Wyatt said.

"That's not what I meant and you know it. What are you up to? How come you're not back home?"

"How come you're not?"

"For fuck sake, 'cause of baseball, you know that," Dub said. "Answer the question."

"I'm staying here."

"Why?"

"It's a good school."

"Since when do you give a shit about school?"

Wyatt shrugged. In fact, and to his surprise, he was starting to get more interested in school, English especially. He'd even done the homework last night, reading all of Act Three, Greer sitting nearby, playing her acoustic guitar.

"You're throwing your life away, man," Dub said.

"How's that?"

Dub stared at him—more of a glare, really—and shook his head. "Talk to Aunt Hildy," he said.

"About what?"

"I mean if your stupid-ass mind is really made up about staying here," Dub said. "Apologize. Be nice. Maybe she'll take you back."

"To her place?" Wyatt said. "Uh-uh."

"What do mean—uh-uh?"

"I'm fine where I am."

"You're an idiot."

"Hey, easy."

Dub was getting flushed; the welt caused by the baseball disappeared in the general redness. "She went to this school," he said. "Graduated two years ago."

"I know that," Wyatt said. "So?"

"So word is you're not the first."

Now Wyatt felt himself reddening, too. "What's that supposed to mean?"

"No big secret," Dub said, sticking out his chin, an aggressive habit he'd had since they were little boys. "She fucked half the football team."

Wyatt didn't think, just threw the hardest punch he could,

right smack on the stuck-out chin. He felt the jolt all the way back down his arm and into his shoulder. Dub's head snapped to the side and he staggered backward, almost fell. Wyatt was just starting to feel a bit bad about what he'd done, pretty close to a sucker punch, when Dub yelled, "Son of a bitch," and came roaring at him, both fists flying. Wyatt blocked one but not the other, which landed on his nose, exact same spot where Rusty had connected. Blood spurted out and Wyatt sank to his knees.

"Maybe that'll knock some sense into you," Dub said. "Sure as hell need it." He turned and walked away.

Wyatt sat on the pavement, leaning against the Mustang. He felt his nose—crooked again. He took a deep breath, counted a silent one-two-three, and snapped his nose back into place. That hurt, but not as much as the first time.

Wyatt found a sweatshirt in the trunk of the car, changed into it. When the bleeding stopped, he picked up his books and went into the school. The hall monitor wrote him up for tardiness, two demerit points, and glanced once or twice at his nose.

Ms. Grenville passed quiz sheets down the rows.

"Quiz?" said the funny kid in back. "Can't just give a quiz with no warning."

"Warning's a bit dramatic for a mere quiz, don't you think?" said Ms. Grenville. "I made an announcement at the end of class yesterday, but perhaps not loudly enough."

"What does it count for?" the funny kid said.

"The usual," said Ms. Grenville. "Five percent of your final grade."

"Two and a half," said the funny kid. "That's my final offer."

Wyatt looked over the quiz. There were three questions.

*1. What is the title of the play within the play? When the King asks Hamlet for the title, what does Hamlet tell him?*

Ms. Grenville demanded whole sentences. Wyatt wrote:

*The title of the play within the play is* The Murder of Gonzago. *Hamlet tells the king it's* The Mouse-trap.

*2. At the end of Act Two, Hamlet says, "The spirit that I have seen may be the devil: and the devil hath power to assume a pleasing shape." What does he mean, and what does this have to do with the play within the play?*

Wyatt wrote:

*It means the ghost can't be trusted, so Hamlet thinks up this plan to trap Claudius. The idea is about getting a——*

Wyatt couldn't think of the word he wanted, stopped right there, went to the next question.

*3. What is the result of Hamlet's plan? Do you consider it a success?*

Wyatt wrote:

*When the poison gets poured in the player king's ear,*
*Claudius, the real king, sort of loses it, so Hamlet knows to*
*trust the ghost. Claudius is for sure the killer of Hamlet's*
*father. So it's a success.*

Although maybe you couldn't really say, not until the end of the whole thing, and Wyatt hadn't read past Act Three. Wyatt was wondering whether to add something about that when Ms. Grenville said, "Time."

He passed in his sheet, realizing two things. First, he hadn't gone back and erased the unfinished sentence on number two, where he'd been stuck on a word. Second, the word he'd been looking for: *confession*. He'd wanted to say: *The idea is about getting a confession out of the king.* But too late. Had he blown the quiz completely?

When Wyatt got back to Greer's, she threw her arms around him and said, "How was school?"

"I'm going to go visit him," Wyatt said.

"Sonny Racine?"

"Yeah."

"Good idea," Greer said. "What changed your mind?"

"I guess you were right."

She took a long look at him. "Hey! What happened to your nose?"

"Nothing."

"Were you in a fight?"

"No."

She stroked the side of his nose, very gently.

# 17

YOU COULD WALK INTO A PRISON, no problem. A sign over glass double doors read PUBLIC ENTRANCE. Wyatt entered and approached a desk where a woman in an olive green uniform was gazing at a computer screen.

"Uh," he said. "The visitors' room?"

The woman looked up. "You have an appointment?"

"Yes, ma'am."

"Name?"

"Wyatt Lathem."

The woman tapped at the keyboard, nodded slightly. "Visiting?" she said.

"Yeah," said Wyatt. Like what else would he be doing here?

"Visiting who?" she said.

"Oh," said Wyatt. "Sonny Racine."

The woman made a mouse click. "Hours start at three today," she said. She handed Wyatt a clipboard. "Fill this out."

An unoccupied row of plastic seats, the kind all molded

together, stood along one wall. Wyatt sat at one end, filled out the form—his name, his address (he used Greer's), his arrest record (never), his relationship to the inmate. He thought for a long time, then wrote "family friend" and handed in the clipboard.

"Have a seat," said the woman at the desk. "We'll call you."

Wyatt returned to his plastic seat and opened a magazine. A fragment of a potato chip fell out, the ruffled kind. Wyatt set the magazine aside.

At 2:45 a woman came in. She wore a jogging suit but didn't look like a jogger. She was short and heavy, had a baby in her arms; another kid, maybe Cammy's age, trailed behind. The woman sat down with a grunt, not at the far end of the row, what Wyatt would have done in her place, but just three or four seats away. The baby was sleeping—a girl; she already wore earrings. The other kid, a boy, kept going, headed for a fountain in the corner. The woman called out to him in Spanish, obviously telling him to come back, but he ignored her. When he got to the fountain, he found he was tall enough to push the lever that started the water flowing but too short to drink. He turned and said something to his mother. He had a very loud voice. The mother again told him to come back. The baby awoke and started fussing. The uniformed woman tapped her fingernail on the desk and said, "If you can't keep it down, you'll have to wait outside."

Wyatt didn't get to see how that played out, because a man in an olive green uniform came through a door on the other side of the room, picked up the clipboard, and said, "Wyatt Lathem?"

Wyatt rose and approached him. The man was short and muscular, had a neatly trimmed mustache and wore a badge that read SHIFT SUPERVISOR. "This way," he said.

Wyatt followed him through the door and down a short corridor to a glassed-in booth. The uniformed man inside said, "License."

Wyatt slid his license through the slot. The man took it, ran it through a scanner, checked a screen, tossed the license into a tray. "Wallet," he said. "Keys, belt, anything metal."

"Get it all back when you leave," said the shift supervisor.

Wyatt nodded, but there was a problem already. The $200 was in his wallet, the plan being to give it back during the visit. How was he going to do that now? He had no idea, but he sensed that raising the issue wasn't the way to go. In fact, he wanted to get out of the place already.

Wyatt handed everything over. The man in the booth dropped it all in the tray.

"This way," said the shift supervisor, leading him to a metal detector. Wyatt walked through. Another green-uniformed man stood on the other side. "Arms up for the corrections officer, please," said the supervisor. Wyatt raised his arms, got wanded.

He followed the supervisor down the corridor. A pool of water was spreading across the cement floor. "Plugging the toilets never gets old, for some reason," the supervisor said. They avoided the wet section, came to a heavy steel door. The supervisor punched keys on a keypad and the door swung open. They went inside.

VISITING ROOM read a big notice on all four walls.

No physical contact of any kind. No food or drink. Appropriate clothing must be worn at all times. No miniskirts, halter tops, tank tops, short shorts. No exchange of any objects whatsoever. Violators will be arrested and prosecuted to the fullest extent of the law. This room is under constant video surveillance.

"Take a seat," said the supervisor. Two rows of plastic seats, each backed against a wall, the seats a little different from in the first room—farther apart, three feet or so, and each row bolted to the floor. There was no one else in the room. Wyatt sat in the middle of the row opposite the door he'd come in through. The supervisor went to a second door, used the keypad, and left. As the door swing shut, Wyatt caught a snatch of someone yelling in Spanish.

He waited. It occurred to him that he actually couldn't get out of this room on his own. He glanced up, into the lens of a video camera. His heart rate speeded up. He took a deep breath, thought about getting up, maybe pacing around a bit. At that moment, the second door opened and a man dressed in inmate khaki entered, followed by a green-uniformed corrections officer, a big woman with short dreadlocks. They both looked at Wyatt. The CO sat in a corner. The man in khaki crossed the room, his movements slow, even halting, and approached Wyatt.

Wyatt rose, probably in a slow and halting way also, although he was barely aware of that. All he was really aware of were his beating heart and this fantastic resemblance. The genetic bond was impossible to miss. Father and son: what could be more obvious?

Sonny Racine stopped about a yard away. Was this a moment for handshaking? Wyatt didn't know; and then he remembered the sign: No physical contact of any kind.

"Wyatt," Sonny Racine said. "Thank you for coming."

In his mind, Wyatt had rehearsed a few things he might say first, but now he couldn't remember any of them. He just nodded.

Sonny smiled. He had a nice smile, his teeth big and white, none missing. Wyatt would have expected bad teeth in prison. Also: no visible tattoos or scars, no evasiveness in the way he looked at you, no tics or twitches.

"I know it's not the most pleasant atmosphere," Sonny said.

"That's all right," said Wyatt.

Sonny gestured toward the plastic seats. He had strong, well-shaped hands, very much like Wyatt's but older-looking, maybe because one or two of the fingers weren't perfectly straight. Sonny was strong and well shaped in general, Wyatt's height to the inch, a little thicker in the chest and shoulders.

They sat in adjoining seats about three feet apart, each half turned to face the other. Wyatt was relieved to sit down: a sudden feeling of weightlessness had overcome him.

"My heart is beating pretty fast right now, I can tell you,"

Sonny said. "But not your problem. First, I want to say how much I appreciate this visit."

"That's all right," Wyatt said for the second time, feeling a little foolish about the inane repetition; but if it struck Sonny as foolish, he gave no sign.

"Second—I—" Sonny broke off, turned away, brushed the back of his hand over his eyes. When he turned back to Wyatt, his eyes were clear. "The natural thing is to say something about you being a fine-looking young man," he said, "but it's almost like giving myself a pat on the back."

"Because of the resemblance?"

"Exactly. It's . . . it's uncanny."

A silence fell over them, kind of awkward, at least for Wyatt, but he couldn't think of what to say. He glanced at the CO with the dreads, seated in the corner. She was gazing off into space. Even sitting down, he felt weightless.

"You don't have to stay," Sonny said. "If this is too uncomfortable or anything."

"No, no," said Wyatt.

"But if it gets . . .," Sonny began, then noticed a speck of dust on his knee and brushed it off. His khaki pants were spotless, with sharp creases down the fronts of both legs. He looked up at Wyatt and said, "Do you like the name?"

"What name?"

"Yours—Wyatt."

"Yeah." He did like his name, always had.

"Good," said Sonny. "It was either that or Derek."

"What do you mean?"

"In our discussions about what to name you," Sonny said.

"I'm talking about Linda. Your mom. We'd narrowed it down to those two, when . . . when . . ." His voice trailed off.

Derek? That was news to Wyatt. So was the whole idea of this man's involvement in the choice of his name. Wyatt had always just assumed his mom had picked it on her own.

Sonny was watching him. "Hope that doesn't bother you," he said, as though reading Wyatt's mind. "My being in on the naming and all. Obviously not my right, looking back from later events. Linda's, but totally."

"No," said Wyatt. "It's, uh . . ."

Another silence. Sonny rubbed his hands together, maybe trying to warm something up, like the room. "Is the Chuckwagon still around?" he said.

"Chuckwagon?"

"Guess not," Sonny said. "It was a diner on Fremont Street, across from that little park."

Wyatt knew the spot, back in East Canton. "A Laundro-mat's there now," he said.

"Yeah?" said Sonny. "I didn't know that." He turned back toward Wyatt. "It was tricked out to look like a covered wagon. Linda and I went there a lot. Does she still like BLTs, the bacon nice and crisp?"

"Yeah."

"She ordered it every time, always with a chocolate shake." Wyatt had never seen his mother drink a shake. "That's where we had these name discussions," Sonny went on, "at the Chuckwagon. Once—might have been the last time, now that I think about it—you kicked. I felt it, you know, in the womb. Linda kind of went still for a second, her mouth full of BLT. I can practically see it." He shook his head. "But enough of that. You didn't come all this way to hear an old guy get sentimental. Main point is—you like your name. Got a middle one, by the way?"

"Errol." A name he didn't like and never used, not even on official forms, like his license. Also: it was impossible to think of this man as an old guy, and Wyatt wouldn't have minded hearing more about the Chuckwagon.

"Errol—that would be after Linda's dad," Sonny said. "How's he doing?"

"He died a long time ago." So long that Wyatt had no memories of him.

"Errol was a good guy," Sonny said. "Loved baseball."

"Did he go to any of your games?" Wyatt said, taking a guess.

"Yeah, he did. How'd you know I played?"

"Coach Bouchard told me."

"What a character. Hope he's doing all right."

"They had to cut baseball, on account of the economy."

"I heard. No economy in here—one of the silver linings."

"What's another one?" Wyatt said; a question that came blurting out, mostly on its own.

Sonny laughed. He had a nice laugh, low and musical. "I'll have to think about that," he said. He gave Wyatt a quick sideline look. Wyatt had seen Mr. Mannion give Dub a look just like that, one day back in middle school when Dub had surprised everyone by winning honorable mention at the science fair.

"You heard the baseball story from Greer?" Wyatt said.

Sonny nodded. "She says you've got a nice compact swing. Interesting a girl would notice something like that."

"I was hitting at the cage," Wyatt said.

"Even so," Sonny said. "You miss it?"

"No," Wyatt said. "A little."

"What position?"

"Center field."

"Meaning you can run."

"A bit."

"More than that, I'll bet. Coach Bouchard always wanted a burner in center—doubt that changed over the years." He took a deep breath. "I still love baseball."

"Uh," said Wyatt, "do you get to throw the ball around and stuff?"

Sonny laughed again. Yes, a happy laugh. How was that happiness possible? "A baseball in the wrong hands is the kind of thing they try to avoid in here. But there's a lounge with a TV. We've got a game pretty much every night during the season." He smiled. "Not all the guys are baseball fans, of course, but we work it out."

The visitors' door opened and the heavy woman in the jogging suit came in with her two kids. They sat at the opposite wall, the baby in the woman's lap, the little boy beside her but almost at once slumping down to the floor, then crawling under the seats.

"Hey," said the CO with the dreads.

The heavy woman reached down, grabbed the boy by the pant leg, and pulled him out. The baby began to slide off the woman's lap. She grabbed him, too. The baby started crying.

The boy sat back down on the seat beside his mother, crossed his arms over his chest, looked angry. At that moment, the other door opened and an inmate in khaki entered, followed by another CO, this one white and male. The CO was big, but the inmate was even bigger, a huge guy with a shaved head, goatee, a tear tattoo under one eye, and another tattoo—Jesus on the cross—taking up most of the other side of his face.

He glanced at Sonny and gave him a curt nod. Sonny gave him one back. Then the huge guy walked toward the woman and the kids. The woman and the baby didn't take their eyes off him, but the boy kept staring straight ahead. The woman said something in Spanish. The man shrugged. He took a seat next to the boy, who still had his arms folded across his chest.

"Hey, what's wit' you?" the man said to the boy. The boy didn't answer. The man looked over him at the woman. "What's wit' him?" he said.

The woman answered in Spanish. She sounded annoyed.

"That's not what he needs," the man said. "I'll tell you what he needs." Wyatt noticed his hands: enormous, tattoo covered, half curled into fists.

Sonny saw where Wyatt was looking. "Best not to make eye contact with Hector," he said. "Among other things, he doesn't appreciate baseball."

Wyatt looked quickly away.

MORE VISITORS CAME IN, plus three inmates. It got a little noisier. Sonny Racine leaned forward so he wouldn't have to raise his voice. "How's Linda?"

"Good," Wyatt said, but the mention of his mother's name suddenly took him back to Hilltop Breeze: *Your mom was involved?*

"What's wrong?" Sonny said. "She's not having difficulties?"

"No."

"Is she sick?" Sonny said.

"No, nothing like that."

"Money problems?"

"No."

"What does she do?"

"Works in an insurance office."

"Married?"

"Yeah."

"What's the guy like?"

Wyatt shrugged. "I've got a half sister—Cameron, but we call her Cammy."

"You get along with the guy all right?"

"No complaints."

"So what's wrong?" Sonny said. "I got the feeling you had some kind of bad thought back there."

Wyatt shook his head, and as he did his gaze passed over the little groupings, Hector's and the others, all giving off waves on tension, unhappiness, even desperation, and nobody touching anybody else. "It's only," he said, "that you seem kind of happy."

Sonny's face changed, didn't become hard, just unreadable and still. "Is that a crime?" he said.

"No. Sorry. I didn't mean . . ."

"Go on."

Wyatt took a deep breath. What was the point of coming into this horrible place and not asking the big questions? He plunged ahead. "I never expected you'd be happy."

"Wouldn't push that too far, the happiness thing," Sonny said. "I'm happy to see you, of course, but we're still waiting for a day at the beach in here."

"Yeah, but, um, speaking of crimes, any innocent person in here would be . . ." Wyatt searched for the word, couldn't find it.

"Beside himself?" Sonny said.

"Yeah."

Sonny was watching him carefully. "You're getting at something, I can sense it," he said. "Problem is these visiting sessions have a time limit." He smiled; a nice smile, with the eyes joining in, no longer probing. And even as he spoke, the CO with the dreads was glancing at her watch.

Wyatt made himself look Sonny right in the eye; that had to be the way to deliver information that might be unpleasant. "The thing is, we saw Mr. Wertz. Me and Greer, I mean."

Sonny sat back. "Morrie Wertz is still around? Hasn't drunk himself to death by now?"

"He's at Hillside Breeze."

"What's that?"

"A nursing home behind the hospital."

"In Silver City?"

"Yeah."

"Don't know Silver City."

Wyatt thought about that. Sweetwater State Penitentiary was across the river but still within the town limit, so Sonny had actually been living in Silver City for seventeen years.

"What were you seeing old Morrie about?" Sonny said. "Not legal advice, I hope."

"Greer told me that everyone in here thinks you're innocent," Wyatt said. "That's why."

Sonny smiled, shook his head. "And every one of them also thinks he's innocent, too. They really wind up believing that, all of them."

"No, but—"

Sonny raised his voice, not a lot, but it carried across the room, and all the other conversations went silent and the COs suddenly looked wide-awake. "Hey, Hector," he said. "You innocent?"

Hector looked up, the light from the overhead fluorescent strips shining bright on his Jesus-on-the-cross tattoo. "Hundred percent."

A few people laughed, including the CO with the dreads; a few people, but none of the visitors. Conversations started up again. Sonny turned to Wyatt, the smile not quite gone from his face. Wyatt found himself reddening, not so much from awkwardness or embarrassment—although there was some of that—but more from anger.

"So what are you saying?" he said. "You're guilty? You did it?" The biggest question of all.

It didn't seem to throw Sonny the slightest bit. "A jury of my peers said so."

"But I'm asking you."

"I know, and you have every right," Sonny said. "What did Wertz say?"

"He thinks you were innocent," Wyatt said. "That you were protecting someone else."

Sonny lowered his voice. "Like who?"

"He didn't say," said Wyatt. "But—but was it Mom? My mother, I mean. Linda."

"Did Wertz say that?"

"No, but I couldn't think of—"

"Because if he did, he must be demented. A woman like Linda could never be involved in anything like that. Out of the question."

Out of the question: the exact same expression that had risen up in Wyatt's mind when Greer suggested the possibility. "So why did you get up on the stand when he told you not to?"

"He went into that?" Sonny said. "Funny how some people's grudges stay strong when there's almost nothing left of the rest of them—seen that more than once in here."

"His grudge is because he thinks you blew the case?"

"Exactly. But it was pretty clear to me at the time that I had a drunk for a lawyer—and the person blowing the case was him."

"What happened on the stand?"

For an instant, Sonny's face twisted up, as though he'd tasted something bad. "The DA made a fool of me. Which is what DAs can do to a kid, guilty or innocent."

The CO with the dreads checked her watch again, rose, and said, "Time's up."

Everyone started getting to their feet. "Which one were you?" Wyatt said.

"Guilty or innocent?" said Sonny. "It's not that simple."

"Let's move it, people," said another CO.

Wyatt talked fast. "But you didn't pull the trigger, did you?"

"Makes no difference under the law."

"But did you or not?"

Sonny gazed at Wyatt. Wyatt could feel him thinking.

"Hey, Racine!" called the big CO, the one who'd brought Hector in. All the inmates were lined up at the inmate door, all the visitors at the visitors' door.

Sonny rose. "Thanks for coming," he said. "Don't worry about me, whatever you do." He gave Wyatt a little wave and joined the line. The inmates filed out and the door closed. From somewhere in the walls came a deep clanging sound, and then softer ones, fading away.

● ● ●

Greer was up early in the morning. Wyatt smelled coffee, opened his eyes.

"You awake?" she called from the kitchen, somehow knowing.

Wyatt sat up, suddenly very awake. He felt different today, different in a way that disoriented him for a moment or two before he realized what this feeling was. Wyatt felt older, more solid, somehow. Could that happen overnight? Being older seemed to be a physical feeling, hard to describe even to himself. Did becoming an adult, a man, just mean accepting one day that that was what you were, and getting on with life?

"Hey, Mister Deep Thoughts," Greer said. She stood at the bedroom door, all dressed, a steaming mug of coffee in her hand.

He turned to her. She looked great, skin clear and glowing, eyes bright.

"Come here," he said.

"You want coffee?"

"Soon."

"Not too soon, I hope."

Not too soon after that, they were at the kitchen table. Granola with banana slices on top, coffee. Whatever Greer put on the table was always so good.

"Now comes Mister Hungry," she said.

Wyatt laughed, finished off his granola, plus half of hers.

"Know what we should do this weekend?" she said. He waited to hear. "Take a drive over to Millerville."

Wyatt wiped his mouth on the paper napkin. "How about today?"

She shook her head. "School day."

He rose. "Today."

"Mister Bossman?" she said. "He's new."

Millerville was about four hundred miles away, the apex of a stubby triangle with the East Canton–to–Silver City line forming the base. They stopped for gas in a tiny flatland town at the halfway point, the wind blowing scraps of paper across the road.

"See if this works," Greer said, pulling out a credit card.

Wyatt glanced at it: a corporate Visa card for Torrance Amusements.

"Maybe they haven't blocked it yet," Greer said.

Wyatt gave it back, went inside, and handed over a twenty. He returned to the car and was pumping gas, hunched against the wind, when his phone rang. He dug it out of his pocket, checked the number: his mom. He almost didn't answer.

"Hi, Mom."

"Wyatt," she said, her voice unsteady with emotion, "this can't go on."

He straightened. "I love you, Mom. You and Cammy. But I'm ready to be out on my own."

"What are you talking about? You're sixteen."

"I'll be seventeen soon. And I'm ready."

"You're not ready. And even if you were, it doesn't matter. You can't leave home without my permission until you're eighteen in this state—I checked with a lawyer."

"Then give me your permission, Mom."

"Absolutely not. I want you home today."

"I just can't," Wyatt said. Inside the car, Greer had her earphones on, was nodding her head slightly to some beat, eyes front.

"Is this about Rusty?" Linda said. "Are you punishing me or something? I've been going to this website on blended families, and they say that often happens in cases like—"

"Aw, Mom, I'd never think about you like that. You haven't done anything wrong."

"Then what? Is it that girl? I wish you'd waited . . . you know, before, um, an intimate relationship, and I know it must be exciting, but there'll be other girls."

*Not like this.* That was Wyatt's thought. He kept it to himself.

"Wyatt? Are you still there?"

"Yeah."

"You know how hard it would be for me to come down there. I can't miss work, not in this economy."

"Why would you want to come down here?"

"To get you. Didn't I just explain? You don't have my permission."

"Sorry, Mom. Please don't worry about me. I'm fine."

"And I'm sorry, too, Wyatt, but it's not your call. In the eyes of the law, you're a runaway. I have the right to notify the police."

"You wouldn't do that."

"Don't test me. I want you home tonight."

"Come on, Mom. I'm no runaway. I—"

She hung up. The pump hit the twenty-dollar mark and shut off. Wyatt tucked his phone into his pocket and replaced the nozzle. Greer turned and blew him a kiss through the window.

# 19

**WYATT GOT BACK IN THE CAR.**

"I've been thinking," Greer said. "What if—"

Her cell phone rang. Greer had a cool ringtone, three resonating Dobro notes. She checked the screen. Wyatt happened to see it, too. HONG KONG, it read, followed by lots of numbers. Greer shrugged her shoulders, flicked the phone shut.

"Hong Kong?" Wyatt said. "That's weird."

"Yeah," said Greer. "So here's my question—suppose he really was innocent, like totally. What are we going to do about it?"

"I don't know," Wyatt said, pulling back onto the highway, which they had pretty much to themselves. The land flattened out and the wind came unimpeded from the west, sometimes buffeting the car. "What could we do?" Wyatt said. "Also, maybe it's not even our problem. It's for sure not yours."

"Oh? What do you mean by that?"

He caught a sharpness in her tone, didn't know what to

make of it. A quick glance at her and he still didn't know: she had her eyes on the road.

"Just that you have your own problems," he said.

"Like what?"

"Like what? Like this whole thing with the bankruptcy, handling that all by yourself."

"Nothing left to handle. They changed the locks—you know that."

They drove in silence for a while. A horse ran by itself in an empty field. Bankruptcy meant the end of something, and big changes—Wyatt knew that from what had happened at Baker Brothers Iron and Metal Foundry. "So what are you going to do next?" he said.

"Huh?"

"Your plans and stuff," Wyatt said.

"What plans should I be having?"

"I don't know." But she was nineteen, smart, good-looking. Was reading to old blind people all she wanted? "Your music, for example. Isn't that something you want to do?"

"Didn't I mention that I sing flat?"

"I liked your singing."

"And my playing is faked," Greer went on, showing no sign she'd heard him. "I mentioned that, too."

"It didn't sound faked to me," Wyatt said.

"What are you really saying?" Greer said. "That I'm not good enough for you as I am?"

"Huh?" All of a sudden they seemed to be fighting; about what, he didn't know.

"Don't play dumb."

"I'm not. I don't understand what—"

"And since you brought up the subject of plans, are you going to divulge yours any time soon?"

Wyatt glanced at her again: still gazing at the road ahead, no expression on her face to indicate she was in a fight. "No secret," he said. "Graduate from high school, go to community college if I can, see what happens after that."

"Graduate from what high school?"

"This one. Bridger."

"Good luck and Godspeed," she said.

"What do you mean? What's wrong?"

"If I have to tell you, that just proves it." She leaned forward, switched on the radio, turned some country song up to earsplitting volume.

Wyatt hit the off button. For a second or two, he thought she would turn it back on, foresaw a quick mutual deterioration back to completely childish behavior. But instead Greer shifted away from him and cracked her window open an inch. Cold air came flowing in.

Some cows went by, then some sheep, and a llama. Only the llama turned to look. There was something about the gaze of the llama, or maybe the angle of its head, that crazily enough seemed scary for a moment. Wyatt took a deep breath.

"What's going on?" he said. "Why are you mad at me?"

There was a long silence. All Wyatt knew was that he wouldn't let himself ask again. A little settlement appeared in the distance, low shapes with lots of right angles in an enormous natural landscape with none. Wyatt parked in front of an old general store with a hitching rail out front.

"I'm getting a sandwich," he said. "Want anything?"

"I'm not hungry."

Wyatt switched off the car. And then a second crazy thing: he almost took the keys with him.

He went inside, got a turkey sandwich on homemade bread, a bag of chips, and a yogurt for Greer; she liked yogurt, could eat it later if she wanted. What was wrong with her all of a sudden? He had no idea. Back outside, he saw that she was on her phone. She closed it and put it away as he entered the car.

"Who was that?" he said, handing her the yogurt.

She put it on the floor. "Just some asshole."

"Who?"

"Nobody you know." She was silent as they pulled away. A state trooper zoomed by in the other direction. Greer sighed. "My landlord," she said. "If it's really that important."

Wyatt felt some of the tension between them dissipate. He tore off one end of the sandwich wrapper with his teeth, took a bite, realizing at the first taste how hungry he was. "What'd he want?" he said, talking with his mouth full.

"What do landlords usually want?"

"Rent?"

She nodded.

"How much is it?" he said. "I should be contributing."

"No," she said. "I'm fine. Fine for money." She reached for the yogurt. "Lemon, my favorite. Thanks." She started eating, shifted back closer to him. The sun came out, or if it had been out the whole time, Wyatt finally noticed.

Both East Canton and Silver City were hilly towns on rivers. Millerville was flat and riverless; as they drove into it, Wyatt couldn't imagine why anyone would have picked this spot for a town in the first place. They followed the main street past a doughnut shop, an auto supplies place, a going-out-of-business gift shop, a boarded-up building, the town hall. The town hall was solid-looking with a round tower on top; most of the windows in the tower were broken.

"What a pit," Greer said. "We better stop and ask."

"Ask what?"

"Directions for thirty-two Cain Street," Greer said. "Shouldn't we have a look at where all this went down? Or do you want to start at Pingree's construction yard, assuming it still exists?"

Wyatt didn't know, hadn't thought much about the steps beyond just getting to Millerville. "How are we going to do this?"

"Look around," said Greer. "Play it by ear. Isn't that the way everyone ends up doing just about anything?"

Wyatt thought that over. People tried to organize the future—for example, Coach Bouchard had come up with the whole Bridger idea, trying to keep baseball in Wyatt's future—but then things had gone wrong, at least partly because Mr. Mannion had been organizing Dub's future at the same time—and since then, yes: Wyatt had pretty much been playing it by ear. Maybe Greer was right and it was the same even at the very highest levels—why else would the economy be like this, boarded up, going-out-of-business,

174

bankrupt? Everyone, from the top right on down to him, here in this crappy flatland town, ended up playing it by ear.

"Okay," he said, "how about thirty-two Cain Street to start?"

"Now you're talking," Greer said. "Pull over—here's a likely citizen."

He pulled over. The likely citizen was an old woman in a pink quilted jacket, tacking a notice to a telephone pole with a small hammer. Wyatt slid down his window.

The old woman glanced over, pausing in midstroke. "You seen Effie?" she said. "Effie's my cat."

"Sorry, no."

"She's missing. White with black feet."

"Uh," Wyatt said, "we're looking for Cain Street."

"Cain Street?" said the woman. "No way Effie'd make it that far, not with her arthritis."

"Where is it?"

"Cain Street? To hell and gone." She waved vaguely. "Know where the bus station used to be? Way past that." She went back to tacking up the notice.

"Thanks," Wyatt said, pulling away.

"I hate cats," said Greer.

"What about dogs?"

"I've always wanted one."

"Me, too."

"Let's get one."

"Maybe sometime."

Greer sat back, folded her arms across her chest. He had another crazy thought: she wanted this dog today. "We could name it Millerville," he said. She laughed, and put her hand on his knee. He placed his hand over hers; it felt cold, and not quite steady. "Are you nervous about something?" he said.

"Always," she said. "Didn't you know?" She raised his hand and kissed it. "But not with you."

They found the old bus station—now padlocked, with a bright orange notice on the door—and came to Cain Street a few blocks later.

"Right or left?" Wyatt said. Greer pointed to the right. Wyatt turned right. The houses on Cain Street were small and low, mostly aluminum sided, a few painted cinder block, plus one or two sagging trailers that looked like they'd never move again. The lawns were brown and weedy, littered with all kinds of things—bald tires, rusted machinery, a yellowed Christmas tree, tinsel fluttering in the wind. A mailbox went by, the number on it—757. No numbers on the next bunch of mailboxes, and then came 921.

"I've always been a bad guesser," Greer said.

Wyatt U-turned, crossed back over the main drag, and continued to the other end of Cain Street. It grew more and more potholey, and finally the pavement petered out completely. Cain Street ended with no warning at a small stand of trees. The nearby lots were all blackened, as though the houses had burned down. The last one standing—a single-story house with two front windows, one big, one small, like mismatched eyes—had the number 32 on the door. Wyatt stopped the car.

They gazed at 32 Cain Street. The blinds were closed on both front windows. Flyers lay scattered outside the front door.

"This is where it happened," Greer said. "Or where whatever happened happened is maybe the way to put it."

Wyatt tried to imagine the scene. Had the blinds been closed that night, too? Probably, with drug dealers inside: Luis and Esteban Dominguez, plus Esteban's girlfriend, Maria, who died, and their baby, Antonia, who got shot in the eye and ended up in foster care. Thirty-two Cain Street was a very small house to contain all that trouble.

"All set?" Greer said.

"For what?"

"Knocking on the door."

"And then what?"

"Playing by ear."

"Can't we do better than that?"

"We could say we're looking for the Dominguez brothers," Greer said.

"Because we want drugs?" Wyatt said.

"Well?" Greer shrugged.

Greer and drugs: he shook his head.

She laughed. "Scared you, huh? How about we're a couple of ambitious students doing a story on the case for the school paper?"

He thought that over.

"Or criminal justice students at the community college, working on a project?" she said.

"Yeah," said Wyatt.

She opened her door. "What are we waiting for?"

**WYATT AND GREER WALKED** to the front door of 32 Cain Street, a white door, the paint peeling here and there, revealing black paint underneath. Greer pressed the buzzer. Wyatt listened, heard no buzzing sound from within, or anything else. Maybe nobody was home; maybe they'd gone for good. Greer tried the buzzer again, then knocked, hard knocks, one-two-three; Wyatt was surprised her fists, not very big or powerful-looking, could make noise like that.

A woman spoke on the other side of the door. Wyatt had heard no footsteps: she might have been standing there the whole time. "Who's there?" she said.

"We're from Foothills Community College," Greer said, so natural and confident Wyatt could almost believe it himself. "We've got a few questions for our school project."

Silence.

"Easy ones," Greer said.

More silence, and then: "Are you here for the rent?"

"The rent?" said Greer. "No. We're from the community college. We just need a minute or two of your time."

"The car's not here," the woman said, "in case you want to repo it."

"We don't want your car. We just want your help."

"My help?" The door opened. A woman stood there, blinking in the light. She was old, wore a threadbare robe, had bare feet, one with a big bunion, the other slender and nicely shaped. She looked at them, her expression puzzled and a little afraid. "What kind of help?"

"Just answering a few questions," Greer said. "Not for attribution if you don't want."

The woman began to look less afraid, more confused. "I don't understand a word you're saying."

"It doesn't matter," Greer said. "How long have you been living here?"

"Almost five years now. But there's no lease or nothin', which is how come the landlord—"

Greer cut her off with a quick chopping motion. "Do you know the Dominguez brothers who used to live here?"

"The place was empty when we moved in. I can't be held responsible . . ." Her voice trailed away. After moment or two, she blinked again and said, "Are you cops? You look too young to be cops."

"We're not cops," Wyatt said. "But a murder was committed in this house."

The woman took a step back. "That was long before my time."

"But you know about it?" Wyatt said.

"Too late. I knew too late."

"What do you mean?" Wyatt said.

"Ever hear of bad luck?" said the woman. "What's badder than living where murder's been done? We'd never have moved in if we'da known. Then it was too late."

"Couldn't you have moved out?" Wyatt said.

"And gone where? It's not so easy."

"What do you know about the murder?" Greer said.

"Nothin'."

"You must have heard something about it."

The woman shrugged. "Drug deal gone wrong or some such. Why are you asking all these questions, anyways?"

Greer's tone sharpened. "We told you. For our project— it's about the murder."

The old woman gave Greer an unfriendly look. "Sounds like a no-good project to me." She turned to Wyatt. "Why don't you take your question to the goddamn landlord—he's owned this place forever."

"Okay," Wyatt said. "Who's the landlord?"

"Slumlord's more like it—owns the whole godforsaken street." She bent down, clasping her robe at the throat with one hand, fishing through a scattering of unopened envelopes on the floor with the other. She picked one up, ripped out the return address from the upper left, handed it to Wyatt.

"Pingree Realty?" he said.

"Bloodsuckers," said the old woman.

"Any relation to Art Pingree?" Wyatt said.

"How would I know? Think I socialize with those people?" She leaned closer to Wyatt. He smelled booze on her breath. "I'm choosey about my friends."

* * *

Back in the car. "Art Pingree's the nephew of Sonny's boss?" Greer said.

"Yeah."

"See what this means? The Dominguez brothers were renting the house from old man Pingree. The nephew found out they were drug dealers and cooked up the plan."

"You should be a detective," Wyatt said.

"Not a bad idea," said Greer. She paused, then raised a finger, brought it down on Wyatt's lips. A charge went through him. She smiled. He'd never seen her look better.

The Pingree Realty office was in a strip mall a few blocks from the town hall, a pizza place on one side and a liquidation store on the other. Wyatt and Greer approached the door. It opened and a middle-aged woman came out, lighting a cigarette.

"Help you with something?" she said, squinting at them through the smoke. "In the market for a cute little starter home, maybe? I happen to have one, several, in fact, and there's never been a better time."

Greer smiled—amused by the idea, Wyatt thought, or maybe she even liked it. "We're looking for Mr. Pingree."

"Mr. Pingree?"

Greer pointed to the gold-lettered printing on the plate-glass window: PINGREE REALTY.

"Oh, that," said the woman, taking another drag. "I kept the name is all. Pingree sold out. I took over ten years ago this summer."

"Where can we find Mr. Pingree?" Greer said.

The woman shook her head. "Cancer, I think it was,

which was why he was selling. What's this about?"

"We're—" Wyatt began, ready to again offer up the community college story, but Greer cut him off.

"We're researching our family tree," she said.

"You're related to the Pingrees?" the woman said.

"That's what we're trying to find out."

"I thought that kind of thing was done online these days."

"Mostly," said Greer, "but sometimes you run into a dead end."

The woman studied Greer's face, then nodded. "Mrs. Pingree and her daughter are still around," she said. "Two-seventeen Willow Street." A phone in the office started ringing. The woman took one last big drag, ground the cigarette butt under her heel, and went inside.

"Family tree?" Wyatt said. "Where did that come from?"

"Isn't it true in a way?" Greer said. "Your family tree, to be specific."

Wyatt could see that; and more: they were researching perhaps the most important incident in the life of that tree.

Willow Street was by far the nicest part of Millerville that they'd seen. Big old wooden houses with lots of porches and turrets lined both sides, separated by broad lawns and tall hedges, although there were no willow trees in sight, and FOR SALE signs poked up here and there. Wyatt stopped in front of 217, a brown house with yellow trim. "Family tree or school project?" he said.

"School project."

They climbed the stairs to the porch, knocked on the front door. No answer.

"What if they've all gone for good," Greer said, "and we just move in and live happily ever after in this great big house?"

Wyatt didn't like that idea, even found it a bit creepy— Art Pingree's criminality maybe being at the root of how Sonny Racine lost his freedom. He was casting around without success for some light or even funny way to put that when a minivan came down the street and pulled into the driveway. A girl about Wyatt's age got out of the driver's side door, slung a backpack over her shoulder, and headed for the porch. She saw Wyatt and Greer standing there and came to a stop.

"Can I help you?" she said. She was short and lean, with dark hair and eyes and light brown skin.

Greer stepped down from the porch, Wyatt following. "Hi," Greer said. "We're looking for Mrs. Pingree."

"That's my mom," the girl said. "She won't be home till six."

"Um, okay," Wyatt said, turning toward the Mustang, parked on the street.

But Greer, as he'd been learning, didn't discourage easily. She gave her hair a quick shake, smiled at the girl, and said, "Maybe you can help us. We go to Foothills CC and we're working on this project."

"Do you know Billy Friel? He goes there, too."

"Don't think so," Greer said. "Is he in criminal justice?"

"I'm not sure. He was a year ahead of me, at Polk High."

She looked at Wyatt, back to Greer. "You guys didn't go to Polk, did you?"

"We're from Silver City," Greer said. "What we're supposed to do on this project is write a report on some real-life crime, from A to Z, kind of like *Law and Order*."

The girl looked a bit puzzled.

"But more analytical," Greer said. "Twenty pages minimum, double-spaced, no fancy fonts."

The girl laughed. She was very pretty, with lively eyes; actually, Wyatt realized, noticing something strange, only one of her eyes was lively. The other didn't seem to be sparkling as much, or at all. "Like Braggadocio," she said.

Greer laughed, too. "Exactly," she said. "I'm Greer and this is Wyatt."

"Hi," said the girl. "My name's Toni."

"Cool," said Greer. "The case we're looking into involved someone named Art Pingree. We wondered if—"

"Oh, my God," Toni said. She turned pale. Her mouth opened and closed, but no sound came out.

"Christ," said Wyatt, putting the pieces together and suddenly feeling sick. "He's your brother."

Toni shook her head, very fast, as though wanting to make that suggestion go away. "Oh, no, no, no. Nothing like that."

"You're not related to Art Pingree?" Greer said.

Toni winced, almost like she'd been slapped. "No," she said.

"We've got the wrong Pingrees?" Greer said.

"No," Toni said again.

184

"I don't understand," Greer said.

"You've got the right Pingrees." Slowly, as though her legs were losing strength, Toni sat on the top step. Greer sat beside her, just as slowly, a couple of feet away. Wyatt stayed where he was, standing at the bottom of the stairs, fighting instincts that were urging him to get back in the car and leave.

"I'm a little lost," Greer said.

Toni nodded, whether agreeing that Greer was lost or because she herself was lost, Wyatt didn't know. "Art Pingree was my mom's nephew," Toni said.

"Was?" said Greer.

"He's dead. He got killed in Western State Prison; didn't last a week, my mom said."

"Who killed him?" Greer said.

"Some inmates, I guess," said Toni. "I'm not sure if they ever found out who." She glanced down at Wyatt. He saw a tiny white scar over her nonlively eye, shaped like an upside-down V. "You didn't know he was dead?"

"No," Wyatt said.

"How much research have you done?" Toni said.

"We're just getting started," said Greer. "Maybe it would help if you just gave us a quick run-through on the whole thing. It was all about robbing some drug dealers, right?"

"I guess so," said Toni. She took a deep breath. "But I don't really want to talk about it."

"No?" said Greer. "I'm not sure I—how old are you?"

"Seventeen."

"Meaning you weren't even alive when the robbery happened. So the trauma couldn't—"

Toni, her voice rising sharply, cut off whatever Greer was going to say about trauma. "That's not true. I was alive. Very much alive." A tear appeared at the outside corner of the lively eye.

"My apologies," Greer said. "But you must have been just a baby."

"Just a baby, yes."

"So you couldn't remember your cousin," Greer said, "or anything about the whole incident, really."

"My cousin?"

"If Art Pingree was your mother's nephew, then don't you have to be his cousin?"

"What a horrible idea," Toni said.

The tear grew too big for her eye to contain, and spilled over her lower eyelid, running down her cheek. Wyatt had an idea—not a real idea, with a foundation of reason and logic, more like simply the final product.

"Were you there when it happened?" he said.

# 21

"YOU WERE THERE?" Greer said. "How could that be? Oh, my God—Art Pingree was babysitting you, took you along on a robbery?"

Toni shook her head. "Toni's a nickname," she said. "My real name's Antonia."

"And therefore . . . ?" Greer said.

"I never talk about this," Toni said. "I have no memory of it at all, of course, but at the same time it's impossible to forget. And even if somehow I could forget, almost every day someone—usually someone I don't know—looks at me funny."

"Still not getting you," Greer said.

Wyatt wished Greer wouldn't say anything, wished she'd simply let Toni tell her story. He shot Greer a quick glance. She shot him back one of her own: first surprised, then annoyed.

Toni turned to Wyatt. "How did you know I was there? Was it in your research?"

"No," Wyatt said. "It was just a wild guess."

"Are you religious?" Toni said.

"Not really," said Wyatt. "Why?"

"Me either," said Toni. "But I used to wish I was—you know, hoping to make sense of things. On the other hand, you could say life's worked out way better for me than it would have." She was gazing at Wyatt's face—one of her eyes inquiring and probing, the other not—gazing as though searching for something. "No one could ask for a better mom, for example. And I've had every opportunity—I got accepted early at Northwestern."

"But?" said Greer.

"I'm sorry?" Toni said.

"I thought I heard a but."

Toni bit her lip. Wyatt gave Greer another look. Greer smiled a mouth-only smile and rose. "Got a few calls to make," she said. "I'll leave you guys to it."

*What's with her?* Wyatt thought. He watched Greer walk to the road and get in the car, aware that Toni was watching her, too.

"It's a kind of group project, where you team up?" Toni said.

"Yeah."

"That sounds interesting. Do you like Foothills?"

"It's all right." Which was probably true about Foothills, and at least not as direct a lie as saying, *Yeah, I like it.* Kind of stupid, since this whole . . . interview, if that was what you'd call it, was based on falsehood.

"The thing is," Toni said, "I'm not sure I'd want this whole story in your project. Not that it's a secret, but it's not really public, either. You know how the internet gets, so out of control."

"We, uh, could change your name," Wyatt said. "Change all the names, and the town, too."

"You could?"

"Don't see why not."

Down in the car, Greer seemed to be watching, although the reflection of the bare treetops on the windshield made it hard to tell.

"In that case," Toni said—she paused, then looked directly at him. "Notice anything about me?"

"No," Wyatt said. "I mean, yeah, you're, you know, nice-looking, but besides that, uh . . ."

She smiled, a very little smile, and shook her head slightly. "About my eyes," she said. "Do you notice anything unusual about my eyes?"

Wyatt nodded.

"I knew you did. I always know."

"Sorry, I—"

"No need to be sorry. I always know—but it doesn't affect me. I don't remember being any other way." She pointed to the nonlively eye, the one with the tiny upside-down V scar above it. "This eye isn't real. It's a very good fake—we went to Denver for it."

Wyatt didn't know what to say. Toni had already ruled out saying sorry, and nothing else came to mind.

"The truth is I'm adopted," Toni said. "My last name's Pingree now, but it used to be Morales. My mother was killed when I was eight months old."

"She was Esteban Dominguez's girlfriend?" Wyatt wanted to be silent, let her tell her story, but he couldn't stop himself.

"That's right," Toni said. "He was my biological father. My real father was Dad—William Pingree, but everyone called him Bud. Kind of a strange situation, the real father not being the biological one."

"It's good that you ended up with a real one," Wyatt said.

"Yes!" said Toni. "Exactly. I've never had the slightest desire to look up Esteban Dominguez or anything like that. William Pingree was my dad, pure and simple. He suffered so much at the end." Another tear formed in her good eye. "Have you ever seen someone die of cancer?"

"No."

"He was so brave." Toni wiped away the tear. "But that has nothing to do with your project. The point is my dad rented out a few houses on the North Side to some of his construction workers. One of them was Esteban's brother, Luis. Of course, Dad didn't know they were dealing drugs on the side. Art Pingree was the one who collected the rents, and he found out about the drug thing. He wasn't a bad guy himself, but he was the follower type and he had these two buddies who *were* bad guys. One was called Doc, the other name I don't remember. They decided it would be cool to rip off the drug dealers. Long story short, there was shooting. My mother got killed and I got shot." Toni spread her hands.

"Who by?" Wyatt said.

"Who did the shooting, you mean?"

"Yeah," said Wyatt. "I know it doesn't matter legally, but . . ."

"That's right. But it kind of does matter, doesn't it? My dad thought so. It turns out that the two shots that mattered came from Art Pingree's gun. He and the other two got sent to jail, and so did the Dominguez brothers, for drug dealing, and later they were deported back to Mexico. I was put in foster care, but after Art Pingree got killed, Mom and Dad adopted me. Nothing's so bad it can't be made a little better— that's what my mom says." She was silent for a moment or two, then looked at Wyatt. "Don't you need to take notes or something?"

"I'll remember," Wyatt said. Down in the car and screened by the windshield reflection of the bare treetops, Greer seemed to be sitting very still.

"Any questions?" Toni said.

"What do you know about the trial?" Wyatt said.

"Not much. The judge gave Art Pingree and one of the bad guys life sentences. The other bad guy—Doc—testified for the prosecution in return for less jail time. He got out last year." Toni's good eye lost some of its sparkle. "The creepy thing is he came back here."

"Here?"

"To Millerville. He's on parole, of course, and the police chief told us they watch him, but still. Even more creepy—I wouldn't even know him if I saw him."

"Where, uh, does he live?"

Toni shivered. "I have no idea," she said. "The police chief will know. Maybe you should be talking to him about your project, but he wasn't the chief back then."

"That's a thought," Wyatt said. Loaded with problems, yes, but maybe the kind Greer could solve. He rose. "Thanks," he said, "for the help."

"No problem." Toni rose, too. "Good luck with the project." She held out her hand. He shook it. Her hand was small, but warm and surprisingly strong.

He got in the car. Greer didn't say anything, or even look at him. They drove off. He was on the main street, almost back in the center of town, when she said, "Well, Mr. Bossman— are you going to share the story or not?"

He pulled over, parked in front of a convenience store. "What's with you?" he said.

"With me? Nothing's with me. Nothing's ever with a third wheel."

"What are you talking about?"

"You know."

"No, I don't."

"Then figure it out," she said. "I'm thirsty." She flung the door open, got out, and entered the convenience store.

He sat there, tried to absorb everything that had come at him, not really succeeding. Maybe pen and paper would help, to get the facts listed in bullet points—and if he got the facts and lined them up right, he'd know whether Sonny Racine was innocent, at least in the sense of not being the shooter. Wyatt was reaching toward the glove box when Greer's phone went off, that ringing Dobro sound. He spotted the phone, wedged between her seat and the console.

Wyatt dug out the phone, checked the screen. HONG KONG, it read, followed by a long number. He remembered Greer saying, *Curiosity killed the cat,* remembered as well what they'd been discussing at the time, namely the arson and her part in it, or not, and all that somehow added up to him clicking the talk button.

He didn't say anything, just listened.

A man spoke. "Hey, baby," he said. "How're you doing?"

Wyatt said nothing.

"Greer?" said the man. "Can you hear me? It's Van. Greer? Greer?"

Wyatt clicked off. The Dobro ringtone sounded again, almost immediately. Wyatt didn't answer. After a minute or so the new-message icon popped up on the screen. Not long after that, Greer came out of the convenience store with an energy drink in her hand, and got in the car.

Wyatt handed her the phone. "I think there's a message waiting."

"You could have checked it. No secrets from you—the voice mail code's seven four times." Greer took the phone, glanced at the screen. "Nothing important," she said, flipping the phone shut. "Where are we headed?"

"Not sure," said Wyatt.

"No?" Greer sipped the energy drink. "I thought you were in command."

"What do you mean by that?"

"The masterly way you took over the Q and A of our pretty

little friend back there," Greer said. "That's what I mean. Ever going to share your discoveries, or is it just between the two of you?"

All of a sudden, Wyatt was angry. It didn't happen often. "All right, let's share," he said. "Who's Van?"

Greer shrugged. "No clue." She took another sip, slightly off-target, so that a few red drops of energy drink trickled from the corner of her mouth. Her eyes shifted toward him. "What's that look for?" she said.

"I'll try again," Wyatt said. "Who's Van?"

"I don't know what you're talking about."

"That won't work."

"Huh?"

"Because you're caught in a lie, Greer. Van just called you from Hong Kong."

"Hong Kong? I don't know anybody in Hong Kong. Must have been a wrong number."

Wyatt's voice rose. He was shouting now. "I answered your goddamn phone. Don't you get it? He called you baby."

She wiped the red trickle off her chin. "My mother's husband's a yeller, too," she said, not raising her voice at all.

"What the fuck?"

"And nothing you do is going to make me change my story. I don't know anyone in Hong Kong, don't know anyone named Van. It was a wrong number, end of story."

Wyatt got a grip on himself, forced his voice lower. But inside he was just as angry, or even more, now that it was bottled up. "You're lying to my face," he said. "He called you by name. What kind of wrong number is that?"

Greer's eyes narrowed, almost closing completely. She came close to looking ugly. "Maybe that'll teach you not to spy on me."

"I wasn't spying on you."

"You answered my phone. That's spying."

"You just said you had no secrets. Who's Van?"

She didn't answer.

"If you're not hiding anything," Wyatt said, "why don't we call that Hong Kong number right now?"

"Know what?" Greer said. "You're just like all the rest. You do sincerity better—that's the only difference. Especially in bed. Lucky you."

"You're making no sense."

"Don't worry your little head about it," Greer said, opening the door. "You're free as a bird." She got out, closed the door—not with a slam, more like the opposite, slow and careful, and walked off down the street. After two blocks she turned a corner and vanished from sight. She'd left nothing behind but the can of energy drink, balanced on the dash.

Wyatt just sat there. Time passed. He cooled down. After a while, he considered driving around, trying to find her, but what was the point? She'd come back when she was ready. And then? Wyatt had no idea.

He finished the energy drink, cooled down a bit more. He began to notice things going on around him, like a thin old man in a tweed jacket and bowtie, coming out of the convenience store. He wasn't one of those bent-over old men; he held himself erect, and moved briskly. The old man walked a few doors down and entered a brick building with a picture window in front. In gold paint on the window:

THE MILLERVILLE BEACON
Established 1849
Your Town, Your News

Wyatt got out of the car.

WYATT ENTERED THE OFFICE of the *Millerville Beacon*. He'd never been in a newspaper office before, didn't know what to expect. The *Millerville Beacon* had a counter in front, bearing a stack of fresh-looking newspapers, and four or five workstations in back, only one of which was occupied. The old man in the bowtie sat there, eating a sandwich, eyes on his computer screen.

"Looking for today's paper, young man?" he said, somehow catching sight of Wyatt peripherally. He turned, pointed with his chin at the stack. "Just drop fifty cents in the dish," he said.

Wyatt took the top paper off the stack, put two quarters in a dish that now held four.

"Don't see many of your generation as customers these days," the old man said, giving him a second look. "I'd be interested in any insights you might have about that."

"Well, uh . . ."

"Simply put—why the hell don't you read the goddamn paper?"

"There's, um, online," Wyatt said.

"Online." The old man practically spat out the word. "You mean free."

"What about advertising? Pop-ups and stuff."

"One, it doesn't pay diddly-shit. Two, no one even glances at the ads, and as soon as the accounts realize that, they're over the blue horizon. So answer me this, young man— what's your name, by the way?"

"Wyatt Lathem."

"Nice name," said the old man. "Mine's Lou Rentner. Interested in palindromes?"

"What's that?"

"Something that's the same forward and backward—like Rentner. Lathem's not a palindrome, of course, but it is an anagram."

"Don't know that one either," Wyatt said.

"Not your fault—blame the education system in this country. An anagram's where you can rearrange the letters and come up with something else. In your case, Lathem turns into Hamlet." Wyatt thought, *Whoa*, and inside he reeled a little. "Ever heard of Hamlet?" said Mr. Rentner.

"A play by Shakespeare," Wyatt said.

"Well, well. Can you tell me a thing or two about it?"

"It's all about whether to believe the ghost or not."

Lou Rentner tilted back in his chair, gave Wyatt a closer look. "Well, well," he said again. "And where do you go to school, young Wyatt?"

Quick-decision time. Wyatt stuck with the story. "Foothills CC."

"Really? You don't look that old. But it's true what they say about us geezers—the older you get, the harder it is to guess the age of the young people. What are you studying?"

What did people study at Community College? "Just taking a little of this and that for now," Wyatt said.

"This and that will get you nowhere in life on planet Earth," Mr. Rentner said. "If you don't mind me sticking my oar in."

"I'm interested in criminal justice."

"Yeah?"

Wyatt nodded. He plunged ahead, the way he thought Greer might have in his place. "Right now I'm working on the story of this old case—it actually happened here in Millerville."

"Did it, now?" said Mr. Rentner. His chair squeaked. "And what case would that be?"

"It was about these guys who tried to rob some drug dealers."

"Thirty-two Cain Street?" said Mr. Rentner.

"Yes."

Mr. Rentner pulled over a chair from the adjoining workstation and patted the seat. Wyatt walked around the counter and sat down.

"An interesting case," Mr. Rentner said. "How did you happen to pick it?"

Was this the moment for starting over, for saying something like, *It turns out that my real father, who I'd never met until very recently, committed this crime, or maybe not, and my girlfriend and I—another maybe not—are trying to find out what happened?* Wyatt's every instinct told him not to. "My partner found out about it," he said.

"Partner?"

"We team up on these projects."

Mr. Rentner shook his head. The skin of his face was shiny and must have been very thin: Wyatt could see purple networks of blood vessels underneath. "Never learn a god-damn thing that way. Real learning means all by your lonesome. But not your fault." He drummed his bony fingers on the desk. "Tell you what let's do," he said. "I'll take you on a quick tour."

"Of what?"

"The crime scene, other places of interest. Nothing beats a firsthand look, and no amount of digital dipsy doodling will ever change that."

"Thanks," Wyatt said, "but I don't want to take up your time." But more important, how could he leave? What about Greer?

"Not an issue—I've actually been considering a follow-up piece, where-are-they-now, ten column inches. A handy space filler in this trade, should you ever choose to go into it, supposing it's still around, which I highly doubt, as I hope I already made clear."

"Won't people always need news?" Wyatt said.

Mr. Rentner rose and took a cap off a wall peg, one of those flat caps with almost no brim. "Need, yes," he said. "But all they want is entertainment. When you're done with Shakespeare, check out the fall of the Roman Empire."

They went outside. "This is my car," Wyatt said. "Did you want me to, uh—"

200

"Nice ride," said Mr. Rentner, patting the hood. "No—we'll take mine." He turned toward a bright yellow minivan. Wyatt quickly unlocked the Mustang so Greer could wait inside. Then he climbed into the minivan.

"Buckle up," Mr. Rentner said. He pulled onto the road without looking, did a too-quick U-turn, and headed back in the direction of the North Side, over the speed limit by ten or fifteen miles an hour. A cop in a patrol car coming the other way made a pressing-down-air gesture with his hand, sign language for "slow down," but Mr. Rentner didn't seem to notice and sped up, if anything. Wyatt glanced back. The patrol car hadn't turned to follow them; from behind, it looked like the cop was shaking his head in resignation.

"What do you know about Millerville?" Mr. Rentner said.

"Not much."

"Where're you from originally?"

"East Canton."

"Did you know Mark Twain once ended up there by mistake?"

"Yeah."

Mr. Rentner looked disappointed. "Bottom line—Millerville's much the same, but in even worse shape. Unemployment rate topped twenty percent last month. Know what that means for people?" He jabbed his finger at storefronts passing by. Jab. "Going out of business." Jab. "Closed down last week." Jab. "Hanging on, but only by the good graces of the landlord." Jab. "Bankrupt." Jab. "In court." Jab. "Skipped town in the middle of the night." Jab. "Tried to commit suicide." They drove in silence for a while. "Town was in much better shape back in the period you're interested in. We just didn't know it, is all."

They came to Cain Street, turned left. Just past the point where the pavement ended, Mr. Rentner pulled over, onto the edge of one of the blackened lots.

"This was always the worst section, going back to frontier days. Know why? On account of the well water tastes skunky. But everyone's been on town water for fifty years, and it's still the bad part of town. Some folks, maybe most, take way too much time to realize things." He pointed through the windshield. "Thirty-two Cain. Inside we had the Dominguez brothers, Luis and Esteban, illegal immigrants from Mexico. Make up your own mind whether the illegal part is germane to the story. The brothers worked construction for a local builder and developer name of Bud Pingree, now developing in the great beyond. Bud wasn't a bad guy, rented out some properties he had on the North Side to some of his workers at a fair price. Thirty-two Cain was one of them. Not sure who owns it now."

Wyatt came close to telling him; a strange situation, and uncomfortable. He realized with an inner start that there'd been too many of these lately.

"Bud's nephew, Art—one of those guys who thinks he's smarter than he is, in other words a born loser—did some of the rent collection. They say he came up with the robbery idea but I doubt it. Much more likely it was one of his lowlife pals—Doc Vitti or Sonny Racine."

"What, uh—I mean how come you call them lowlifes?" Wyatt said.

"In addition to what they did right here?" Mr. Rentner said. "They were all pretty young, of course—mustn't be too judgmental with the youth—but Doc already had a record and a rep as being something of a barroom brawler. The other one, Racine, was clean, as far as I recall, but there was something strange about him."

"Like what?"

"He seemed—this was in court, I'm talking about—very smart, by far the smartest of the three. Not the kind of guy who shows it off, though—maybe he doesn't realize how smart he is, pretty rare in my experience. The Art Pingrees of the world are much more common. Yet in a crime with incomplete forensic evidence and confused and sometimes contradictory testimony, plus no surviving witness other than a pair of drug dealers and an infant—you know about her?"

"Yes."

"Here's something you don't know, the kind of sidebar that's better than the main story—Bud Pingree and his wife ended up adopting her and she turned out to be quite a gal. Good rising out of the stink of evil. Don't see that every day. But back to the main point—the smart thing in a case like this is to make the first deal. So why didn't the smartest guy do the smart thing?"

"Why?" said Wyatt. "Tell me."

Mr. Rentner laughed, an unpleasant sound in his case, like unlubricated steel parts rubbing together. "If I knew, I would." He turned the key, did a U-turn, headed back the way they'd come. "It was chaos in there that night, and chaos leads to incoherence. Luis Dominguez got knocked out with a baseball bat right from the get-go, so his testimony was useless, and Esteban's wasn't much better—he was pretty much occupied grabbing his gun from under a seat cushion and trying to do some killing of his own. Do you have a handle on the forensics?"

"No."

"Good. I mean by that it's good to say you don't know when you don't know. Want to stay short of being an ignoramus, of course. First thing, there were two guns fired that night. One was a thirty-eight revolver belonging to Esteban Dominguez. Two shots were fired from that gun. One slug was dug out of the kitchen wall at thirty-two Cain Street, the other ended up in Art Pingree's leg. Two more shots were fired from a twenty-two handgun that probably belonged to Art Pingree and was never recovered. The first one passed right through the girlfriend's throat, severing her jugular vein, and then striking the baby in the eye. The second shot hit Esteban in the chest, missing his heart by an inch or so. He testified that he didn't see who fired it, also testified that he remembered seeing only two invaders, Art Pingree and Doc Vitti. Pingree swore he wasn't the shooter; Doc made his deal and fingered Racine; Racine took the stand and also denied he'd fired the shot. But then, in response to a question from the DA about what he thought had happened to the gun, Racine did the most amazing thing: he said he'd thrown it into the woods just as the police moved in. What do you make of that?"

Wyatt was totally confused. "The gun was never found?"

"Nope."

"It doesn't make any sense."

"Not without an alteration or two, completely speculative."

"Like what?"

"Naturally the DA had no interest in speculation. What he had was a strong case, just about open-and-shut, that speculation could only muddy up. No gun? They figured Racine had thrown it in some other direction, or a dog had found the thing and run off with it, or that it had fallen into a hole they'd missed."

Mr. Rentner turned down a street that led to the edge of town. They passed a few shabby houses, then stopped outside a trailer park.

"But suppose," said Mr. Rentner, "there'd been a fourth person on that little shindig. Further suppose that said fourth person, perhaps the actual shooter, ran away with the gun just as the police were closing in, maybe was never in the house at all, but outside a window, let's say. Maybe Racine was there, too, at least part of the time. Then his testimony starts to make sense."

"How?" Wyatt said.

"Saying he threw the gun away takes the police off the scent of number four. Therefore, in this scenario, Racine lied to protect whoever that was. Not even much woods back of Cain Street, then or now. Suggests a certain unfamiliarity with the area. I'm not convinced he was even there."

"But why would he do that?"

"*Cherchez la femme,*" Mr. Rentner said.

"I don't understand."

"A basic French phrase like that?" Mr. Rentner said. Then he sighed and said, "Not your fault. Let's put it this way— there were rumors at the time that Racine had a girlfriend."

Wyatt felt the blood drain from his head, like he was about to faint. Yes, Racine had had a girlfriend all right: Wyatt's mom. The girlfriend theory wouldn't go away, threatening Wyatt's whole history.

But there was no time to deal with that. An old black Dodge Ram pickup came driving out of the trailer park, a big-headed man with shoulder-length graying hair behind the wheel.

"That's Doc," said Mr. Rentner.

## 23

"WHEN I HEARD HE WAS BACK HERE, I got it in mind to interview him, gave him a call, in fact," said Mr. Rentner. "He told me no comment, but not in those words. One thing about the news business—we don't like to take no for an answer." He turned the van around—backing into a bush but not seeming to notice—and followed Doc's black pickup.

The pickup led them down a road with boarded-up buildings. After a while they came to a strip mall, a series of stores with dusty windows and no cars parked outside. The sign over the last store read FIVE ACES LIQUOR. The black pickup pulled in there. Mr. Rentner parked a few spaces away. Doc got out of the pickup, a cigarette dangling from his lips. He wore black jeans, a black jean jacket, dirty work boots; a big guy, about the size of Hector in the Sweetwater visiting room, a comparison that might have suggested itself to Wyatt from the top of a tattoo that curled up Doc's neck from under the collar of his jacket. His eyes took in Wyatt and Mr. Rentner, sitting in the front of the van. Then he flicked the cigarette away—the wind pinwheeling it toward a Dumpster beyond the last parking space—and went into the liquor store.

Mr. Rentner raised the console lid, took out a digital camera. "Bet he takes a nice dramatic picture," he said. He got out of the van. Wyatt got out, too. They walked over to the pickup. Mr. Rentner peered through the driver's side window. "Always look for the telling detail."

Wyatt peered in, too. "Like how messy it is?"

"Sure. But what else do you see? What pops out at you?"

"That shoe?" Wyatt pointed to the floor in front of the passenger seat.

"Describe it."

"Well, uh, a woman's shoe."

"Color?"

"Red."

"Style?"

Style? Wyatt knew nothing about women's shoes styles. "High-heeled, you mean?"

"Good enough. It can't help raising questions in anybody's mind, such as—"

Wyatt heard the closing of the liquor store door and looked up. Doc was standing outside, a case of beer under one arm and a muscle twitching in the side of his face.

"What the hell?" he said. "Messing with my truck?"

Mr. Rentner stepped away from the pickup, but not in a hurry. "Mr. Vitti?" he said. "My name's Rentner, from the *Millerville Beacon*. This is my young colleague, Wyatt. Wondered if you had a moment for a few quick questions."

"You the asshole who called me already?" Doc came forward.

208

"Let's just say I called you already and leave it like that," said Mr. Rentner. He was an old man, tiny next to Doc, but he didn't back away and showed no fear. Wyatt didn't back away either, but he felt afraid inside, no question. There was something wrong with Doc—he could feel it in the air. "But," Mr. Rentner said, "these things always work much better in person."

"Things? What fuckin' things?"

"An interview for the *Beacon*. I'm sure our readers would be interested in hearing your side."

"My side of what?"

"Thirty-two Cain," said Mr. Rentner. He wasn't speaking fast, the way most people would be at a time like this, had slowed down, if anything. At the mention of the address the muscle in Doc's face jumped again. "The events of that night," Mr. Rentner pressed on, "and whether you see them differently looking back—how about we start there?"

"See them different?" Doc took a step closer to Mr. Rentner, was at about an arm's-length distance now. "What's that s'posta mean?"

"Is there anything you're now free to add about your testimony?" said Mr. Rentner. "Some information left out at the trial? Was there anything personal between you and Sonny Racine, for example?"

"Get the hell out of my way," Doc said.

"Our readers would also be interested in learning your plans for the future, and how it feels being free after a seventeen-year incarceration."

"You don't hear so good," Doc said. "I got nothin' to say."

"In that case, just a quick picture will have to do." Mr. Rentner raised his camera, pressed the button.

"God damn it," Doc said, and knocked the camera loose with a backhand swipe. The camera fell to the pavement and Doc tried to kick it, but Wyatt scooped it up before he could. Doc moved toward Wyatt. "Give me that fuckin' camera."

Wyatt held on to the camera, backed away. Doc reached inside his jacket.

"Technically," said Mr. Rentner, "you're free on parole, which can be revoked at any time."

Doc glared at him. His hand emerged empty from inside the jacket. "Watch your step, old man," he said, then turned to Wyatt. "Do I know you, punk?"

Wyatt didn't answer.

"I do now," Doc said. "Better believe it." He brushed past Mr. Rentner, climbed into the pickup, slinging the beer inside, and drove off, tires squealing.

Wyatt handed Mr. Rentner the camera. Mr. Rentner peered at the screen. "Not bad," he said, and showed Wyatt the photo: a furious Doc launching that backhand swipe, the letters H-A-T-E clearly visible on his knuckles. "Excellent work on your part, Wyatt. One of the best no comments I've gotten in some time. In fact, what do you think of 'No Comment' as the headline, running the photo right beneath that, and the piece following?"

"Yeah," Wyatt said.

All at once, Mr. Rentner's expression changed, no longer so exhilarated. "Damn," he said. "I forgot to ask about the red shoe."

They got into the van, returned to the *Beacon* office. Mr. Rentner's good humor returned. He smiled and said, "What are your plans for the summer?"

"Not sure."

"But they'll include work."

"Oh, yeah."

"I might have something—more or less an internship, but it'll be paid, if not well. Interested?"

"Yeah," he said, and thought: *Wow*. "Thanks."

"Not well at all, but write down your phone number."

Wyatt wrote his cell number on a scrap of paper. Mr. Rentner parked beside the Mustang. Greer wasn't there.

"I'll be in touch," said Mr. Rentner. They shook hands. Mr. Rentner hurried into his office. Wyatt got into the Mustang, called Greer, went right to voice mail. He sat outside the *Beacon* office, wondering what to do. After a while, Mr. Rentner appeared in the window. He made a questioning gesture with his hand. Wyatt waved good-bye, started the car, and drove off.

He cruised around Millerville, first in the downtown area, where he saw few people out walking, none of them Greer, and then farther and farther into residential areas, where he saw only one walker, a postman on his route. Wyatt pulled over, tried Greer's cell, again got sent to voice mail. He headed back downtown, and was driving slowly along the main drag when he spotted what he took to be the new bus station, the simplest kind of bus station, just a ticket booth and a space in front for a single bus to park.

Wyatt got out of the car and walked to the booth. BACK IN

10 MINUTES read a sign in the window. On the schedule taped up next to it Wyatt saw that a bus for Silver City—last one of the day—had left half an hour before. He got back in the car, formed an incomplete plan involving catching up to the bus at some stop down the road, seeing if Greer was on it, seeing what might happen next. At that moment, the black pickup went by, Doc at the wheel. Wyatt didn't think twice, or even once, really. He followed Doc.

Doc turned left at the next corner, drove for a few blocks, and stopped outside a bar called Good Time Charlene's. Wyatt parked a few spaces behind him, a landscaper's truck in between. Doc didn't get out of the pickup, just sat there. After a few minutes, a woman came out of Good Time Charlene's. She walked past the pickup without a glance, went by Wyatt, too. When she'd first appeared, he'd thought she was in her midtwenties, but now he saw she could be twice that: a middle-aged woman with copper-red hair, lots of makeup, tight jeans, and a tight red sweater. She must have had a great body at one time, still did, in fact, maybe just a little overweight. In his rearview mirror, Wyatt watched her get into a small sedan. She drove away. Doc pulled out and followed her. Wyatt followed him.

A mile or so later, they were in a not-too-bad neighborhood, nicer than Wyatt's in East Canton. The woman parked in the driveway of a well-kept bungalow that backed onto some woods. Doc kept going, turned a corner, stopped by a small park with a swing set, the swings shifting in the wind. Doc parked. Wyatt kept going. In the rearview mirror, he saw Doc get out of the pickup, glance up and down the street, then hurry into the woods, moving in the direction of the bungalow.

Wyatt stayed where he was for a minute or two, then made a U-turn and drove back past the bungalow. The woman was at a window, closing a curtain. There was a man in the room behind her, possibly Doc, but Wyatt couldn't be sure. An electrician's van was parked a few houses farther on. Wyatt pulled in behind it.

He turned, looked back. All the houses on the street had mailboxes out front, some plain black, some big and fancy, decorated with painted flags or ducks. The bungalow had the duck kind, and over the ducks two names in red letters: BOB AND CHARLENE WATERS.

Wyatt sat there. Half an hour later, he thought he heard a door close, possibly the slap-snick of a screen door, but no one appeared. A few minutes after that, Wyatt drove back around the corner to the small park. The black pickup was gone. He returned to the bungalow and stopped right outside.

What now? He could chase after the bus, assuming Greer was on it, or—

The bungalow door opened and the woman came out. She was still wearing tight jeans but she'd changed sweaters, now wore black. She saw Wyatt, gave him a close look. He got out of the car.

"Uh, ma'am?" he said.

"If you're selling something, forget it," the woman said.

"No," Wyatt said. "I'm from the community college. We're doing this project and maybe you can help."

"Project?" she said. "What kind of project?"

He went a little closer, smelled her perfume, also couldn't help noticing the way her breasts stretched her sweater taut. Her eyes were small and watchful.

These things were easier with Greer. He glanced at the mailbox. "You're, uh, Charlene Waters?"

"That's what it says."

"This project," Wyatt said, "it's about a crime that happened—"

That was as far as Wyatt got before the black pickup came around the corner. It seemed about to drive on by, then swerved to a stop maybe twenty yards farther on. Doc hopped out, the red shoe in his hand.

"Hey," he said. "What's goin' on?"

Charlene shot a quick look up and down the street. "What the hell are you thinking?" she said in a very loud half whisper that might have been funny in different circumstances.

"I forgot about—" He held up the shoe. "I was going to park around the—" Doc's gaze went to Wyatt. "What the fuck's he doing here?"

"Some project at the community college," Charlene said, still in that loud half whisper.

"Community college?" said Doc. "He works for the goddamn paper."

Charlene turned to Wyatt. "Is that true?"

"No," Wyatt said.

"He's lying," Doc said. He was on the move now, his stride quick and jerky. Wyatt backed toward the car. "What did you tell him?" Doc said.

"Nothing," Charlene said. She closed in, too. "Who are

you?" No half whisper now, and her tone was aggressive.

Wyatt didn't answer. He slid around to the driver's side of the car, fumbled for the handle, and was opening the door when Doc dropped the red shoe and charged. Wyatt sprang inside—at least in his mind; in real life he was moving in slow motion—and reached for the key. The next thing he knew, an iron hand had him by the arm. And the moment after that he was in midair, flung from the car.

Wyatt landed hard on the pavement, rolled over, started to get up. Doc came forward, big fist poised for a roundhouse punch, H-A-T-E on the knuckles.

"Doc!" Charlene said. "Not here."

"Fuck that," Doc said, the muscle twitching in his face. Doc swung that big fist at Wyatt, landing a heavy blow on the shoulder that knocked him flat. Doc kept coming. He wore heavy work boots with thick lug soles. Wyatt rolled away from those boots. A thought came to him, kind of strange and maybe beside the point: he didn't want his nose broken again. Something about that thought ignited a jet of anger in him, an anger that at least for the moment overwhelmed his fear. He sprang to his feet—not at his fastest, but not in slow motion, either—and got his hands up.

"Boy's lookin' to get his head beat in," Doc said.

Maybe a boy, but the boys from East Canton knew something about fighting. Doc was big and strong, no doubt about that; it didn't mean he was fast. Wyatt watched that big right hand. The twitchy muscle was on the right side, too.

Charlene called out, "Doc! Not here!"

"Shut your fuckin' mouth," Doc said, and he threw that

right hand. Not with a whole lot of speed; Wyatt ducked under it with ease and threw a left of his own, not at Doc's head—he had no illusions about the damage one of his punches would do to a big thick-boned head like Doc's—but at his throat. And yes: square on the voice box; it felt like punching a steak. Doc made a retching, gasping sound and sank to his knees, one hand clutching his throat.

Charlene's mouth opened wide. Wyatt jumped in the Mustang. He sped off and didn't look back.

WYATT DROVE OUT OF MILLERVILLE, soon came to a junction. A right turn led back to Silver City, a slight left to East Canton. He slowed down, and as he did, his phone rang.

"Hello?"

"Wyatt? It's me, Lou Rentner. Can you stop by?"

"I'm sort of on my way back," Wyatt said. Had Doc, in a fury, gone barging into the *Beacon* office? Or had Greer shown up? Wyatt steered onto the shoulder and stopped the car. "What's it about?"

"Have you ever seen a picture of Sonny Racine?" Mr. Rentner said.

Wyatt sensed what was coming. "No."

"I'm talking about the young Sonny Racine, around the time of the trial. This may sound strange, but there's an eerie similarity. Has anyone ever mentioned it?"

"No."

There was a long pause at the other end. Then Mr. Rentner said, "I'm wondering why you didn't ask what was similar to what."

Wyatt gazed at the road sign. SILVER CITY——412 MILES; EAST CANTON——207 MILES.

"Is there something you're not telling me, Wyatt?"

Wyatt didn't answer.

"Maybe I can help." Another long pause. "Fact is, I checked with Foothills Community College. They report no one registered under the name Wyatt Lathem. I'm concerned you're getting into something a little over your——"

Wyatt clicked off. He headed for home.

It was almost fully dark by the time Wyatt drove up through the familiar streets of Lowertown and parked in front of the house he'd lived in all his life. Linda's car was in the driveway, lights glowed in the kitchen window, a bulb was out on one of the two porch lanterns. In short, everything looked the same, except that Wyatt got this strange feeling that the whole house had no secure hold on the ground, just sat there unfastened, and could blow away if the wind rose high enough. He went to the door, took out his keys, and then paused, wondering whether entering in the normal way, just letting himself in, might frighten them. A crazy thought. He let himself in.

Wyatt heard Cammy's voice. "Mom? I think I hear the door."

Linda came out of the kitchen, wiping her hands on her apron. She looked down the hall, saw Wyatt, and smiled. "And just when I was losing hope," she said.

"Sorry, Mom."

"Wyatt?" Cammy called from her bedroom.

Linda came down the hall, threw her arms around Wyatt.

"I'm so glad to see you," she said, her voice suddenly thick with emotion.

Cammy came running, crayons in both hands. She dropped them, clutched Wyatt by the leg. "Me, too," she said. "I'm glad, too. How come you've been gone so long?"

Wyatt patted Cammy's head. Her hair felt like some strange luxury from a faraway place.

Linda had been making tuna casserole. Wyatt didn't like tuna casserole, but tonight it tasted delicious. He found he was very hungry, had seconds and then thirds.

"Are you going to have fourths?" Cammy said.

Wyatt laughed, at the same time realizing he hadn't laughed much recently. Cammy climbed up on his lap and showed him some drawings.

"That's a dog I want, here's another dog, and another one, and another one."

"Don't you draw anything besides dogs?"

"Here's a puppy."

Cammy wanted him to put her to bed.

"First a story," she said.

He lay down beside her. "What story do you want?"

"*Go, Dog, Go.*"

"Isn't that a bit young for you now?"

"So what?"

He read *Go, Dog, Go* three times.

"Let's do fourths," Cammy said.

"Cammy?" Linda called. "That's it. Night night."

"Give me a kiss, Wyatt."

He gave her a kiss. She gave him one back.

"Walk me to the bus tomorrow?"

"Sure."

"Night."

"Night."

"Tell me sweet dreams."

"Sweet dreams," Wyatt said.

"Leave the door open a crack."

He left the door open a crack.

"Two cracks."

He opened it a little more.

"Night, Wyatt."

"Night."

Wyatt went into the kitchen. "Tea?" his mom said. "Soda?"

"I'm good."

Linda poured herself a cup of tea. They sat at the table, now cleared, the dishes all done. He saw how tired his mom looked, her face kind of sagging, dark patches under her eyes.

"How's work, Mom?"

"Not too bad."

"Where's Rusty?"

"Cheyenne tonight, I think it was. He'll be home next week."

"And it's, uh, working out?"

"No complaints." Linda sipped her tea, gazed at him over the rim of the cup. "What about you?" she said.

"I'm okay."

"That's good to hear," Linda said. "Is your stuff in the car?"

"No."

She put down her cup. "What does that mean?"

"I don't know, Mom."

"Are you home or not?"

"I'm home right now. But there are things I've got to take care of."

"Like what?" Linda said. Wyatt looked at her. Could he imagine this decent and kind person at some earlier stage in life firing a gun at 32 Cain Street? No. But Mr. Wertz the lawyer suspected that Sonny Racine had been covering for someone, and Mr. Rentner had heard rumors of a girlfriend. His mom had been the girlfriend, pregnant with him, waiting on a marriage that never happened.

"What's wrong, Wyatt? Is it that girl Hildy was telling me about? Greer something-or-other?"

Wyatt gazed down at the table.

"Listen to me," his mom said. "There's a big, big difference between sixteen and nineteen. A girl of nineteen—any girl, she could be perfectly nice—is coming from a place you know nothing about, Wyatt, way past your ability to handle. I'm not talking about just you, but any sixteen-year-old—"

He looked up. "All right, Mom. I get it."

Linda sat back a bit. "You're in some kind of trouble."

"I'm not."

"Is she pregnant?"

"No." But even as he spoke, Wyatt realized he really had

no idea of the answer to that question, also had no idea what Greer would want to do about it if she was. "What are you thinking?"

"Nothing."

Linda shook her head. "It's so weird that anyone could change this fast."

"What are you talking about?"

"You. I used to trust you completely, believe every word you said. What's happened?"

"Nothing." He got up, opened the fridge. Cammy's lunch box—blue with a pattern of red dogs—was on the top shelf, tomorrow's sandwich already made. Wyatt took out a soda, drank it down, suddenly very thirsty. He turned to Linda.

"Where were you the night of the crime?" he said.

Her forehead wrinkled in puzzlement. "What crime?"

He gazed at his mom. Sonny Racine's girlfriend, yes, but there was just no way. He started to think, *If I can't trust her, who can I trust?* but then the fact of Rusty intervened, complicated things. Could he trust her when it came to Rusty? Maybe there wasn't one single person who could ever be trusted completely in anyone's life. But no matter what, he couldn't play investigative reporter or detective or anything like that with his mom.

"I've seen him," Wyatt said. "Sonny Racine."

Tea slopped over the rim of Linda's cup. "What are you talking about?"

"In the visiting room at Sweetwater State Penitentiary."

She put the cup down; it rattled in the saucer. "Why would you go and do a thing like that?"

"Why wouldn't I? He's my father."

"Haven't we been through this? He's not a father to you. Rusty's the one who—"

"I don't want to hear about Rusty."

"Don't raise your voice. Cammy's sleeping."

They were both silent for a few moments. Coyotes shrieked, not too far away.

Linda's eyes narrowed. "This . . . this visit of yours," she said. "How did that come about?"

"It's complicated. He found out I was in the area and called me."

"How would he find out something like that? How would he get your number?"

"I told you it was complicated. But that's what happened."

"How? I don't understand. Take me through it."

"Why, Mom? That's not what matters."

"This girl's involved, isn't she?"

"So?"

"So? Just the fact you can say that means you don't know what you're doing. I don't want you going back there, on no account."

"Don't you want to know how he is or anything?"

"No."

"Why not?"

"I'm not interested."

"But you were interested in him back then."

"That was before I knew what he was really like, obviously."

"What was he really like?"

"How can you even ask that question? An innocent woman got killed and her baby got mutilated. What more do you need to know?"

What more did he need to know? That was the question, right there. "Suppose he was innocent?" Wyatt said.

Linda dismissed the idea with a backhand wave. "Of course he told you that. They never admit guilt."

"That's what he said—that inmates never admit guilt."

"A kind of admission, then? Is that what you're saying? I don't get it."

"No. It's really the opposite, you know, like practically telling me to doubt. I guess that's why I'm starting to believe."

"Believe what?"

"That he was innocent. Maybe he wasn't even there."

"Not even there? Did he say that?"

"No."

"He admitted he was there—that was never in question," Linda said. "And even if he didn't do the actual shooting, he's every bit as guilty."

"Come on, Mom. That's just what the law says."

"And I say it, too. Think of that poor mother. Think of the baby."

Wyatt met his mom's gaze but couldn't hold it. If she'd been at 32 Cain Street, if Sonny had covered for her, then she was a gifted liar and he didn't know her at all. "How did you find out about that night?" he said.

Linda closed her eyes. "I'll never forget," she said. "I was asleep. This was in the apartment I had then over on Bates Street—Sonny stayed there when he got weekends off from the construction. Knocking woke me up. I answered the door and there was a cop with a search warrant. Donnie Reeves. He'd been three years ahead of me in school."

That was that. The whole protecting-the-girlfriend theory was out.

Her eyes were open now, and watching him closely. "By the way," she said, "you asked me that same question two different ways. Any explanation?"

Wyatt almost laughed. He had a smart mom. And—he almost went further, almost found himself thinking he had a smart dad, too. The urge to laugh disappeared fast. "I'm just trying to understand."

"I got together with a guy I didn't really know," Linda said. "That's all there is to understand."

"Why don't you want to hear how he's doing?" Wyatt said.

"I just don't."

"He had nice things to say about you."

"I don't care. That's all in the past and it's no good to live in the past, not for me, not for you."

That had the sound of good, sensible advice, but not the feeling. All at once Wyatt remembered a line from *Hamlet*—so weird, because he wasn't good at remembering stuff like that, even when he tried to memorize it, and in this case he hadn't. Actually he didn't remember the line exactly. "Do not for ever" something something "seek for thy noble father in the dust." Spoken by Hamlet's mother, the queen, to Hamlet. *Whoa*. He felt a lurch inside, as though the ground had abruptly lowered itself. "I saw that baby," he said, the words just popping out.

"What baby?"

"The baby who got shot."

Linda covered her mouth with one hand. "My God," she said.

"Her name's Toni." Wyatt told his mother about Toni—how she'd been adopted by the Pingrees, was going to Northwestern, seemed happy. Linda's face, worried and irritated when he started, had softened by the end, and her eyes were damp.

"Thank you, Wyatt," she said. "That's good to know." She reached across the table, took his hand. "But that's enough now. Promise me."

"Promise you what?" said Wyatt, who was wondering whether to bring Doc into the story.

"That this is over," Linda said. "That you're back home."

Wyatt rose, went around the table, put his arms around her, and kissed her cheek. "It's good to be home, Mom." That was true, but it promised nothing, not in his mind. She gazed up at him with worried eyes.

Wyatt slept in his own bed that night, had no dreams, sweet or otherwise. He fell deep, deep down into a state of perfect rest, sleeping, yes, like a baby.

**25**

"HEY, WYATT—IT'S A NICE DAY."

"Shh—he's sleeping."

"But I want him to take me to the bus."

"You've been going to the bus on your own."

"But now Wyatt's home. I want him to take me to the bus."

Wyatt opened his eyes. For a moment he felt great; lighthearted, energized, rested. Then memory awoke. His mother was wrong about the past: it returned every morning.

"It's okay," he called. "I'll take her."

His door burst open. Cammy ran in and jumped on the bed, then kept jumping, higher and higher.

"No jumping on the bed," Linda said, watching from the doorway. She was dressed for work but hadn't finished with her makeup, one eye still undone. Something about that sight touched him. He was lucky to have a mom like her.

Cammy landed on her knees beside him. "Mommy says are you going to school today."

Wyatt looked past Cammy to his mom. "Maybe tomorrow," he said.

"Tomorrow sounds good," said Linda.

Linda left for work soon after. She was going in a little early these days—the boss had laid off one of the girls, as they were called, saving one salary and making the others nervous at the same time. A two-fer, she told Wyatt on her way out.

Wyatt and Cammy had cereal for breakfast.

"Do you ever just eat sugar right out of the bowl?" she said.

"No."

"I do."

He walked her to the bus stop.

"Where's your jacket?" he asked her.

"Don't need it. The sun's out."

"Doesn't mean it's warm."

"I'm warm."

The bus rolled up. The door opened, and Mr. Wagstaff looked out. "Hey, Wyatt—ain't seen you in a while. Been sick or something?"

"No."

"Lost some weight, buddy."

Cammy climbed onto the bus. Before the door closed, Wyatt heard her starting to tell Mr. Wagstaff about the three helpings of tuna casserole.

Wyatt walked back home. A bank foreclosure sign hung in front of the house across the street, and someone had spray-painted JOHN 3:16 on the front door. The wind rose, and Wyatt thought it carried the distant sound of a baseball smacking into a glove, and was listening for it again when his phone rang. UNKNOWN CALLER.

"Hello?" Wyatt said.

"Hi, Wyatt. It's Sonny."

"Hi."

"Just thought I'd give you a call. How's everything?"

"Not bad."

"Been up to anything interesting?"

"Not really."

"Me neither," Sonny said. He laughed. "Rude to laugh at my own joke, I know, but humor gets you through sometimes. There are some funny guys in here, believe it or not. One even did the Laugh Factory before his bail got revoked." There was a silence. "Ever been to a comedy club?"

"No."

"I took your mother to one in Fort Collins. We laughed so hard our stomach muscles hurt."

"She never mentioned that."

"No?"

There was a silence. Wyatt heard a man speaking Spanish in the background. His hand tightened on the cell phone. "Where was she the night of the—that night in Millerville."

Pause. "That's a strange question. What's on your mind?"

"Nothing." He waited for an answer.

"Just a strange question out of nowhere," Sonny said. Another pause. Boys from East Canton, especially boys like Wyatt, learned the value of keeping their mouths shut at an early age. "Where are you right now?" Sonny said.

"Out walking," Wyatt said, avoiding a precise geographical answer.

"A nice day for it?"

"Yeah."

"It's raining here," Sonny said. "In Silver City, I mean. Fair weather in Millerville and East Canton—at least according to the weather report."

Wyatt felt himself turning red, kind of crazy all by himself, the other person hundreds of miles away.

"But what's more boring than talking about the weather?" Sonny said. "The answer to your question is that Linda was at the apartment we had at the time—Bates Street in East Canton. They woke her up in the middle of the night with a search warrant. I always felt bad about that." Another pause. "Any other questions?"

"No."

"You're sure? Take a rain check if you like—I'm not going anywhere." Another joke? If so, Sonny wasn't laughing this time. "I enjoyed your visit—hope it wasn't too unpleasant for you."

"No," Wyatt said.

"You're welcome to come back whenever you like—goes without saying."

"Thanks."

"No problem. Nice talking to you—enjoy your walk."

"Okay."

"Take care. Oh—almost forgot—had a quick word with Bert today. He's got some concerns about his daughter."

"What concerns?"

"Not the kind I'd like to discuss on the phone."

"But is she all right?"

Wyatt heard voices in the background. "Sorry, Wyatt. My time's up."

Click.

He called Greer, once more got sent straight to voice mail. "Greer? It's me. Are you all right? Where are you? Call."

Wyatt went back inside the house, his mind racing. He was halfway finished making his bed before he realized what he was doing. Making his bed? He straightened, gazing at nothing. He never made his bed. His eyes focused on his baseball trophies glowing dully on a shelf. Maybe because of a trick of the light, the trophies looked old, like antique trophies from some long-ago era of baseball.

Wyatt finished making his bed, closed the door to his room, and went into the kitchen. He found pen and paper and wrote a note.

*Dear Mom,*

*It was great to see you. And Cammy. Don't worry. There's nothing to worry about. I want to come back here and live at home all the way through high school, but there's one or two things to take care of. First I have to—*

He paused, scratched that out.

*I'll be back soon. Want to go to the water park, Cammy? I'll take you when I get home. Love, Wyatt*

He left the house, making sure the door was locked behind him, got in the car, and drove down out of Lowertown. The gas gauge needle was quivering halfway between one quarter and empty. He checked his wallet—found he had $37 left—stopped where he always did for gas, Low Low Gas. It was boarded up. He hit the Exxon station two blocks down and filled up. Mr. Mannion drove by in his Caddy. He didn't look Wyatt's way, but in those few moments, Wyatt took his eye off the pump. By the time he checked, it read $41.10. He let go of the handle, too late.

Wyatt went inside to pay. A quick plan sketched itself in his mind, something unimaginative about returning later with the $4.10 but the attendant looked unfriendly, even a bit aggressive, possibly one of those old guys who hated kids. Opening his wallet, Wyatt saw Sonny's $200 stuck in one of the slots for credit cards, still waiting to be returned. He took a twenty from that slot and added it to his own money. The attendant licked his fingertip before making change.

Wyatt drove to Silver City, losing the sunshine at about the halfway point, heading into rain not long after. By the time he got to Greer's apartment building, the wipers could hardly keep up. Wyatt pulled his jacket up over his head and ran to the door.

He pressed the buzzer for her apartment, waited for a response, dry under the overhang. Water poured off the strange stone creature over the door, seemed to be coming from its open mouth. A taxi rolled up the street, stopped behind the Mustang.

A man with a suitcase and an overnight bag got out, fumbled with an umbrella, and came hurrying up the path to the door. Wyatt stepped aside. The man groped in his pocket, produced a set of keys, stuck one in the lock, and paused. He turned to Wyatt. "Help you with something?" he said.

A man of about Wyatt's height, maybe ten or twelve years older—Wyatt had trouble guessing the ages of older people who weren't yet old—wearing small oval eyeglasses with expensive-looking frames.

"No," Wyatt said.

"Visiting one of the tenants?" the man said.

Wyatt shrugged. It was none of this guy's business. The guy shifted the garment bag on his shoulder impatiently. A soft leather garment bag, also expensive-looking, and on the side a sticker: CHECK ROOM, HOTEL DYNASTY, HONG KONG.

"The reason I ask," the man said, "is that I happen to own this building and I've spent a lot of time and money making it safe for my tenants."

"Your name's Van?" Maybe not the smartest move— maybe no move at all would have been smarter—but the question just came out on its own.

The man put down his suitcase. "That's what some people call me. Who are you?"

Wyatt felt his chin tilting up. "A friend of Greer Torrance's," he said.

Van's face flushed slightly. "What kind of friend?"

"That's for her to say."

"Is it?" Van said. He looked down his nose at Wyatt and said, "Fine." Then he ran his finger down the row of buzzers and jabbed it at Greer's. No answer. Van turned to him. "Your friend Greer, whatever kind of friend she happens to be, doesn't seem to be in at the moment, so I can't see you've got any reason to be hanging around my door." He turned the key and let himself in, shoving the suitcase along with his foot, then banging the door closed with his elbow. Wyatt jabbed his own finger at Greer's buzzer and kept it there. He thought he heard it sounding up above.

Wyatt backed away from the door, right under the water pouring from the mouth of the stone creature, soaking his head. He ran to the Mustang, water dripping down the back of his neck, and jumped inside. Looking up, he saw Van watching him from Greer's front window. He overcame any stupid impulses, like giving him the finger, but he didn't drive off until Van backed away from the window. Owned the goddamn building: a few gaps in his understanding of Greer began filling themselves in.

Wyatt headed for the bowling alley. Any chance she'd be there? Probably not, but where else could he look? He was almost there when his phone rang.

UNKNOWN CALLER. Wyatt answered on the first ring.

"Wyatt? Sonny here. Hope I'm not disturbing you."

"No."

"Good," Sonny said. "I'd hate to be intrusive. The thing is I'm available at visiting time today." Wyatt was trying to think how to respond when Sonny continued, "And I understand you're back in town."

The back of Wyatt's neck, already wet, now felt cold as well. "How do you know that?"

"I just do."

"But I'm asking you how." Was he being followed somehow? Wyatt looked around, saw normal-looking traffic moving in normal-looking ways.

"It's nothing nefarious," Sonny said. "Why don't I explain in person?"

**26**

WYATT WALKED THROUGH the metal detector. "Arms up for the corrections officer, please." Wyatt raised his arms, got wanded. A CO led him down the corridor. The cement floor was still wet, or wet again. "Never gets old, for some reason," the CO said, "plugging the toilets." They stepped around the slowly spreading pools; the smell couldn't be avoided.

The visiting room was empty. Wyatt took a plastic seat in the same row he'd occupied before. He read the visiting room notice about what not to wear and what not to do, and counted the video cameras—nine. He heard a clang, distant and muffled, and felt a faint vibration in the floor.

The inmate door opened and Sonny came through, followed by the big female CO with the dreadlocks. Sonny was dressed as before in spotless unwrinkled khakis. The CO glanced at Wyatt, then sat at the end of the row against the opposite wall, as far from them as she could be. Sonny smiled and sat next to Wyatt. He looked rested and relaxed, and somehow stronger than before; maybe the first time Wyatt hadn't really noticed how Sonny's muscles stretched his shirt.

There wasn't a hint of gray in his dark hair, and the few lines on his face were shallow and very fine, hardly visible at all.

"Hi, Wyatt," he said. "Thanks for coming."

"How did you know I was in Silver City?" Wyatt said.

"Direct and to the point—I'm getting the idea that's your style," Sonny said, his smile still there, just not as broad. "The answer is Bert told me."

Meaning Greer must have told Bert, and therefore Greer had to have been up in her apartment the whole time he was outside at the buzzer. Was there another explanation? Not that Wyatt could see. "So what's wrong with her?" he said.

"Not quite following you," Sonny said.

"You told me something was wrong," Wyatt began, then lowered his voice. "Something you couldn't talk about on the phone." He glanced at the CO. She was gazing off into space. Wyatt felt a moment of anger, directed at himself. Why had he lowered his voice? He wasn't a criminal, had done nothing wrong, didn't need to get stealthy in front of someone in a uniform.

Sonny turned to the CO, raised his voice. "All phone conversations are recorded, right, Taneeka?"

Taneeka nodded. "In and out."

"Which is why it's best not to discuss a lot of personal details on the phone," Sonny said.

"I sure as hell wouldn't," said Taneeka. She unwrapped a stick of gum.

Sonny nodded, turned back to Wyatt. Wyatt felt lost, and stupid, too. "No need to feel stupid," Sonny said, lowering his voice down to normal volume. "How can you be expected to know our little ways? The point—all according to Bert, of course—is that Greer got a bit upset when you ditched her someplace, never did get the precise details. Where was it, again?"

"Millerville," Wyatt said. "And I didn't ditch her. Is she okay?"

Sonny nodded. "As it turned out."

"What does that mean?"

"Don't have all the details," Sonny said. "Something about hitchhiking and being picked up by the wrong kind of driver. Always a danger with a looker like Greer." Looker? Wyatt didn't like that, wasn't sure why. "But she managed to extricate herself from the situation," Sonny said, "no harm done."

"I never meant anything like that to—she jumped, for God's sake, and I looked all over for her and everything."

"I'm sure you did—no need to blame yourself," Sonny said. He waved his hand, as though dismissing the whole topic and asked, "What did you think of Millerville?"

Wyatt shrugged.

"Yeah—that's the way I feel about the place myself."

Wyatt laughed, couldn't help it. Sonny laughed, too. They laughed together. Tears appeared in Sonny's eyes.

Taneeka looked over. "Hey, Sonny, what's the joke?"

Sonny wiped the corner of one eye with his sleeve. "Wouldn't know where to begin," he said.

"Uh-huh." Taneeka nodded. Something in her tone and in that nod gave Wyatt the idea she respected Sonny, possibly even admired him. She went back to gazing into space and chewing her gum.

"I met this newspaper guy in Millerville," Wyatt said. "An old guy—he covered the trial."

"Why are you doing this?" Sonny's voice had softened.

"Because there are so many questions."

Wyatt waited for Sonny to ask what they were, but he did not. Instead his voice softened even more and he said, "I don't want you asking them. I don't want you getting into any of it."

"Why not?"

Sonny sat back, folded his hands in his lap. "I'm content," he said.

Wyatt glanced around the horrible room. "Content about what?"

"Content to take my punishment."

Wyatt leaned forward. "Punishment for what? Esteban Dominguez testified he only saw two people—Pingree and Doc. Why didn't you fight the charges?"

"I did fight," Sonny said. "I pled not guilty."

Their eyes met. "But you didn't do a good job," Wyatt said. For a brief moment, Sonny's face changed, became thinner and harder. "Why did you take the stand?"

Sonny shook his head. "I'm telling you not to go there."

"Why?" Who would help put themselves behind bars, or not do whatever they could to get out?

"I already explained."

"But this newspaper guy thinks you might not have even been there. And Mr. Wertz said only an innocent man wants to take the stand."

"That just proves his incompetence. This place is full of

guys who took the stand and were guilty as sin."

Taneeka cracked her gum.

"Were you there that night?" Wyatt said.

"Front and center."

Wyatt couldn't believe that. It felt wrong, if not completely then at least partly. "Was my—was Linda involved in any way?"

"I've answered that. Why do you keep asking?"

"Because Mr. Wertz—"

"I told you he's a drunk."

"—and the newspaper guy both said there might have been a fourth person, someone you were—"

Sonny held his hand up in the stop position. They gazed at each other. "Don't look so angry," Sonny said.

Wyatt hadn't been aware of his anger, but it was there, all right. He tried to tamp it down. "I'm moving back home," he said. "Back to East Canton."

"Sounds like a plan."

"Yeah." No baseball? It really wasn't important; Wyatt could now see a life beyond baseball, not clearly, but a life that included interesting work, maybe the kind Mr. Rentner did. "But before I go, I just want to know the truth."

"Why?"

"Because," Wyatt said, "you're my father."

Sonny's eyes closed and stayed closed for a moment or two. When he opened them, the expression had changed in a way that was hard to define: less guarded, maybe; and all the hardness was gone from his face. "Don't think that way," Sonny said. "I don't deserve the name."

"But it's a fact anyway. Look at us."

Sonny smiled slightly and shook his head. "For one thing, I'm not as smart as you. For another, that may be a fact, the DNA part, but other parts, all the missing ones, are more important."

"Okay," Wyatt said, "that's what I want to know—the missing parts."

Sonny gave him a long look. Was there admiration in it, even pride? Wyatt didn't know—but whatever was in that look made him feel good. "That's not what I meant by the missing parts," Sonny said.

Wyatt could sense Sonny thinking, got the impression he was about to say more, and kept quiet. A silence fell over the visiting room, a comfortable sort of silence, like this was a cozy place and they were simply two guys long accustomed to each other's company.

"The missing parts," Sonny said. He glanced over at Taneeka. Her face was slack, like the face of a sleeper, although her eyes were open. "What do you want to know?"

"Who fired the gun?"

Sonny let out his breath, long and slow. "Art Pingree," he said. "It was his gun, of course, this little snubnose twenty-two, but Art shouldn't have been the one packing—just not reliable in a crisis."

"Why didn't you say it was him at the time?"

"I'd like to think it's because I'm not a rat," Sonny said. "And maybe that's true. But it's also true that Doc Vitti cut his deal first. The DA only takes one."

"What happened to the gun?" Wyatt said.

"No idea."

"Then why did you say you threw it in the woods?"

Sonny shook his head. "I don't know. That whole part—my testimony—is just a fog now. Was then, too, to be honest."

"What was the point of getting on the stand at all?" Wyatt said.

"It was pointless in retrospect. Back then, I thought . . ." His voice trailed off and he got a distant look in his eyes.

"What? What did you think?"

Sonny shrugged. That shrug of his—almost teenage-like, and Sonny had been hardly more than a teenager at the time of the trial.

"You weren't even there, were you?" Wyatt said.

Sonny looked up, confused. "In court?"

"At thirty-two Cain Street."

Sonny reached out as though to touch Wyatt's knee, stopped with his hand inches away. "I was there, Wyatt. No getting around that."

"I meant inside. You didn't go in. You weren't part of the home invasion."

"It's the same under the law. Let's not go over that again."

"Not if you went there to stop it," Wyatt said. "Arrived too late, or something like that." Sonny was watching him, mouth slightly open. "That's the real story, isn't it?"

"I wish it was."

"You're still protecting someone."

Sonny gave him a long look. "Any idea what you're going to do in life, after school and all that?"

"No."

"Give it some thought. You've got the brains to go all the way in something."

"No, I don't."

"You're wrong about that," Sonny said.

Wyatt waved that away, at the same time realizing the gesture was exactly like Sonny's. "This is about filling in the missing parts," he said. "Who are you protecting?"

"Nobody. I can't make it any clearer. You've got all the missing parts, all that matter. I hope it helps." He smiled. There was something sweet about Sonny's smile, and maybe brave as well. "This has really been something," he said, "getting to know you a bit. I can't help thinking that if—"

Whatever Sonny couldn't help thinking remained unspoken, because at that moment the visitors' door opened and Greer walked in. She glanced at Wyatt and Sonny, then sat at the far end of Taneeka's row. "Hey, Greer, how's it goin'?" Taneeka said.

"Great," said Greer. She took a book from her pocket, started reading. She looked great, completely undamaged except for a scab on her biggest knuckle.

The inmate door opened and a pale, heavy man entered. He was dressed in rumpled khaki, had a bandage over one eye. Greer jumped up. "Dad—what happened?"

The inmate approached her. Greer rushed forward and threw her arms around him.

"Hey!" Taneeka said.

Greer and her father separated.

"Hi, Greer," Sonny said.

Greer turned to him. "What happened to my dad?" she called across the room.

Now Taneeka, too, was watching Sonny. "I actually don't know," he said.

"Was it that horrible man, Hector?" Greer said. "The one with Jesus on his face?"

"Couldn't tell you," Sonny said. But out of the corner of his eye, Wyatt had seen Greer's dad flinch at the mention of Hector's name.

"It was an accident," Greer's dad said. "In the shop."

"You're sure?" Greer said.

"Yeah. I'm fine."

"Accidents happen all the time in the shop," Sonny said. "Isn't that true, Taneeka?"

"True enough," said Taneeka.

"I'm fine," Greer's dad said again, not looking at anyone in particular, in fact gazing down at the floor, a cement floor painted the color of cement.

"Bert?" Sonny said, rising. "Like you to meet Wyatt. Wyatt, Bert Torrance."

Bert looked up. "Heard a lot about you," he said.

"Hi," Wyatt said. He stood up, tried to think of some good follow-up. "I, uh, liked the batting cage."

"Thanks," Bert said.

Wyatt felt Greer's glare at the same time.

"Come on, Dad," she said. "Let's sit down."

They sat in the far corner, began to talk in low voices. The visitors' door opened and more visitors entered, lots of them, maybe a dozen. More inmates came through the inmate door, and more COs. In less than a minute, it got pretty crowded. Taneeka sat up straight, plucked the gum from her mouth, and stuck it under the seat. Two women took the spots where Wyatt and Sonny had been sitting. Wyatt and Sonny moved toward the inmate door, stood near a CO with sergeant stripes on his sleeve.

"Looks like we're in for one of those busy days," Sonny said. "I'll say good-bye."

"There's one more thing," Wyatt said, keeping his voice down. Sonny leaned in to hear. "Why did Doc name you as the shooter?"

The sergeant's eyes shifted toward them.

"Have to ask him," Sonny said.

"I didn't get the chance."

Sonny went still. "You're telling me you saw him?"

"In Millerville. Didn't you know he was out?"

"I did," Sonny said. "But Millerville? Why would he go back there?"

"Isn't that where he's from?"

"No. He came from Wichita originally."

"Maybe it's because of this girlfriend," Wyatt said.

"What girlfriend?"

"It's kind of strange," Wyatt said. "I got the idea she might be married to someone else."

"That wouldn't stop Doc," said Sonny. "More of an incentive, if anything. What makes you think she's married?"

"I kind of followed him to her place. He parked far away and then must've snuck in the back. And later when I was talking to her, he came back, and she wasn't happy about being out in public with him. She's actually kind of a tough lady—I think she owns a bar."

There was a pause. "A bar?"

"Good Time Charlene's," Wyatt said. "Her name's Charlene Waters—I read it off her mailbox."

Sonny swayed backward slightly, as though having a little trouble with his balance. He leaned against the wall. Beside him, the inmate door opened and more men in khaki came in. Voices rose all around them.

"Gonna have to clear some of these folks out of here," the sergeant said. "Sonny? You about done?"

Sonny nodded, pushed himself off the wall. He left through the inmate door.

# 27

WYATT SAT IN THE PARKING LOT at Sweetwater State Penitentiary. The parking lot lay in the shadow of the front wall, the wall facing the river. A dark rectangle of a shadow with a dappled margin at the end: that pretty topping was the razor wire. In the distance, a school bus was driving across the bridge; the river water looked black and viscous, almost like something solid and reptilian. Soon Wyatt would be crossing that bridge himself, then following the river road to the state highway, heading home. All that remained was saying good-bye to Greer in a way that closed things off as near to nicely as possible. Was it shameful to admit there were things you weren't ready for? Yeah, probably.

The main public door of the prison opened and visitors walked out—almost all of them women and children, none of them talking. Greer was at the end. Some visitors moved toward their cars, none of the cars the kind anyone would want to own. The others, including Greer, headed for a waiting bus. Wyatt got out of the Mustang and approached her.

"Greer?"

She turned. "What do you want?" He noticed that the eyebrow ring was back in place.

"Is your apartment rent free?" he said. Not close to nice, not the kind of thing he'd had in mind to say at all, instead a nasty and mean dig he wanted to take back right away. Jealousy was new to him; he was jealous of Van, no doubt about it. He knew deep down he still wanted Greer, and wanted her all to himself.

"None of your fucking business," she said.

What if Van was some sort of bad person, screwing up her life? Not his problem. "I'm going home," he said.

"What are you waiting for? Have a good trip."

The last two or three visitors climbed on the bus, maybe twenty or thirty feet away.

She wasn't his problem and he was going home, so, yes, what was he waiting for? "Is your dad okay?" he said.

"What do you care?"

The bus sat there, engine running, door open.

"I care."

"Bullshit. You just called me a whore."

"I didn't mean it that way."

The bus door closed with a long sniffing sound.

If Greer noticed, she showed no sign. "What else could it mean?"

Their eyes met. Wyatt was reminded of other times that this meeting of eyes had happened, especially in bed with her, when he'd thought he'd seen deep inside. How weird that you could be so close to a person at one time and that at another she was almost a complete stranger. "I'm jealous, that's all," Wyatt said.

"Jealous? Jealous of who?"

"Who do you think? Van, of course."

"You're jealous of *Van*? That's all over."

"It is?"

The bus made a wide turn and drove out of the lot.

"Since I met you," Greer said. "It was shaky to begin with. Then you came along."

But Van had called her *baby* on the phone. "It's over between you and him?"

"All but the shouting," Greer said.

"What does that mean?"

"And he's my landlord, true," she went on, "but I paid rent every single month, just about."

Silence. They gazed at each other. The look in Greer's eyes changed, and something changed inside Wyatt, too, and all at once they were laughing. Her arms came up, and then they were embracing—laughing and holding on to each other in the shadow of the prison wall.

She spoke in his ear. "No matter what happens, we fit."

Yeah, they did. Wyatt was about to say that, to agree with her, when he felt like someone was watching him and glanced up. A guard was looking down from one of the towers. "Let's go," he said.

They got into the Mustang. He could smell her. She smelled good.

"Where to?" she said.

*Play it by ear.* "Ever been to East Canton?" he said.

"Never wanted to."

"But now?"

"Now?" she said. "I still don't want to. But I'm willing to discuss it."

"Okay," Wyatt said. "How about coming back to East Canton with me?"

"I'm willing to discuss it, but not here."

"Then where? Your, um, apartment?"

She laughed. "Let's not push our luck."

"Meaning what?"

"Meaning you only get so much luck in life," Greer said. She pointed ahead. "Drive. Turn right after the bridge."

Wyatt drove out of the shadow of the prison wall, crossed the bridge, turned right; left led to the highway and home. A dog sniffed at something by the water's edge; on the other side of the street stood small clapboard houses, some with FOR SALE signs out front. A little boy on a tricycle watched the Mustang go by.

"Some get more than others," Greer said, "when the luck's handed out. Ever dreamed about winning the lottery?"

"Sure."

"They say lottery winners don't end up happier than anyone else."

"I don't believe that," Wyatt said.

"No?" said Greer. "What makes you happy?"

Wyatt thought about that.

"Nothing comes to mind?" Greer said. "We're in trouble."

"Wait—I didn't—"

"Hang a left."

Wyatt turned left, onto a street that climbed away from the river.

"Stop here."

Wyatt parked in front of a brick house, the only brick house on the street; all the rest were clapboard.

"Fucking hell," Greer said.

"What?"

"They cut down the tree."

Wyatt noticed a low stump on the front lawn. Greer got out of the car.

"Why the hell would they go and do that?" she said.

Wyatt got out, too, stood beside her, gazing at the stump. A sign standing nearby read: BANK FORECLOSURE SALE—NO REASONABLE OFFER REFUSED. Greer walked over to the stump and knelt beside it, running her hand over the wood, smooth from the saw's cut.

"Like the tree didn't pay its bills or something?" she said. "So they had to punish it?"

Wyatt watched the back of her head, didn't speak.

"A beautiful willow," Greer said. "I played in it all the time."

"You lived here?" Wyatt said.

"And nowhere else till last year," Greer said, "when everything went to shit." She rose. "Want to see inside?"

"Can we?" Wyatt said. "They didn't change the locks?"

"Sure they did—this is boom time for locksmiths." Greer walked around to the back of the house; Wyatt followed. "But I know this place like those assholes never can," she said. She went past the back door to a double-hung window. "All you need to do is—" She stuck her finger into the space where the top and bottom frames met and pushed. "Even when it looks latched from inside, it never is." The top half dropped down, and Greer climbed through in one easy motion. "What are you waiting for?" she said from inside. Wyatt climbed through, not as smoothly.

He was in a small bare room, empty except for a poster on the wall and a bare mattress on the floor.

"Welcome to Greer's childhood bedroom," Greer said.

"Who's that?" Wyatt pointed to the poster.

"Jean Harlow."

"Who's she?"

Greer closed the window. "An old-time movie star." She turned, put her arms around him. "Want to see the rest of the house?"

"Sure."

"I don't," she said.

"What do you want to do?"

She kissed him, ran her hand down his back, two powerful stimuli coming at him from different directions. "Whatever you dream about," she said. "That's what I want to do."

Soon they sank down on the mattress. A while after that, the light began to fade. Up on the wall, Jean Harlow seemed to hold on to it a little longer than the rest of the room.

They lay in darkness, the empty house quiet.

"So," Wyatt said, "about coming to East Canton."

"You really want to talk about that?"

"Yeah."

She took a deep breath, let it out slowly. He felt the tiny warm breeze on his chest. "And where would I live? Is there room for me with Mom, Stepdad, and Little Sis?"

Wyatt hadn't gotten that far, in fact hadn't really thought this out. "Maybe we could get a—" His phone rang. He fumbled for it on the floor. The tiny screen glowed. UNKNOWN CALLER.

"Don't answer it," said Greer.

But he did. "Hello?"

"I never answer unknown caller," Greer said.

Wyatt sat up, turning away from her.

"Wyatt?" Sonny said.

"Yeah."

"Thought I heard someone else."

Wyatt stayed silent.

"Is this a bad time?" Sonny said.

"No. It's okay."

There was a pause. "You're a fine young man," Sonny said. "I'm proud of the connection, no matter how distant it is in the actual life sense, if you see what I mean."

"Yeah."

"I know you're going back home, might be there already."

"No."

"Where are you? None of my business, of course."

"Still here—in Silver City."

"At Greer's apartment?"

"Her old house, actually."

"Patching things up, I hope?"

Wyatt didn't answer.

"Don't have to answer," Sonny said. "Withdraw the question, in fact—again, none of my damn business. I want the best for you, is all." He was silent for a moment. "Funny, to be thinking of the welfare of another person. In here we get used to thinking of only numero uno, and I'm no exception, believe me. Which, ah . . ." He paused, breathed out, one of those long, self-calming exhales. "Which brings me to something I want to say before you go. This is probably the last time we'll talk, Wyatt, so—"

"Why?"

"Because you've got a life to live," Sonny said. "I don't. I'm alive, sure, but there's no life to live in here. That's pretty much what *lifer* means. No one needs a millstone and I'm not going to be yours. That's why I want to settle your mind."

"What do you mean?"

"It's no good to be worrying and wondering about the past. You agree with that?"

Wyatt wasn't sure he did, at that moment found himself leaning the other way.

"Even if you don't," Sonny said, "I want you to know the truth. Unless you don't want to know—that's different."

"I want to know."

"The funny thing is I believe you already do."

Wyatt didn't speak. He thought he could hear his own pulse beating inside him.

"You can say anything you want," Sonny said. "This isn't a recorded line."

"It's not?"

Sonny spoke softly. "I'm on a cell phone—just for emergencies."

Were the inmates allowed cell phones? No way. But another thought immediately pushed that one aside. "This is an emergency?"

"Maybe not," Sonny said. "Or maybe just psychologically. I spent my first three or four years in here reading psychology and nothing but. Did I mention that yet?"

"No."

"Since then I've branched out. You can educate yourself in here, no question about that."

"Did you read *Hamlet*?" Wyatt said.

"Tried," Sonny said. "I got nowhere with that one. Why do you ask?"

"No reason."

"Have you read it?"

"I'm in the middle," Wyatt said. "What did you mean— you believe I already know?"

"You want me to say it right out?" Sonny said.

"Yes."

"Then here goes. Your theory about me arriving late, trying to stop the whole stupid thing? That's the truth, one hundred percent."

Wyatt felt Greer's hand on his back. "That means you're innocent?" he said. Innocent: and spending life in prison.

"No human being is innocent," Sonny said. "But what went down at thirty-two Cain Street? I'm innocent of that."

"Then we've got to do something."

Sonny laughed; he sounded genuinely amused. "First, it's

not your problem. Second—do what?"

"Get a lawyer, a good lawyer this time."

"And what would he do?"

"Start over. Reopen the case."

"Based on my say-so? Every loser in here would be reopening his case if it worked that way. Standing room only in every courthouse in the land."

All the facts, everything Wyatt had learned about the case, shifted slightly in his mind, and suddenly he had an answer to Sonny's last question. "What if a new witness came forward?"

"And who would that be?"

"Whoever you're covering for," Wyatt said. "The fourth person."

Silence, and in that silence, Wyatt thought he could feel Sonny's presence, as though he were in the room. "You're very smart," he said, "but we're not going there. Told you before—I'm content. More content than ever, now that we've had this talk. Good-bye, Wyatt. Just know one thing— you've done me a great service, simply by the way you are."

"Wait, don't hang up," Wyatt said. He wanted the name of that fourth person.

Click. And no way to call back—that was one of the features of "unknown caller."

**28**

"ARE YOU COLD?" Greer said. They lay in the darkness on the bare mattress in her childhood room.

"No," Wyatt said.

"You're shivering."

"I'm not."

She wrapped herself around him. "Do you believe him?" she said.

"I don't know."

"I think you do," Greer said. "And I do—I believe him."

"Why?" Wyatt said.

"I trust my dad."

"What's that got to do with anything?"

"Trusting your parents? Isn't that central?"

Maybe, Wyatt thought: but not so easy, since they came in twos.

"What are you thinking?" she said.

"Nothing."

"I don't believe you," Greer said. "You always hold something back, don't you?"

Did he?

"See—there you go again," Greer said. "But nobody's perfect, including me. The point I was making is I trust my dad and he thinks Sonny is innocent."

"You told me that already," Wyatt said. "Based on what?"

"Can you imagine how hard this has been for my dad, being locked up? But Sonny looks out for him and they got to know each other. My dad's a real smart judge of character— he says Sonny's the only good man in the whole goddamn place."

That didn't strike Wyatt as a lot to go on.

Maybe Greer was reading his mind, because she went on, "But the main thing is, I know you."

"So?"

"So you're just like him and you could never do what they say he did or anything close."

"I'm not like him at all."

She laughed, a quiet laugh, quickly shut off.

"And if I am, then doesn't that mean he holds things back, too?"

"You can be a complete jerk sometimes, you know that?" she said.

They moved apart.

"And why now," Wyatt said, "does he all of a sudden confess the truth?"

"What could be more obvious? You're his son."

During the night—under a blanket now, which Greer must have found somewhere while he slept—they came together again, and in the morning woke up side by side. A little later, the room full of light—had to be midmorning, at least—she said, "Know what I've never had?"

The words *peace of mind* occurred to him at once; a strange, disturbing thought Wyatt kept to himself. "No," he said.

"Breakfast in bed."

"That's what you want?"

"Real, real bad."

He mussed her hair. "Okay." A siren sounded, faint and far away.

"There's a doughnut place half a mile down the street. Chocolate glazed, please, and coffee."

A few minutes after that, he was dressed and in the Mustang. A fat raindrop splatted on the windshield, then a few more. Wyatt crossed a busy street—busy for Silver City—then passed a gas station with a sign on the pumps reading NO GAS, and came to Dippin' Donuts. By that time it was raining hard. He ran inside, bought doughnuts and coffee, headed back to Greer's old house, the windshield wipers going their fastest. Was there some way they could live together in East Canton? He'd have to juggle school and a part-time job, and she'd have to find work, too. But doing what? Wyatt was trying to imagine some future life for them as he recrossed the busy street. A police cruiser was going by. The cop at the wheel glanced over at him, then squealed around in a hard U-turn, siren on, lights flashing.

Me? Wyatt thought. He checked the speedometer. Wasn't speeding, had done nothing wrong: he kept going. The cruiser zoomed right up behind him; in the rearview mirror

Wyatt saw the cop making angry pull-over gestures. Wyatt pulled over.

The cop got out of the cruiser, came to Wyatt's door with his gun drawn. Gun drawn? What was going on? Were you supposed to have your lights on when it rained? Wyatt reached for the switch.

"Hands up high," the cop yelled, rain dripping down off the brim of his hat, and the gun pointed through the glass right at Wyatt's head.

Wyatt raised his hands.

The cop took a quick glance into the backseat, then threw open Wyatt's door. "Get out real slow."

Wyatt started getting out.

"Hands! Get 'em up or I'll blow your fucking head off."

Wyatt raised his hands as high as he could, stepped out of the car. The cop grabbed his shoulder, spun him around, and shoved him against the car.

"Any weapons on you?"

"No. What's this—"

"Shut your goddamn mouth."

Wyatt shut his mouth. Rain soaked his head, ran down his face.

"Spread your legs."

Wyatt spread his legs. He felt the cop's hands patting him down, starting from his armpits, working to his ankles.

"Don't move a goddamn muscle."

Wyatt didn't move a muscle. He heard the ripping sound of a Velcro seal opening, and then the cop was talking on his radio. Moments after that, sirens started wailing and more cruisers came barreling up the street from both directions. Cops jumped out, some of them dressed SWAT-style in body armor and armed with rifles or shotguns. One reached into the ignition, grabbed the keys, and moved to the trunk.

"Anybody in there—move and you're dead," he said.

Two of the SWAT guys took their stances, long guns aimed at the trunk. The cop with the keys opened the trunk and stepped back. From the corner of his eye, Wyatt could glimpse them peering in. But he knew there was nothing to see except the spare, his bat, his cleats, maybe some old towels.

Someone behind him said, "Turn around."

Wyatt turned. A bunch of cops stood in front of him, guns still drawn but pointed down. In the middle, unarmed and wearing the only green uniform in all the blue, was Taneeka, the CO from the visitors' room at Sweetwater State Penitentiary.

"This him?" said a cop with gold braid on his hat.

Taneeka nodded.

"Wyatt Lathem?" said the cop.

"Yes," Wyatt said.

"You can lower your hands."

Wyatt lowered his hands. The rain let up a bit and things got quieter. Wyatt heard water running in drains under the street.

"Where were you headed?" the cop said.

"To my friend's place," Wyatt said. He gestured toward the car. Guns came up right away. "I was bringing breakfast."

The cop with the gold braid made a pointing motion with his chin. Another cop reached into the car, brought out the Dippin' Donuts bag, handed it over. The cop with the gold braid looked inside.

"Where's your friend's place?" the cop said.

"Just down the street," Wyatt said. "What's this about? I don't understand."

"How about we go pay a call on him?" said the cop.

"Who?"

"This friend."

"It's a she," Wyatt said. "What's happening? What's going on?"

"Take a guess."

"I don't have any idea."

The cop gave him a long look. "You a good liar, son?"

"I'm not lying about anything," Wyatt said. "I don't know what you're talking about."

"No?" the cop said. "Then how about we pay a call on your friend?"

"Cuff him, chief?" said one of the SWAT guys.

The cop with the gold braid shook his head. At that moment the Dippin' Donuts bag, soggy with rain, came apart. The coffee cups splatted on the pavement, and coffee and doughnuts got washed away down the gutter.

Wyatt ended up riding in the back of the lead cruiser, one of the cops driving the Mustang. "Here," he said, when they came to the brick house with the foreclosure sign.

They approached the front door, two SWAT guys first, then Wyatt and the chief, followed by the rest of the cops.

"This friend got a name?" the chief said.

"Greer," Wyatt said. "Greer Torrance."

"Come again?" said the chief.

Wyatt repeated the name. "She hasn't done anything, either. You're making a mistake." Then he realized that breaking into the foreclosed house was probably a crime. But the kind of crime that brought out the SWAT team? He didn't know.

One of the SWAT guys kicked at the door with his boot. "Open up."

The door opened at once, and there was Greer, fully dressed. She took everything in fast, her eyes widening. "Wyatt? What's wrong?"

"Remember me, Greer?" said the chief.

Greer nodded.

"No more playing with matches, I hope?" the chief said.

She looked him in the eye. "I never played with matches, so there's nothing to give up."

At that moment, Wyatt realized—or decided—that he loved her.

"Maybe we can discuss that further one day," the chief said. "For now, we're going to search this house."

"Don't you see the sign?" Greer said. "It's empty. And what about a warrant?"

"Not necessary in a hot-pursuit situation," the chief said.

"Hot pursuit?" Greer said. "I confess. The house belongs to the bank now but we spent one night in it anyway. Guilty as charged."

"You trying to be funny?" the chief said.

"About what? Wyatt? What's happening?"

"I don't know." His heart was pounding. He noticed for the first time a blue vein in the almost translucent skin at Greer's temple: it was pounding, too.

The cops pushed past Greer and entered the house. Wyatt, Greer, the chief, and a uniformed cop waited in the doorway, out of the rain. Wyatt heard doors opening and closing, heavy footsteps on a staircase and down in the basement, nightsticks tapping on walls. One by one the cops came back, shaking their heads. They got in the cruisers and took off, lights flashing but sirens off. Only the chief and his driver stayed behind.

The chief turned to Wyatt. "You spent the night here?"

Wyatt nodded.

"Then went out for coffee?"

He nodded again.

"When was the last time you saw Sonny Racine?"

"Yesterday."

"Where?"

"Where? In the visitors' room at the prison, of course. Has something happened to him?"

"You wrote 'family friend' on the visitor form," the chief said. "Elaborate."

So that was it. "It's not a lie," Wyatt said. "I just didn't know what to put."

"Why's that?"

"Because it turns out he's my biological father—I'd never met him in my life before I came here."

The chief nodded. "Not as uncommon a situation as you

might think—lots of the inmates are that way, like animals," he said. "Any reason why you decided to look him up at this point?"

Greer spoke first. "Why shouldn't he? Wouldn't you be curious?"

The chief looked at her. "Maybe," he said. "At that age. Which is kind of what I'm getting at here. At your age it's easy to make mistakes that change your whole life. Wouldn't want to see that happen. You follow?"

"No," Greer said. "I don't understand a word you're saying."

"First, I was talking to young Wyatt here," the chief said. "Second, I believe you. If I didn't, the two of you'd be in a cell right now."

"Why?" Wyatt said.

"Because," the chief said, "Sonny Racine's on the loose."

"Oh my God," Greer said.

"On the loose?" Wyatt said. "He escaped?"

"Not from the prison," said the chief. "That's never happened yet. But they were taking him to the hospital and he broke out of the van. Called for help and when they stopped and opened up he just sprang. Apparently wasn't cuffed— totally against procedure—on account of his injuries and long peaceable record."

"What injuries?" Wyatt said.

"He took a beating of some sort—don't have the details as yet. But the point I'm making—if he tries to contact you, get in touch with us right away. You'll be doing him a favor. Escapees never get away, but they often die trying, if you see what I mean." His eyes went to Greer, back to Wyatt. "I'll take that for a yes," he said. "Aiding and abetting are felonies, probably so obvious it's a waste of breath to mention." He turned and walked away, the driver following. They got in the cruiser and rode off, the chief glancing back just before they turned a corner.

The wind picked up, whipped a curtain of rain into the house. Greer closed the door. They stepped into each other's arms. Wyatt had a bad, bad feeling inside, and her embrace didn't take it away.

"This is horrible," he said.

"Yeah."

"Why would he do it, after all these years?"

"Haven't got a clue," Greer said. "Let's find out."

"Find out? How?"

She took him by the hand, led him up the stairs. The cops had left their damp footprints on the bare treads. "There used to be a nice soft carpet," Greer said. "I loved sitting on these stairs when I was a kid, seeing the tops of people's heads. Lots of parties in those days."

At the top they turned right, walked down a hall. The wall had light rectangular patches at picture-hanging level. They entered a room at the end of the hall.

"My dad's bedroom," Greer said. "Mom and Dad's, in ancient times; then he moved to the couch, then she moved out and he moved back." The closet door was open; she walked toward it. "I used to search the house from top to bottom before my birthday," she said, "trying to find the presents." She went into the closet, a completely empty cedar closet with a bare rail for hanging clothes and three brass hooks on the back wall. "I never did find my dad's hidey-hole—he ended up telling me where it was after they put him away, on account of some papers he needed." Greer reached for the top right-hand hook. "Some papers he needed burned, actually."

Greer twisted the hook. Wyatt heard a faint click. A portion of the wall swung open. This was a cleverly concealed door, its edges hidden in the grooves between the cedar planks, the hinges on the inside, and also padded so tapping wouldn't produce a hollow sound. On the other side of the cleverly concealed door was a space big enough for a man to stand in. The man standing in it was Sonny Racine.

## 29

ALL AT ONCE, THE ROOM, a normal-size bedroom, seemed too small, hardly big enough to hold the three of them. Wyatt had never experienced this sensation before, people overwhelming their physical space, obliterating it. Wyatt could feel danger, like a toxic contaminant escaping from the walls. He backed away from Sonny. What was Sonny doing here? That thought was quickly pushed aside by the sight of Sonny's messed-up face. Both times Wyatt had seen him—the only times he'd seen him in his life—Sonny had looked good, but he didn't look good now.

"What happened to you?" Wyatt said.

Sonny smiled. One of his two front teeth was gone; the other was chipped in half. "Not as bad as it looks," he said.

But it looked bad. Sonny's left eye was swollen almost shut and his left cheek, under the eye, seemed hollower than the right one, as though the bone around the eye had caved in; Wyatt had seen that happen to a kid who'd been hit by a pitch. His upper lip was swollen, too, and there was lots of blood on his khaki inmate shirt, now torn and missing buttons.

He stepped out of the closet, wincing slightly.

"Were you in a fight?" Wyatt said.

"Hector and his boys went a little overboard," Sonny said.

"Oh my God," Greer said. "That guy with the Jesus tattoo?"

"He's actually quite religious," Sonny said. "Just one of those misunderstandings."

"About what?" Greer said.

"Nothing. The wrong look, the wrong word, the wrong stance—inmate stuff. What would be nothing in the outside world, is I guess how to put it." He looked around the empty room, went toward the edge of the window, shot a quick sidelong glance outside. "Cops gone?"

"Yes," Greer said.

"Good job," Sonny said. "Both of you."

Wyatt hadn't done any job at all, hadn't known Sonny was in the house. But Greer had. He turned to her.

She seemed to know what he was thinking. "He came to the window maybe two minutes after you left. I hid him as soon as I heard the sirens. What did you want me to do? Turn him in?"

"Of course not." But almost at once Wyatt had second thoughts about that—what had the police chief said? *Escapees never get away, but they often die trying.* So what was the right thing to do?

"No need to give that a second thought, either of you," Sonny said. "I'm planning to turn myself in."

"You are?" Greer said.

"After I take care of business." Blood appeared at the corner of his mouth. "This sure feels good, can't tell you—first time outside those walls in seventeen years."

"What kind of business?" Wyatt said.

"Funny question coming from you," Sonny said. "You're the one who unsettled me. I told you—I was content. Now I'm not. I intend to prove my innocence."

"But how will this help?" Wyatt said. "Don't you need a lawyer?"

"We're long past the lawyer stage," Sonny said.

"So what are you going to do?" Wyatt said. He was aware of his voice cracking, like a pubescent kid's.

"What I should have done long ago," Sonny said. More blood seeped out of the corner of his mouth; he felt there with his fingertips. Wyatt noticed again how strong and well shaped his hands were. And something else: they were completely unmarked, unscratched, unswollen. Hector and his boys must have jumped him, overwhelmed him; he hadn't landed a single blow.

"What do you want us to do?" Greer said.

Sonny smiled at her, a once-nice smile now made ugly; with the blood and swelling, there was even something animal about it. "You, sweetheart?" he said. "I want nothing from you. And from Wyatt—I'd just like to borrow that sweet pony for a short time. The two Cs might come in handy as well."

"Uh," said Wyatt, "I spent twenty."

"Yeah?" Sonny sounded surprised. "On what?"

"Gas."

"A necessity," Sonny said. He paused, as though waiting for something. Wyatt took out his wallet and handed over the $180. Sonny tucked it away in his waistband. Wyatt saw that his khaki inmate pants—now wrinkled and bloodstained—had no pockets. "You'll get it back, I promise," Sonny said. "With interest."

"I don't want it," Wyatt said.

"We'll call it a down payment on all the birthday presents you never got." He approached the window again, took another sidelong glance. "What a beautiful day." It was raining harder than ever now, the sky a solid roof of low, dark cloud. "Hear that sound? Rain on the roof? You forget there are sounds like that."

The three of them stood silent in Greer's father's old bedroom, listening to the rain. Sonny dabbed with his sleeve at the corner of his mouth.

"Maybe you want to take a shower or something," Wyatt said.

"No water," said Greer.

"How about some ice?" Wyatt said.

"No fridge."

Sonny laughed, a strange sight with his teeth the way they were, hard to get used to. "I'm all right, kids."

"I could go out for ice," Wyatt said.

"I'll do it," said Greer.

"No," Sonny said, his voice suddenly sharp. Then, softer, he went on, "I'm all right, really. We'll just lie low here until dark, nice and quiet."

"And then?" Greer said.

"Then I'll hit the road in that borrowed pony."

"Hit the road for where?" Wyatt said.

"Probably best if we stay away from the specifics."

But there was one thing Wyatt absolutely had to know. "Are you going to see my mother?"

"No."

"Is she the person you're protecting?"

"No, for the millionth time."

They gazed at each other, an uncomfortable second or two for Wyatt; he couldn't help focusing on the swollen eye and bashed-in cheek.

Sonny put his hand to his heart. "I swear. Your mother had nothing to do with this. It's just not in her. She's a good person, through and through."

"Then who is it?" Wyatt said. "Who are you protecting?"

"No one anymore," Sonny said. "Took me a long time to learn, but it's true what they say—you can't protect people from themselves." He put his hand on Wyatt's shoulder, the first time they'd touched. Wyatt felt a tremor, very slight, pulsing inside Sonny. "I want to prove my innocence and that's all."

"How?" Wyatt said.

"Still got time to think about exact measures." A little more blood leaked from his mouth.

"I'll go get some ice," Wyatt said.

Sonny paused for a moment, then nodded and said, "And maybe some paper towels." Wyatt turned to go. "Don't be too long."

A remark that first struck Wyatt as almost parental, the kind of thing his mom might say: but as he drove away from the foreclosed house another possibility—that Sonny didn't quite trust him—rose in his mind.

He found a convenience store about a mile down the cross street. There were no other customers. The clerk was watching a TV mounted above the scratch tickets. An onscreen reporter stood in front of the visitors' entrance at Sweetwater State Penitentiary, the volume too low to be heard. Wyatt took a five-pound bag of ice from the freezer, grabbed a roll of paper towels, and went to the counter.

"Got any sandwiches?" Wyatt said.

"No more sandwiches," the clerk said. "New policy. You could try the Lunch Box." He pointed down the street.

Wyatt drove a few blocks farther, bought three turkey sandwiches and a six-pack of soda. The TV at the Lunch Box was tuned to a business show; numbers and symbols streamed across the top and bottom of the screen. Wyatt went back to Greer's old house. No one was on the street or at any of the windows in the nearby houses, two of which also had bank-sale signs on the front lawns. Wyatt parked, walked to the front door, and knocked.

The door opened, whoever was doing the opening staying out of sight behind it. Wyatt went in. "That was quick," Sonny said, closing the door. If anything, he now looked worse than before, a thin sheen of sweat on his upper lip.

Wyatt handed over the bag of ice. "I've got sandwiches, too."

"Great," said Sonny.

They went into the kitchen. No appliances, but the sink was still in place. Sonny pounded the ice bag in the metal basin, wrapped a few chunks in paper towel, pressed them lightly against the bashed-in side of his face and his swollen eyelid.

"Ah," he said. He leaned against the wall, closed his good eye, took a deep breath.

Wyatt snapped two sodas from the six-pack. "Greer upstairs?" he said.

Sonny's good eye opened. "Actually, no," he said. He pushed himself off the wall, stood straight. "She left."

Wyatt, almost at the door, turned back. "Left?"

"She got a call," Sonny said, "and two minutes later she was out the door."

"A call from who?"

"Don't know. But, uh . . ."

"What?" said Wyatt. "Tell me."

Sonny exhaled a long, slow breath. "I peeked out through the window upstairs. Some guy came to pick her up."

"What guy?"

"Didn't get a good look at him," Sonny said. "He stayed in the car."

"What kind of car?"

"A Lexus, I think, something fancy like that. Haven't kept up with cars all that well. But I caught the plate number, one of those vanity plates, easy to remember—VAN 1. I didn't get the impression she was coming back."

Wyatt set the two soda cans on the counter, very gently, as though they were fragile. He just stood there, feeling hollowed out inside. Either Greer had been outright lying to him or she'd been going back and forth in her own mind, playing fair with nobody. Was there a third possibility? None that he could see.

He felt Sonny's hand on his shoulder. "There'll be other girls, son. Maybe with a more honest approach, if you don't mind my opinion."

Wyatt turned, stepped away. "What does that mean?"

Sonny sighed. "Take the arson, for example—that was her."

"But you told me it wasn't."

"Probably a mistake, in retrospect. But I didn't see myself as the bad-news messenger, not when we were just getting to know each other, you and me. Plus she pretty much begged me not to tell, one time in the visitors' room. The truth is she might have been a little impulsive, but she was only trying to help her old man."

"What about Freddie Helms?"

"Who's he?"

"The firefighter who got his face practically burned off."

"I didn't know about that," Sonny said.

There was a long silence. The ice in the paper-towel ice pack melted and water ran down Sonny's face.

Wyatt had a sudden thought. "What if she tells Van you're here?"

"She won't do that," Sonny said. He went to the sink,

prepared another ice pack, held it to his head. "Do I smell turkey?" he said. He went to the counter, opened the bag. "Is one for me?"

"Yeah, sure."

Sonny took out a sandwich and unwrapped it. "Real food." He picked it up. Wyatt wondered: how was he going to eat it with his teeth like that? But he managed, no problem. "How about you?" Sonny said between mouthfuls.

"I'm not hungry."

Sonny cracked open a soda, drank it down in two swallows. "You okay with lending me the car? I'll bring it back, promise."

"Before you turn yourself in?"

"Exactly."

"What if you get spotted?"

"A risk I'll have to take," Sonny said.

"I'll drive," Wyatt said. "I want to help."

Sonny bowed his head. "Thank you."

"Where are we going?"

"Millerville."

"And then?"

"I'll explain on the way," Sonny said. "Right now I'm going to grab a little shut-eye. You should, too."

"I'm not sleepy."

"Suit yourself."

Sonny turned, went upstairs. Wyatt heard him moving down the hall toward Bert Torrance's old bedroom.

● ● ●

A few minutes later, Wyatt realized that in fact he was very tired. He entered Greer's old bedroom, gazed at the mattress on the floor, finally lay down on it. After a while he took out his cell phone and called her, without the slightest idea of what he would say. He got sent straight to voice mail, and left no message. Rain hammered on the roof.

# 30

WYATT SMELLED GREER, opened his eyes. It was dark, and for a moment he had no idea where he was. Then it came back: Greer's old bedroom, no Greer.

He got up, rubbed his eyes, looked out the window. Dim lights shone in the windows of a neighboring house or two; other than that, nothing but darkness and the rain falling steadily. He flicked a light switch and nothing happened.

Wyatt left the bedroom, moved carefully down the dark hall and into the kitchen, slightly lit by a streetlamp halfway down the block. The bag of ice, split down the middle, still lay in the sink, most of the ice melted. He dipped his cupped fingers in the bag, splashed cold water on his face. The rain slanted past the streetlamp in black streaks. Wyatt flipped open his phone, checked the time: 7:13. He was hungry. He opened the sandwich bag and found it empty.

Wyatt climbed the stairs, walked down the hall to Bert Torrance's old bedroom. Light from the same streetlamp came through the window, somewhat brighter than downstairs. Sonny lay on the floor in the corner, curled in the fetal position, the undamaged side of his face showing. As Wyatt watched, Sonny shifted slightly and let out a sound very close to the whimper of a dog.

Wyatt, standing in the doorway, said, "It's getting late." Sonny showed no reaction; his chest rose and fell with his breathing.

Wyatt went closer, stood over him. A small pool of dried blood had formed on the floor, under the bad side of his face. He made the whimpering sound again. "Dad?" said Wyatt. The word came out all by itself, shocked him. Sonny slept on, chest rising and falling, a sleep so deep and intense it was almost palpable, a thickness in the air.

Wyatt bent, reached down, touched Sonny's arm. And got his second shock: before he realized what was happening, Sonny had sat up and grabbed him by the wrist—a grip so hard it hurt—and was cocking his other hand into a fist, a wild look in his good eye. Then, at the last moment, recognition dawned in that eye, and he seemed to deflate, his grip on Wyatt's wrist relaxing, his other hand opening, sinking to his side.

"Christ," he said. "Sorry." He gave himself a little shake. "Force of habit," he said. "Bad, bad habit. I'm not used to . . . to . . ." He extended his hand. Wyatt took it and helped him up. He felt his father's physical strength renewing as he came to his feet.

There was hardly any traffic on the Millerville highway. The rain still fell, perhaps no harder than before, but the wind had picked up, driving it sideways across their path, almost horizontal.

"You're a hell of a driver," Sonny said. He sat beside Wyatt, his hands folded in his lap, the bad side of his face showing.

"Thanks."

"I mean it—a natural."

Wyatt sped up a bit.

"But let's not get crazy," Sonny said.

Wyatt laughed, came off the pedal an eighth of an inch or so. Sonny laughed, too. Their laughter sounded—to Wyatt's ears—much the same. It petered out together in a comfortable way.

"No craziness tonight," Sonny said, his voice going quiet. Headlights appeared—in the distance, but coming fast. Sonny shrank down in his seat. The headlights came closer, with a reflector strip glowing up above: a truck. It flashed by, buffeting the Mustang and sending a wave of water across the windshield, but doing nothing to disturb Wyatt's sense of complete control. "Hell of a driver," Sonny said, sitting up.

A wild night outside; inside, a small zone of warmth and quiet. "When are you going to tell me what happened at thirty-two Cain Street?" Wyatt said.

"How's never?"

Wyatt whipped around to stare at him.

"Just kidding," Sonny said, touching Wyatt's knee.

In the green light from the dashboard indicators, Wyatt saw that Sonny's hand was damaged, the knuckles skinned and swollen and one fingernail snapped right off, the flesh beneath dark with congealed blood. Sonny must have put up

a fight against Hector and his boys after all, although Wyatt didn't remember seeing these wounds before, must not have looked closely enough.

Sonny removed his hand, sat back. "In all this research you've been doing—Wertz, the newspaper guy, all that—did the money come up?"

"What money?" A road sign flashed by, blurred by the rain. MILLERVILLE—10 MILES.

"The drug money—whole point of the exercise. Turned out to be thirty grand, more or less. No time for a careful count, but I had it in my hand, outside that window. A small fortune, I realize now, or maybe no fortune at all, but at the time it was like striking it rich." He gazed through the windshield, where the wipers could barely keep up with the rain. "So what's your next question? Maybe what happened to the money?"

"Yeah," Wyatt said, thinking: *Outside the window.* Mr. Rentner had been right.

"My guess is it got used for a down payment," Sonny said.

"On what?"

"A bar, but that's not what bothers me."

"What bothers you?"

"Nothing. Shouldn't have said that. What would I have done in the same place? Who's to judge?" He went silent. The dim glow of a midsize town rose in the distance.

"The same place as the person who got away, is that what you're saying?" Wyatt said. "The one you protected?"

"Yeah."

So that was that: absolutely no way Linda had anything

to do with this. She had no interest in bars, didn't go to bars, hardly ever even had a drink.

"But," said Sonny.

"But what?"

"But even in that person's place," Sonny said, holding up one finger, not quite steady, "there's one thing I'd never have done."

"What's that?"

"Hook up with a rat." Another sign: WELCOME TO MILLER-VILLE, A KIDS-COME-FIRST COMMUNITY. Several of the letters were missing; that reminded Wyatt of the current state of Sonny's mouth, a crazy thought. "Let's go pay a call on the rat," Sonny said.

"We're talking about Doc Vitti?"

"You're a real smart kid. Can you get me to where he lives?"

"What are you going to do there?"

"What you've been asking me to do—prove my innocence."

"And hurting him wouldn't do that," Wyatt said, glancing at Sonny, the bad side of his face unreadable.

"Right you are—wouldn't help the slightest goddamn bit, would only hurt my chances, if you want the truth. But he's the key to getting the statement we need."

"From the other person, the one you protected?"

"You're way ahead of me."

"But I still don't have the name."

"I'll have to think about that," Sonny said. "Don't want you involved in any legal ramifications."

"I don't understand." Wyatt came to an ill-lit street lined by shabby houses, the street that led to the trailer park, and turned onto it.

"Even though I'm innocent and will prove it," Sonny said, "the fact is I'm kind of AWOL right now, in a legal sense."

Wyatt thought about that as they came to the entrance to the trailer park. "What would have happened if you hadn't gotten into the fight with Hector? You'd just have stayed there, getting old in jail?"

"No idea. But seize the day."

Wyatt didn't quite buy that explanation, but the time for questions was running out. He slowed down as they entered the trailer park. "He lives somewhere in here."

"What's he drive?" Sonny said.

"An old pickup, Dodge Ram, black." The pickup appeared in the headlights, parked in front of a silver trailer on wheels, the kind that could actually be towed.

"Cut the lights," Sonny said. "Stop the car."

Wyatt cut the lights and stopped the car. They gazed through the rain at the trailer, a glow showing in a side window.

"Pop the trunk," Sonny said.

"What for?"

"I'd like to borrow your tire iron. Just for deterrence— never hurts to be prudent. Doc, at least in the old days, had pigheaded tendencies."

The trunk didn't open from the inside. They got out, into the pelting rain, and walked around to the trunk. Wyatt unlocked it, raised the hood.

"Well, well," Sonny said, peering inside. He reached in and took out Wyatt's bat. "What a beauty." He assumed a batting stance—a very good one, balanced and comfortable—and swung the bat gently two or three times. "You'll get it back, I promise," he said. He lowered the bat, held it loosely in his left hand, extended his right. "This is good-bye," he said, "at least for now."

"Good-bye?"

"Shh. Can't have you implicated—in case anything goes wrong. You haven't seen me, know nothing about this."

Wyatt hesitated.

"Don't worry," Sonny said. "If all goes well, I'll be down at the police station in an hour, presenting my evidence."

"The police station here? In Millerville?"

"Sure." Sonny smiled his broken smile. His lips were wet with a mixture of rain and blood.

"Your evidence meaning the twenty-two that was never found?" Wyatt said. "Is that why we're here?"

Sonny laughed. "My kid the genius," he said. "Take good care of yourself. I'll call as soon as I can."

"But—"

Sonny's smile vanished. "Hey, Wyatt—please don't mess this up. I'm trying to get my life back here."

Wyatt nodded. They shook hands. Sonny's grip was strong and warm—almost hot, in fact. Then, as Wyatt stepped around the car, a powerful light flashed on from a point ten or fifteen feet from the trailer, framing Sonny in a white circle. Doc—his rough voice instantly recognizable to Wyatt—called out: "Don't fuckin' move, Sonny. Got a twelve-gauge pointed at your head."

But Sonny did move—so fast Wyatt wasn't clear exactly what was happening—diving out of the white circle and at the same time hurling the bat at the source of the light. Wyatt caught the gleam of the spinning bat, and then came a thud and a cry of pain, and next the beam pointed wildly in several directions and finally went still, aimed straight up at the sky. Sonny was already on the move, running toward the light and the dark form beside it, shaped like a man on his knees. The man on his knees was reaching for something on the ground, but before he could get it, Sonny was on him. Another thud, another cry of pain, and then Sonny rose. Wyatt went closer, close enough to see Doc lying on his back, bleeding from the side of his head, blood and mud clotting in his long graying hair; and Sonny standing over him, one foot resting on Doc's throat, the shotgun in his hand.

"Can't say the years have been kind to you, Doc," Sonny said. "You look like shit."

Doc gazed up at him, eyes full of hate. "Seen yourself lately?"

Sonny flashed his messed-up smile. "All fixable," he said. "Just part of the plan—a disguise, you could call it." He took his foot off Doc's throat and said, "Up."

Doc rolled over, got back on his knees, then suddenly bent forward and puked.

"That's just the fear talking," Sonny said. "You're not hurt that bad." He grabbed Doc by the collar and pulled him up. "Let's get out of the rain," he said.

At that moment, Doc noticed Wyatt. He blinked. "You?"

Sonny glanced at Wyatt. "Weren't you on your way, son?"

"But—"

"Doc and I need to go inside and straighten things out, and there's only so much time. I'll be in touch, like I said." Sonny smiled. His face was hard, and shiny with rain.

# 31

WYATT GOT INTO THE MUSTANG, turned, and drove out of the trailer park. In the rearview mirror he saw Sonny stomp on Doc's searchlight, bringing back the darkness with a quiet smash, and then two shadowy forms were moving toward the trailer.

Wyatt pulled over, not far from the entrance, and parked by the side of the road. He tried to make sense of what he'd just seen, tried to make it fit with everything he'd already learned about that night at 32 Cain Street; and was still trying when headlights appeared down the street. A car came nearer, a small sedan. As it passed under a streetlamp—the only one on the block that was working—Wyatt caught a glimpse of the driver, a middle-aged woman with copper-red hair: Charlene. Charlene of Good Time Charlene's bar, married to Bob Waters with whom she lived in that well-kept bungalow, at the same time having a secret affair with Doc Vitti. She drove by, gaze straight ahead, hands tight on the wheel, and turned into the trailer park. Wyatt got out of the Mustang and followed on foot.

The rain began to let up. Wyatt ran down the lane that led to the silver trailer, saw Charlene getting out of the sedan, fumbling with an umbrella. She walked to the trailer, adjusting a small purse she carried on her shoulder, and knocked on the door. Wyatt moved closer, staying in the shadows.

The door opened and Sonny looked out; he had the bat in his hand, now reddened at the end.

"Oh my God," Charlene said.

"Surprise," said Sonny.

Charlene backed away. Sonny grabbed her wrist. She dropped the umbrella, tried to get to her purse. Sonny yanked her close with one hand—his other still held the bat—and kissed her mouth. She squirmed and struggled, but couldn't get away. Finally he let go. Charlene wiped her mouth with the back of her hand.

"You used to kiss better than that," Sonny said. "Maybe you don't love me anymore."

"What have you done to him?" Charlene said.

"See," Sonny said, "that's where we reached the tipping point. Covering for you—no problem, I was cooked anyway. Heard you got married to some little fellow. Well, life goes on. But spreading your legs for Doc, who was always sniffing after you and you wouldn't give him the time of day? When I heard that"—he shook his head—"it had a big effect on me, let's put it that way. Do I have to explain why? Doc fucked me over big-time, and now again he's fucking me right through you, if you see what I mean."

"You're out of your mind," Charlene said.

Sonny gave her a good one with the back of his hand.

Charlene's head snapped back but she didn't fall. Instead she said, "Fuck you," opened her purse, and took out a gun.

"Same goddamn twenty-two?" Sonny said, showing no fear at all. "But you're a lousy shot, Charlene—proved that a long time ago, outside the window at thirty-two Cain."

"I've been practicing," Charlene said, stepping back.

Sonny came out of the trailer, moved toward her.

"Not another step," Charlene said.

Sonny took another step. The gun went off, the orange flash bright, the sound enormous. Sonny rocked back, a red stain appearing on his left shoulder at once. The expression on his face turned from fearless to murderous with nothing in between. Charlene tried to take another step back, stumbled a bit, and before she could squeeze the trigger again, Sonny swung the bat—with just his right hand, but so fast Wyatt could hear the whoosh of air—and struck her on the side of the head. The sound was sickening, and so was the sight. Charlene toppled over and lay still. Sonny dropped the bat, picked up the gun, and went back into the trailer. Wyatt turned and puked, just like Doc.

Sonny came out of the trailer almost at once, keys in one hand, a towel pressed to his shoulder. Wyatt stood motionless in the shadows. Sonny climbed into Doc's pickup and drove out of the trailer park.

Wyatt didn't take another glance at Charlene or what was left of her head, didn't even think of going into the trailer. He just panicked, running to his car as fast as he could, jumping in, turning the key. But at that moment, before he'd had a single coherent thought, a cell phone rang. Not his, but

Greer's: he recognized that Dobro ringtone. Greer's? How was that possible? It rang again and stopped, just before he found it in the glove box.

Wyatt held Greer's phone in his hand. Van had come to the foreclosed house, taken her away while Wyatt was getting ice and sandwiches. He could see her not waiting for his return just so she could retrieve her phone—not worth the potential scene—but why not leave a note about sending it along, or a message with Sonny? And then came another thought, a thought that chilled his whole body: If Greer's phone had been in the car the whole time, how had Van called her at all?

Wyatt checked the screen on Greer's phone: two new messages. He went into her voice mail: 7777#.

Message one: "Hi, honey, this is Dad." Bert Torrance was speaking fast and sounded scared. "Sonny Racine's escaped. Hector beat him up—but it's a complete scam: Sonny actually paid him, just so he could get past the walls. Don't go anywhere near him—and warn Wyatt, too."

Message two, the one that had just come in: "Greer? Van here. I'm terminating your lease at the end of the week. Better get back here and clean out your things if you don't want to lose them."

Wyatt started shaking, so bad he could hardly hold on to the phone. He took a deep breath, and another, then jammed the car into gear, spun it around in a shrieking one-eighty, and tore off in the direction Doc's pickup had gone.

A half mile or so later, he came to a highway, a right turn leading east, toward East Canton, a left heading west, out of state. He saw nothing to the east; a single set of far-off taillights was just visible in the west. Wyatt swung left and put the pedal to the floor. Somewhere behind him a siren started up.

The rain had stopped now and so had the wind. The road was almost dry, a straight highway, no traffic: Wyatt hit 105 and kept it there, reeling in those red taillights. Soon he was just a few hundred yards behind; black Dodge Ram pickup, no doubt about it. He flashed his high beams. The pickup didn't slow down; sped up, if anything. Wyatt flashed his lights again, then crossed the yellow line and roared up alongside the pickup. He looked over, saw Sonny looking over at him. Wyatt held up his hand in the stop sign.

Sonny didn't stop. Instead he swerved slightly, just enough to bump the side of the Mustang. Wyatt felt the Mustang's rear end sliding out from under him, threatening to fishtail. He backed off the gas, went with the slide, let it take him farther to the left, almost to the edge of the shoul-der—the night flashing by—before traction returned, the Mustang again grabbing hold of the road. And when it did, he steered back across the road and clipped the pickup behind the left rear wheel, just hard enough.

Sonny lost control immediately. The pickup shot side-ways off the highway, spun round and round, flipped, and skidded to a stop in a bare field, lying on its roof, one head-light shining up at a forty-five-degree angle. Wyatt came to a stop a few hundred feet down the road, turned, and drove back. He parked on the shoulder, got out of the Mustang, pocketing the keys, and walked into the field. The howl of many sirens was in the air, and the clouds glowed with a pulsing blue reflection.

Sonny crawled out of the pickup's cab and rose, one hand pressed to his shoulder.

"What have you done to Greer?" Wyatt said.

"Nothing."

"Don't come any closer."

"I'll come as close as I like," Sonny said. He reached into his pocket and took out the .22, held it by his side. "She shouldn't have slapped me is all. It was just a proposal—a simple 'no' would have done."

Wyatt didn't stop to think, just charged. The gun came up, but Wyatt crashed into Sonny before he could fire. They wrestled in the muddy field, first, for a brief moment, Wyatt on top, then Sonny. His strength was tremendous, even with one arm practically useless. It was over very fast, no contest at all. Sonny straddled Wyatt's chest and raked the barrel of the gun across Wyatt's face. The sirens grew louder.

"Stupid fucking kid," Sonny said. He raised the gun to do it again. "I'm taking your car."

Wyatt gazed into Sonny's eyes and felt nothing, no kinship at all. Fear, which had been threatening to take over completely, now shrank inside him; still there, but not in power. "Then you'll need the keys," Wyatt said. "They're in my pocket."

Sonny smiled that messed-up smile. "That's better," he said, getting off Wyatt.

Wyatt rose, reached into his pocket. Then, in one quick motion, he took out the keys and threw them across the field with all his strength.

"God damn you." The murderous look was back on Sonny's face. He raised the gun. But at that moment, a cruiser skidded to a stop behind the Mustang and two cops with rifles jumped out. A searchlight shone down, capturing Wyatt and Sonny in its blinding beam: frozen in place, Sonny pointing the .22 at Wyatt's head.

"Drop it," one of the cops shouted.

Sonny didn't drop it. Instead he grabbed Wyatt, spun him around, and darted behind him, the .22 still pointed at Wyatt's head, his arm around Wyatt's chest.

But: the wounded arm, the one with no strength in it. "Shoot!" Wyatt called out, and he bolted free.

Actually not free—a slight separation was all he managed: somehow Sonny held on. But the cops fired anyway, one bullet making an insect sound close to Wyatt's ear, the other making a red hole in Sonny's forehead. His eyes went dead as he fell.

More cruisers arrived. An amplified voice spoke from one of them, but the sound seemed to come from way above. "Hands up high."

Wyatt raised his hands.


Doc's body was found in the tiny bathroom at the back of the silver trailer. And then came something too awful to think about, although for a long time after, Wyatt could think of nothing else: Greer's body was in Bert Torrance's secret bedroom closet hidey-hole in the foreclosed house in Silver City. Wyatt came away with only one sure thing, a sure thing that didn't help, actually hollowed him out all the more: He'd been right to love her.

Wyatt faced a number of felony charges, including aiding and abetting the escape of an inmate from a state prison and harboring a fugitive, but after a month's deliberation and consultation with a prominent attorney hired by the Mannions, the DA decided not to bring the case. They made a deal that Wyatt would join the Army as soon as he turned seventeen. He probably would have done that anyway: he had no other ideas; and inside he felt he deserved much worse.

One funny thing—this was in the period before Wyatt went away to boot camp—he now got a lot more respect from Rusty. Rusty took him fishing on the river whenever he was home. Wyatt had never been particularly interested in fishing, but Rusty really knew what he was doing and Wyatt began to enjoy it. Sometimes they all went, Linda and Cammy, too. Cammy liked fishing, as long as the fish got thrown back. Linda just liked sitting beside Wyatt, not talking much, but making sure of things, like he wasn't hungry or thirsty, and was wearing sunblock.

"This family excels at fishing," Cammy said.

"Excels?" said Wyatt. How would she ever have friends, talking like that?

"It means doing real, real good," Cammy said.

PETER ABRAHAMS is the *New York Times* bestselling author of *Delusion*, *Nerve Damage*, *End of Story*, *Oblivion*, *The Fan*, *Behind the Curtain*, *Into the Dark*, and *Reality Check*, as well as *Lights Out* and *Down the Rabbit Hole*, for both of which he received Edgar Award nominations. Writing as Spencer Quinn, he is also the author of the *New York Times* bestseller *Dog on It*. Peter makes his home in Falmouth, Massachusetts, with his family and a dog named Audrey. You can visit him online at www.peterabrahams.com.